Praise for

Shadows on a Cape Cod Wedding
by Lea Wait

"Wait has now written six novels in the Shadows series. Opening any one of these is like coming back home where everyone welcomes you and you know you're in for a good time."

—*Bookloons*

"This cozy…has a very good puzzle at its core. The setting is excellent and the story well-written…. One thing I liked very much was the catalogue-style listing of an antique print, complete with pricing, that headed up each chapter. A reader could learn a lot from this alone. Kudos."

—Creatures 'n Crooks Books

"Stormy weather and threats of violence lead to a far-from-cozy situation—and if Maggie can actually solve the issues for her friends and for the family of the dead man, there's no guarantee it will solve her own. A good read, sweet with a smoky edge of intrigue and suspense."

—Kingdom Books

"Memories of Jessica Fletcher and Miss Marple. How I have longed for someone in that vein to resurface. 'Nice' murders surrounded by interesting people you can care about and an unexpected bad guy or bad gal…. Enough twists and turns add a nice touch and I was surprised at the ending."

—*I Love a Mystery*

Shadows on a Maine Christmas

BOOKS BY
LEA WAIT

Shadows on a Maine Christmas

AN ANTIQUE PRINT MYSTERY

Lea Wait

2014 · PERSEVERANCE PRESS | JOHN DANIEL & COMPANY
PALO ALTO | MCKINLEYVILLE, CALIFORNIA

A Perseverance Press Book
Published by John Daniel & Company
A division of Daniel & Daniel, Publishers, Inc.
Post Office Box 2790
McKinleyville, California 95519
www.danielpublishing.com/perseverance

Distributed by SCB Distributors (800) 729-6423

Book design by Eric Larson, Studio E Books, Santa Barbara, www.studio-e-books.com

10 9 8 7 6 5 4 3 2 1

LIBRARY OF CONGRESS CATALOGING-IN-PUBLICATION DATA
Wait, Lea.
Shadows on a Maine Christmas : an antique print mystery / by Lea Wait.
    pages cm
ISBN 978-1-56474-547-7 (pbk. : alk. paper)
1. Man-woman relationships Fiction. 2. Murder—Investigation—Fiction.
3. Christmas stories. I. Title.
PS3623.A42S5348 2014
813'.6—dc23
                        2014008706

To the many readers
who have become Maggie's friends and followers

Shadows on a Maine Christmas

1

Poinsettia pulcherrima. Plate XXXI from Volume I of *Les plantes à feuillage coloré,* written by English botanist Edward (E.J.) Lowe (1825–1900) assisted by W. Howard, and translated from the English by publisher K. Rothschild: Paris, 1867. Beautiful detailed color lithograph of a single poinsettia flower and two leaves. Based on Lowe's *Beautiful-Leaved Plants, being a Description of the Most Beautiful-Leaved Plants in Cultivation in this Country,* London: Groombridge, 1864. 7 x 10.5 inches. Price: $60.

CHRISTMAS ON THE coast of Maine with the man she loved. It sounded like an ad for a 1940s romantic movie starring Cary Grant and Katharine Hepburn.

Maggie's students and colleagues who'd heard her holiday plans had immediately assumed engagement bells as well as Christmas bells were in the offing. She'd found herself fending off everything from knowing smiles to slightly off-color jokes to well-meaning high fives.

Three people volunteered to take Winslow, her cat, for the holidays. Neighbors had promised to watch her house, and even plow her driveway and shovel her sidewalk should Somerset County, New Jersey be blessed with a white Christmas. Some days even Maggie herself had felt she was getting into the spirit. Admittedly, a few bedtime glasses of sherry had also helped with late-night nerves.

And after all, she told herself on those sleepless nights, she loved Will. He said he loved her. And wasn't this the season for love to conquer all? (Or was that Valentine's Day?)

Okay. So they had a few issues to iron out.

She was set on adopting a child. In fact, last week she'd heard she was now officially on her agency's waiting list for "one girl or two sisters between the ages of five and nine." Not news she'd shared with Will. Not yet.

Because although he might love her, he'd been clear that fatherhood was not for him.

And then there was the little issue of geography. He'd moved to Maine to care for his ninety-two-year-old Aunt Nettie. Maggie lived in New Jersey.

So, yes, they had a few lifestyle issues to work through.

Maggie kept replaying the moment he'd asked her to marry him when they'd been on Cape Cod in October.

And even more vividly, the moment after that when she'd told him she was having her adoption home study done. The moment he'd backed off. Way off. As in, slamming the door and leaving, off.

Nothing—not even the death of her husband two years ago—had felt as awful. But of course, Michael's accidental death had also been the end of his philandering. Death had just made a dying relationship officially over. Her experience with Michael was one of the reasons it had taken so long for her to finally trust Will.

Trust him to love her. But whether their love could survive their both being independent individuals with separate dreams and responsibilities? That was still open to question.

Her right hand, which was clenched on the steering wheel, still wore the R-E-G-A-R-D ring Will had given her. It was their private token of friendship; a Victorian ring with stones spelling out the sentiment they'd felt when they were two antique dealers (she specialized in prints; he in kitchen and fireplace wares) getting to know each other. The Ruby, Emerald, Garnet, Amethyst, Ruby, and Diamond still glittered, despite today's low December clouds.

She'd offered the ring back to him in October. Her heart raced remembering that moment. What if he'd taken it? What if he'd driven back to Maine and they'd never seen each other again?

He'd refused the ring. But she'd almost had to beg for another chance. Promised she'd never keep a major secret, like her adoption plans, from him again. Promised she wouldn't put crazy distractions like trying to solve murders ahead of being with him.

Now it was two months later. No murders had presented themselves, thank goodness, but she hadn't given up her dream of opening her home and heart to a child who needed her.

This visit, this Maine Christmas, would be their test. Was their relationship going to work?

Could she give up her desire to be a parent? Or could Will find it in his heart to love a child?

No; this wasn't going to be a simple, romantic Christmas in Maine. But she was on her way.

2 | **Home For The Holidays.** Wood engraving from January 2, 1869 *Harper's Weekly.* Illustrator: JW. (Full name unknown.) Black-and-white illustration of wooden suburban railway station ("Valley Station") platform filled with elegantly dressed people of all ages greeting each other; stacks of trunks and carpetbags are waiting to be picked up. Train in distance pulling away from station. 15.5 x 11 inches. Price: $55.

YEARS AGO, when Maggie had first started her antique print business, she'd named it "Shadows." That's what old prints had always seemed to her: shadows; reflections; treasured pictures that gave today's viewers a window to the past. A glimpse, perhaps, of the people and places they'd come from.

Tonight, as Maggie first saw Waymouth, Maine in Christmas attire, it seemed as though the classic holiday scenes in her print inventory had come to life.

Despite its being close to midnight, the little town on the Madoc River was bright with holiday lights. The Congregational church overlooking Main Street was illuminated, and cascading lights on the Christmas tree on the Green were reflected by the snow below it. Pine trees strung with tiny white lights tied to the bases of street lamps leading down toward the river made the simple drive into town magical. Windows and doors of homes on both sides of the street were decorated with wreaths, many illuminated with welcoming candles or lights.

Disney couldn't have planned it better if he'd designed this town for the Magic Kingdom. The perfect New England village. Although everyone knew the Magic Kingdom's perfection was a façade. Not everyone behind those doors was following a script with a happy ending built in.

Maggie turned left on a side street, toward where Will would be waiting.

She pulled into the driveway in back of Aunt Nettie's familiar small sedan, and hardly had time to remove her keys before Will was outside her van door.

"Where have you been? I expected you two hours ago. I wanted to call or text, but I didn't want you answering while you were driving if the weather or the traffic—"

And then she was in his arms, his soft beard against her cheek, and the end of the sentence didn't matter.

At least for a minute or two. Then reality set in. "It's freezing cold and snowing!" Maggie said, shivering despite his arms around her.

Will laughed. "It's actually below freezing—about five degrees. And of course it's snowing. You're in Maine, in December. Where're your bag and your coat? We'll get you in the house. Don't worry. We're fully equipped for the modern world. We even have central heating."

Central heating? She hadn't considered the possibility they wouldn't have it. What other possibilities about this week hadn't she thought of?

"How about hot chocolate?" Maggie shivered, as she pointed out her duffel bag and her coat, and balanced six large tins of Christmas cookies in her arms.

"Chocolate's possible. I know my lady. I've even got the Maine solution to all things winter—Allen's Coffee Brandy," said Will, as he hustled Maggie up the steps to the porch.

Maggie wrinkled her nose. "No coffee. Even in brandy. Hot chocolate, please. Maybe with cognac?"

"You didn't think to wear boots?" Will stared at her sneakered feet.

"They're in the van," she said. She focused on getting to the front door before she froze to death. "I'll find them tomorrow."

"Good," said Will, close behind her. "I was afraid I might have to totally outfit you."

The kitchen was as welcoming as it had been in summer, and almost as warm.

"Merry Christmas, Maggie! Welcome to Waymouth." Matriarch Aunt Nettie was sitting in her usual chair at the kitchen table, cozily dressed in a gray wool sweater and slacks, a warm red-patterned shawl wrapped around her shoulders. "I couldn't let Will sit up alone to wait for you. He's been pacing and looking out the window for hours. Thought certain he'd wear a hole in the floor."

"Merry Christmas, Aunt Nettie!" Maggie put her boxes of cookies on the counter and bent down to give the old woman a gentle hug. Aunt Nettie had lost weight since her stroke in August. "Thank you so much for including me in your Christmas. I've never been to Maine in the winter."

"So Will tells me. Hope you brought warm underwear. It gets a mite chilly around here this time of year. It's not the temperature, you know. It's the wind, coming over the river. Gets me in my bones, especially since I can't move around the way I used to."

"You're looking in good spirits, though," said Maggie.

"I am. And pleased you're here. Will needs more company than an old woman, and it's nice to have a guest over the holidays. You always keep us on our toes, Maggie Summer."

Maggie hung her coat on one of the iron hooks on the wall near the door. Will had already produced a large mug of hot chocolate, put it at her place at the table, and was reaching for a bottle of cognac. "That sounds like an order."

"It is. Life was beginning to get a bit dreary around this place. We need some livening up. Right, Will?"

"Something like that," Will answered. "Now, Aunt Nettie, you've stayed up until Maggie's arrived. Don't you think it's time for you to go to bed?"

"In a few minutes," she said, brushing him off. "I know you young folks want time to yourselves. I'm not a fool. We can wait until tomorrow to make plans. We have a few days before Christmas, so there's plenty of time."

"I thought we'd go and cut our tree tomorrow," Will said, as he and Maggie sat down at the table. He looked at Maggie for confirmation. "Christmas isn't really Christmas until there's a tree in the house. Have you ever cut your own tree?"

Maggie shook her head. "In New Jersey they're shipped in from places like Maine and Vermont, and sold at horribly high prices. Or people have artificial ones."

Aunt Nettie shuddered. "The bank in town has one of those. Fire regulations, they said. On the television they even showed one that was pink! Horrid thing. Abnormal, if you ask me. Wouldn't even smell of pine or fir. Give me a nice real tree any day."

"You can buy trees off lots here, too, but not many people do," Will added. "You remember Nick Strait? His family has a few acres and he said we could find a nice Douglas fir there."

"Sounds like fun," Maggie agreed, sipping her chocolate and beginning to warm up. "How is Nick?" She tried to stifle a yawn. "Never mind. You can tell me about Nick tomorrow. I guess I really am tired."

"So—what's in the boxes?" He pointed at the metal tins she'd put on the counter.

"I wanted to contribute a few things to Christmas," Maggie said, smiling. "Those are cookies. Mincemeat-filled, lemon sugar, regular sugar, shortbread, chocolate chip, butterscotch, snickerdoodles, oatmeal, molasses, ginger, raspberry-filled…you name it. I didn't know if we'd have time to bake while I was here. And for me, Christmas isn't Christmas without cookies."

"I knew there was a reason I'd invited you!" said Will. "Is there a rule we can't sample now? Or would you like something more substantial to eat? What about a ham sandwich?"

"A sandwich would be good. On the way here all I've nibbled on are carrot sticks and chips. But you can have cookies." Maggie opened one of the boxes and reached in the cupboard above for a plate. "When I was a little girl cookies were only for Christmas Eve and after. But I think under the circumstances we can start our Christmas now."

"Will, why don't you get up and make this woman a sandwich? We don't want her driving all the way here and then starving to death. While she's eating it, you can help me to bed. Then, after she's had her food, you two can have time together." Aunt Nettie actually winked at Maggie, who grinned back, as Will got up and went to the refrigerator. "Will can check out those cookies of yours tonight. I'll look forward to tasting them tomorrow. I'll admit I'm a bit weary. This is past my bedtime."

"Of course. I understand." Maggie put the plate of cookies down on the table. "Would you like me to help you get ready for bed?" Last summer she'd done that.

"Not tonight. You've just arrived. And Will and I've gotten used to each other." Aunt Nettie leaned over and whispered confidentially, "At first I wasn't too comfortable with his helping me. His being a man and all, you know? But he's not so bad, after all. And they have male nurses nowadays. So an old lady has to be flexible." She sat up and said, louder, "We've learned to cope with each other in the past months, haven't we, Will?"

"We have, indeed," Will said, smiling, as he put a thick sandwich down in front of Maggie. "So, my fine lady, let's head off to bed. You'll have plenty of time to talk with Maggie in the morning."

He handed his great-aunt a cane Maggie hadn't noticed leaning against the wall and helped her to her feet. She expected them to head for the stairs to the second floor, but instead, they walked slowly toward the living room and turned toward the dining area.

In their telephone calls and emails Will had mentioned he'd made changes in the house to make it more comfortable for both of them. He hadn't been more specific, and caught up in her teaching, her print business, and her adoption home study, she hadn't asked. Now she wished she had. Was Aunt Nettie now sleeping downstairs? At the end of August she'd been having a hard time climbing the stairs to her bedroom, but they'd assumed her strength would return.

As Maggie sipped her chocolate and ate her sandwich she listened to the muffled voices coming from the other room.

Will had gotten a cousin to stay with his aunt when he'd come to Cape Cod for Gussie's wedding. She hadn't realized how necessary that had been. No wonder Will cancelled out of the antiques shows he'd usually done in New York and New Jersey this fall.

By the time he'd returned she'd finished eating, washed up the dishes, and nibbled on a couple of her own cookies.

Will smiled at her appreciatively and offered her a snifter of cognac, sans chocolate, which she accepted, poured himself one, and then focused on the cookies. "I've never had mincemeat cookies before. These are terrific."

"Aunt Nettie's weaker than I imagined," Maggie said cautiously, not knowing how sounds would carry in the old house. "How is she, really? And how are you managing? You didn't tell me she was sleeping downstairs."

"I didn't want to bother you with our problems." He reached for another cookie. "Physically, Aunt Nettie's fine, considering she's ninety-two and had a minor stroke four months ago. Mentally, she still has it all together. But she's lost a lot of strength, and her doctor says chances are she won't get it back. Climbing the stairs was too hard for her, and installing a stair lift in that narrow old stairway wouldn't work. So, over her strenuous objections, I convinced her to move downstairs. In case of an emergency it would be a lot easier to get her out of the house if she's on the first floor."

"But there's no bathroom downstairs," Maggie thought out loud.

"There is now. You're forgetting all those years I taught carpentry in high school." Will half smiled. "Tomorrow you'll see. I built a wall to separate the dining room from the living room to give her some privacy—and me, too, if I have guests. When he wasn't on duty Nick helped me build a handicapped bathroom in the corner of her room."

"Wow!" Maggie said. "You've done all that this fall?"

"That's the only construction, other than the ramp I added to the outside steps in the back. Aunt Nettie didn't want a ramp out front. Her room is just big enough for a bed, even a hospital bed should she ever need one, and a bureau and closet. I'll warn you, although I bought a TV for her room, and she rests there a lot, she spends most of her time in the living room, or here in the kitchen, instructing me on how I should cook or clean the house."

"Oh, Will."

He shrugged. "It's really not so bad. Fixing the house has kept me busy, and I do love the lady. And once a week or so Nick comes by and pulls me out to have a beer, which is good. And you'll remember I have cousins in the vicinity, too."

"I remember," said Maggie, choosing a piece of shortbread for herself. Will's cousins were idiosyncratic Mainers, for sure. But they'd come through in past emergencies.

"None of them makes cookies this good, though," said Will. "How have you kept talent like this hidden so long?"

"This is the only year we've spent Christmas together. My cookie-making skills only emerge in December," Maggie answered.

"Hmm. Well, if we spent more time together that might have to change. My only problem is deciding which kind I like best—the mincemeat-filled, or these lemon ones. The ones with the sprinkles are pretty good, too. I'll have to have another, to check it out." He reached toward the plate, which was now almost empty.

"If we spent more time together"? What did he mean by that? She swirled the cognac in her glass and took another sip. It was too early in her visit to start analyzing. So far she was pleased at the reception her cookies had received (maybe six tins of cookies weren't going to be enough) but shocked at the amount of care Aunt Nettie needed.

"So what have you done with all your stuff? From your business, and your home in Buffalo?" she asked.

"I've moved a few of my things into Aunt Nettie's old bedroom upstairs, which I've turned into my office."

"Your office?" Maggie interrupted.

"I'm trying a couple of new ways to make money from my antiques. Anyway," Will continued, clearly allowing no time for questions now, "we'll have time to talk about that later. My business inventory is divided between a storage unit outside town and the barn here. Which means shoveling out any vehicles I'm using, since there's no space for them undercover in winter."

"I noticed Aunt Nettie's car was the one closest to the road."

"I've been using it. She hasn't fully accepted that she shouldn't drive, so she hasn't gotten rid of her car, and it gets better mileage and is more practical for driving locally than my RV. I've about decided to let the RV be snowed in. I won't be doing any antiques shows this winter. I was tempted by a couple of local ones, but I'm not ready to leave Aunt Nettie for a twelve-hour day, much less two or three. And shoveling out both an RV and a car almost every day is getting to be a hassle."

Will had his hands full. She hadn't thought about details like snow. "One positive change, though," he added, smiling at her. "The bedroom you used in August is still the guest bedroom, but with Aunt Nettie downstairs…my dear, you have your choice."

"You mean," she said, coyly, "you're offering to give me your bedroom while I'm visiting?"

"In no way," he said, reaching out, and stroking her hand, now well-warmed from hot chocolate, cognac, and his presence. "I'm offering to share. After all, Maine nights can get wicked cold."

"So I've heard," Maggie replied, as seriously as she could manage under the circumstances. "That would be the more practical plan, now, wouldn't it?"

"And you and I have always been two uncommonly practical people," he said, standing and pulling her up toward him.

3 | **A Winter Morning–Shovelling Out.** Wood engraving by Winslow Homer (1836–1910), major American nineteenth-century artist, for newspaper *Every Saturday*, January 14, 1871. Three members of family outside their snow-covered home standing in a path perhaps four feet deep. The two men are digging with wooden shovels; the woman is throwing seeds or crumbs to birds on top of the drifted snow. 9 x 11.75 inches. Price: $400.

MAGGIE WOKE to the smells of Will's aftershave on the pillow beside her and coffee brewing downstairs. She glanced at the clock on the bedside table. Eight-thirty.

She hadn't asked when he and Aunt Nettie usually got up in the morning. She stretched and smiled. Somehow, the subject hadn't come up.

But he hadn't been kidding about cool temperatures. Her toes were warm under several blankets and a quilt, but her nose was definitely frosty. She sat up and pulled the quilt around her. Good; her duffel was by the door. Will must have brought it upstairs this morning. She didn't remember them thinking of it last night. Reluctantly she put her feet on the chilly pine-plank floor. Time to get going.

Downstairs, she found Aunt Nettie happily dunking a sugar cookie in a mug of coffee and nibbling the edges. "Good morning, Maggie. If all your cookies are as good as the ones I've tasted this morning, I'll have to ask for your recipes."

"More hot chocolate this morning, or your usual Diet Pepsi?" Will asked after a quick hug.

"Hot chocolate is tempting…but with all the calories in holiday cooking, I think I'd better start out with Diet Pepsi," said Maggie, moving toward a heating vent on the floor. "It is chilly this morning, though." Despite her turtleneck, wool sweater, and jeans she was shivering.

"You'll get used to it," Will assured her. "I'll turn the heat up a bit until you do. We keep it at sixty during the day."

"Sixty?" she managed to choke out. "Fahrenheit?"

"At night I turn it down a few degrees," he added, obliviously. "You wouldn't believe what it costs to heat this place."

"What's the temperature outside?"

"Last time I looked it was almost zero," Will said. "Early weather report said it hit nine below in Portland last night. So it'll be a good day to cut our tree. Supposed to get up to twenty or so, and not much wind. It's the wind that'll get you." He looked over at Maggie. "You did say you'd brought boots?"

"They're in the van. With my hat and scarf and gloves. I knew I was coming to Maine." I just didn't know I'd need all that gear inside the house, she thought, pulling the sleeves of her sweater down over her hands.

"Then you're set. Cheddar-and-parsley omelet okay? After that, while I'm getting out the saw and the sled, you can unpack. We'll head over to the Straits' and look at trees in the middle of the morning, when it's a little warmer."

Maggie nodded. "An omelet sounds good. You have our day all planned."

"I have lots of plans for your visit," Will continued as he reached for the eggs and cheese. "We'll be home in time to get lunch, and then we can put the tree up while Aunt Nettie rests, and decorate it later tonight, or tomorrow. After the branches thaw. But first—three omelets coming up."

"You haven't eaten?"

"We didn't want our guest to eat alone," added Aunt Nettie, who was munching on another cookie.

Maggie looked from the half-empty pot of coffee on the stove to the cookie crumbs on the plate. "When do you usually get up?"

"Depends," said Aunt Nettie. "I wake up about five, but I wait for Will to come and help me get out of bed. He's a late sleeper. Some days he doesn't come downstairs until six-thirty or so, do you, Will?"

"You've got me pretty well trained now," Will replied, raising his eyebrows behind her back. "Once in a while I sleep a bit later. If I do, Aunt Nettie rings her cowbell to wake me up, don't you?"

They both laughed. Maggie managed a smile. They'd been up for hours, waiting for her. This was not going to be a lazy Christmas vacation lying in bed.

Aunt Nettie picked up the last cookie from the plate in the center of the table. "We mustn't gobble all of Maggie's cookies. They'll be wonderful refreshments for my party."

"Your party?" Will turned around from the bowl he was stirring. "What party?"

"You just finish those eggs, Will, and I'll tell you both. I wasn't sure about it, but with the two of you here to help, well, I think it'll be fine. And, after all, it's my turn. I can't very well not have it this year, can I?"

The kitchen was silent for a moment.

"What can I do, Will?" Maggie asked.

"Why don't you put plates on the table," he said. "I already have bread warming in the oven. You remember Borealis, the bakery you liked when you were here last summer? I got a loaf of their onion rye yesterday, so it's still fresh. You could get that out and slice it."

"Yum!" Maggie complied, easily remembering where everything was in the kitchen. She had butter and a board of warm sliced bread on the table before Will served the omelets.

"Delicious, Will," said Aunt Nettie. "Maggie should come to visit more often. Our breakfasts aren't this elegant every day."

"That's because every morning you ask for oatmeal with blueberries," said Will, a bit tartly. "If you'd like eggs some days, I'd be happy to cook eggs."

Aunt Nettie only ate a little of her omelet, Maggie noted, but she did eat a slice of bread and butter. Wonderful fresh bread, as she'd remembered. She had two pieces, and found it hard to resist taking a third. So she didn't.

As soon as they'd cleared the plates and refilled the coffee mugs (for Will and his aunt) and the cola glass (for Maggie), Will sat back down.

"Now, Aunt Nettie. What's this about a party?"

"Every year the girls and I have a little Christmas gathering, just ourselves, before any family gatherings any of us might have. We take turns being hostess. And this is my year." Aunt Nettie turned to Maggie. "It's not a fancy shindig. And it's gotten smaller every year, sadly. This year, of course, we'll be missing Susan."

Last summer Susan Newall's death had set off a chain of events that had led to a murder, and to Aunt Nettie's stroke. But the death of her friend had been the hardest part for Aunt Nettie.

"Our Christmas party's a tradition with us, and I wouldn't like it to end when it's my time to pour the wine and put out nice things to eat." She looked from Maggie to Will and then back to Maggie again. "Friends are so important, and old friends are the most important of all, especially when you don't know how much time you'll have with them."

"Who are 'the girls'?" asked Maggie.

Will answered. "Aunt Nettie, you mean the friends you used to go out to dinner with sometimes, or to the movies? The ones you grew up with here in Waymouth."

"We did a great deal more than that together over the years," Aunt Nettie said. "We shared our lives in ways you wouldn't understand. But only four of us are left now. Ruth Weston and Betty Hoskins—they're sisters, Maggie, and they live together. Betty's doing poorly, but I'd hope Ruth could still bring her. And Doreen Strait. You've met her son, Nicky, who's a state trooper. Doreen's mother, Mary, used to be one of our group, but she was sickly, and Doreen took care of her for years, and brought her to our gatherings, so when Mary died we kept including Doreen. She's the youngest of us." Aunt Nettie counted on her fingers. "So it would be three people coming, to share a little wine or tea and maybe a few of these nice cookies. Perhaps we could get a box of that fancy ribbon candy or make plates of little tea sandwiches. The kind with the crusts cut off that are so elegant? I love those. And they're easy to eat when you've got dentures, too."

Will pushed his chair back a little.

Maggie avoided looking at him. "We'd be happy to help you host your party, Aunt Nettie. It sounds like fun. And the tree will be up soon, and the house decorated so everything looks very Christmassy. When did you have in mind?"

Aunt Nettie hesitated. "We can't wait too long. Ruth and Betty often have family coming to visit over the holidays and we'd want the party before then. What about two days from now, at about four in the afternoon? Will that give you two enough time to get the tree ready and do the shopping?"

Will nodded. "Two days it is. Call your friends and invite them and write up a menu. We'll take care of the food and drinks. You don't have to worry about anything, Aunt Nettie."

"Thank you. So much." Aunt Nettie looked from Will to Maggie and back again. "It's going to be the best Christmas this old house has had in years. I just feel it."

4 **Gathering Christmas Greens.** 1870 black-and-white wood engraving for *Harper's Weekly* by Felix Octavius Carr Darley (1822–1888). Darley was a well-known nineteenth-century illustrator and artist. He was the first illustrator of Washington Irving's "The Legend of Sleepy Hollow," illustrated James Fenimore Cooper's works, and worked for Edgar Allan Poe's journal, *The Stylus*. This illustration shows several men pulling a cut Christmas tree toward a horse-cart already loaded with trees and greens. 9 x 12 inches. Price: $70.

AN HOUR AFTER breakfast they were headed north along a lightly traveled road, a two-person saw, ropes, and a sled in the trunk of Aunt Nettie's small blue car.

"How far is Nick's house from town?" asked Maggie. They'd briefly discussed taking Maggie's van, until Will had seen that the back was still packed with the tables, racks, table covers, and portable wire walls she'd used at her last antiques show.

"It seemed such a pain to unpack all that stuff," Maggie admitted. "And I knew I was heading into snow country. They say it's good to weigh down your rear end so you don't skid."

Will glanced at her rear end admiringly. "I'd say there's just the right amount there," he commented with a straight face, giving her a swat on the mentioned area before she reached over and lightly punched his arm. "Nick lives a couple of miles north of here."

"We weren't going to get a twenty-foot tree anyway, were we?" Maggie asked, pretending to ignore him. "The living room isn't that big."

"No. Especially if we're going to leave room for company. And presents. Santa might visit, you know, so we should leave space under the tree."

"So. How much land does Nick have?"

"I'm not sure. He's lived in the same place his whole life. They don't farm it themselves anymore, the way his grandparents did, but they lease a couple of fields out to a neighbor for haying."

"'They'? I didn't know Nick was married," said Maggie.

"He's not," said Will. "Hasn't been in years. He lives with his mother, Aunt Nettie's friend Doreen, and his daughter, Zelda." He shot a sideways look at her. "He's a single parent. His wife left Zelda with him after they'd only been married a few months."

"I never knew that," said Maggie. She'd met Nick several times, and knew he was Will's closest friend in Maine. No one ever mentioned he had a daughter.

"Guess it never came up. Every time you've met Nick he's been investigating a murder. Not exactly on-the-job conversation."

"So his mother helps him take care of Zelda."

"Yup. Always has. She was a nurse, like her mother before her, but gave it up to stay home with Zelda so Nick could go to college and become a state trooper."

"And he never married again? I'm surprised. He's a good-looking guy."

"I never noticed. Besides, marriage takes more than good looks."

"Usually divorced guys with young children remarry pretty fast."

"I don't know about that. But come to think of it, I don't remember Nick's ever dating anyone after Emily." He reached over and patted Maggie's leg. "Never found the right girl, I guess. Or maybe he's been too busy between his job and his family to look very hard. He and his mom are pretty close. And from what I hear, Zelda's been a bit of a handful recently. He can use all the help he can get."

"How old is she?"

"Seventeen, eighteen. Senior in high school. Old enough to give Nick headaches."

What kind of headaches? Typical teenage-angst headaches? Drug or alcohol or boyfriend problems? Maggie wanted to ask. But single parents with problems? Probably on the "too sensitive to discuss" list now. Before she could figure out a way to bring the subject up delicately, Will turned into a narrow side road that hadn't been well plowed.

"Nick's probably working today, and Zelda'll be at school. His mom might be in the house, but Nick told her we'd be by. We'll park by the barn and take off for the woods. He said to take any tree we wanted." Will parked the car in a wide plowed area along the ell, the series of small connected rooms between the barn and the small farmhouse. "Here we are."

He tied the saw onto the sled and picked up the sled's rope.

"Where's the path?"

He grinned. "You're in Maine, m'dear. We'll make our own path. Not to worry. We don't have to go far." He pointed past the barn at trees that edged an expanse of white. "The snow in the field may be over the top of your boots, but once we get into the woods it won't be as deep."

Maggie turned her coat's collar up and tied her scarf tighter. "It's cold."

"The trees'll block most of the gusts in the woods. Let's go, city girl!" He smiled down at her. "I'll go first with the sled to break a trail."

Maggie'd imagined a romantic walk along paths lined with snow-covered pine trees. Instead, she followed Will, slogging through knee-to-thigh-high snow drifts, getting colder and wetter at every step.

She was no wimp, she kept telling herself. But the snow was deeper than the top of the boots she'd thought perfectly adequate for a walk in the country. Plus, although she was following in Will's larger footsteps, she was beginning to breathe heavily. Crossing an uneven field in knee-high snow wasn't easy.

She focused on the woods. There'd be less snow in the woods. She wasn't going to let on she was having trouble just walking across a field.

"Almost there!" he cheerfully called to her over his shoulder.

Thank goodness, she thought. Her nose was dripping, her face felt as sweaty as though she'd run a marathon, her hands were frozen in their gloves, and her feet were already sloshing in the melted snow inside her boots.

When Will finally stopped, she took a deep breath. True, the air was clear and smelled of pine, and the sky was clear Parrish blue, the color named after the artist Maxfield Parrish, who'd used it so lavishly.

But it required all her energy to focus on the positives and not on her frozen feet and hands and the burning in her chest and thighs.

Will looked down at her. "Those drifts were pretty deep, even with me opening a path. Next time we go for a walk we should wear snowshoes."

Next time? "I'm fine. Just need to catch my breath a little."

"I can see that." Will was clearly trying not to laugh. "Luckily, there are a lot of trees not far from here."

"Good!"

He bent down and untied the saw on the sled. "Let's leave the sled here. When we find our tree we'll carry it back this far and then put it on the sled to pull it over the field."

"How much further are the trees?"

"These," Will gestured at the woods in front of them and to the sides, "are trees."

"I mean—where are the trees we're going to cut?"

"Oh? You meant *those* trees," Will teased. "True, most of these are a little high for the living room." He looked up at the thirty- to fifty-foot pines surrounding them. "These are the old-timers. Been here for decades. We're probably looking for one about, oh, ten years old. We can trim the branches, here or at home, if the shape isn't quite right, or we need to top it, or take a few inches off the bottom to fit in Aunt Netttie's old Christmas tree stand."

"Any other lessons? Before I freeze to death?"

"Well, I'm about six feet tall, so I'd say a tree a foot or so taller than I am would leave space for a stand at the bottom and a star at the top. How does that sound?"

"As though you're ordering a suit or a car. I think we're better off just walking and seeing if we can find a tree we like, no matter how tall or short or wide or narrow it is. One that has personality."

"Okay. Personality. And a little over six feet tall."

"So—onward! Now," ordered Maggie. This could be is a test for our possible future life together, she thought as they started walking. Can we even agree on choosing a Christmas tree?

"When I was growing up in New Jersey I remember reading books about people cutting their own Christmas trees," Maggie said, determined to let Will know she was enjoying what he'd planned. "I always envied them. It sounded so traditional."

"Then I'm glad we're doing this. Now you can cross it off your bucket list. I'll admit I've only done it a half dozen times myself, when I've been in Maine for Christmas. When I lived in Buffalo we used to buy our tree at a lot, like you probably did."

We. That would have been Will and his wife. The wife he'd loved so much. The wife who had died because of an ectopic pregnancy.

They were silent long enough so they knew that's what they were both thinking of. There was no way they were going to avoid their pasts, and their previous marriages. Christmas itself was entwined with memories.

"If we cut extra branches, we could use them to decorate the tops of the kitchen cabinets," Maggie said. "Or make a centerpiece for Aunt Nettie's party. You can't have too many pine boughs around during the holidays."

"You and Aunt Nettie can be in charge of decorating. I volunteer to put the lights on the tree."

"Good. I hate having to untangle them and check all the bulbs and then make sure they're distributed artistically on the tree. Tree lights are all yours!"

The trees in the woods were free spirits. They hadn't been raised on a Christmas tree farm with plenty of space to spread their branches. None were perfect cone shapes. Branches had been trimmed by deer, slanted by storms, and pushed downward by heavy snows. In areas the sun reached, many had grown together, their branches woven between them into random paths for squirrels and birds.

"We're probably going to put the tree in the corner of the living room," said Maggie, wondering if they'd ever find a tree that was suitable. "So we only need one with branches good enough to decorate on one or two sides."

"You're probably right," agreed Will reluctantly. "It doesn't have to be perfect."

A little further in, highlighted by a beam of sunlight, they found the tree they'd been looking for.

It was a smidgen taller than Will, and its branches weren't too wide. One side had hardly any branches at all. And in one place its trunk made a short twist sideways before turning skyward again.

"I love it," Maggie declared. "It has personality. And," she added practically, "it won't need much trimming."

They hunkered down on each end of the two-person crosscut saw and began moving it rhythmically back and forth through the pine more easily than Maggie had anticipated. She and Will worked as well together sawing as they did setting up an antiques show booth.

Even adding a few lower branches from a nearby tree to use for decorating, it didn't take long to get both the tree and the extra boughs to the sled, and then to the car.

As they were tying the trunk down over the tree a trim gray-haired woman wearing jeans, L.L. Bean boots, and a long knitted scarf over her sweater came out of the farmhouse to join them.

"Will! Good to see you! And this must be the much-spoken-of Maggie."

"It is," Will agreed. "Maggie, meet Nick's mom, Mrs. Strait."

"Will, at this point in life you might as well call me Doreen, same as your aunt Nettie does. I've known you practically your whole life. Nettie called to invite me to the girls' Christmas party. Thank you both for helping her to host this year. It means a lot to her. To all of us, really."

"It's not a problem, Mrs. Strait. Um, Doreen. She just told us about it this morning, or we could have planned it earlier."

"If I can bring anything, you let me know."

"I think Aunt Nettie has it all figured out already. But thanks. And thank you and Nick for letting us have one of your trees. Maggie'd never cut her own Christmas tree before."

"It was fun, Mrs. Strait. Cold, but fun."

"Doreen, please. Glad you enjoyed it. Wish Zelda felt that way. She did when she was little. Guess if you've been doing something all your life it's more a chore than a privilege. I think Nick's going to get after her tonight to get ours cut. Or more likely, he'll do it himself."

"Teenagers, Doreen." Will shook his head in understanding.

Will had spent years teaching high school. Maggie worked with college students, but he probably knew at least as much about teenagers as she did.

"Don't I just know it. If he'd let her take the saw and go out to choose a tree with Jon Snow, the young man she's sweet on, why then she'd be out there as excited as she was when she was six. But no, Nick's told her she can't even see Jon, so she won't let him see her happy about anything." Doreen shook her head. "Nick's stricter than he needs to be, but she's his baby girl. And Zelda's not at an age when she wants to listen to her daddy. Wish I remembered how old Nick was when he got sensible again. I suspect it was after Zelda was born, more's the pity. Anyway, wanted to say Merry Christmas to the both of you, and thank you for helping Nettie host the party." Doreen reached over and took Maggie's hand in hers. "Thank you, too, for sharing your time with Will with us old ladies."

"We'll see you in two days, then," said Will.

"You most definitely will," Doreen said and waved, heading back to her house.

"Merry Christmas!" Maggie called after her. She turned to Will. "Sounds as though Nick has a problem with Zelda's boyfriend."

"I told you. Zelda's been a challenge recently."

But her grandmother hadn't made it sound as though the problem was only Zelda, Maggie thought. Fathers and daughters… Maybe Nick was being a little overprotective. Teenage years weren't easy for anyone.

She settled back and enjoyed the ride. Thank goodness she wasn't adopting a teenager. She'd have a few years to get used to motherhood first.

5 **Christmas Out Of Doors.** Winslow Homer wood engraving for *Harper's Weekly*, December 25, 1858. One of Homer's illustrations showing disparities in American culture. On a snowy city street corner two drunks hold each other up, a boy with a shovel asks for work, and an old woman looks troubled. Above them, in a private home, though a wreath-decorated window, two wealthier women are celebrating Christmas. 5.75 x 9.15 inches. Price: $225.

THE REST of the day sped by. Aunt Nettie happily announced that all three of her friends had accepted her invitation, and she refused to take her after-lunch nap until they'd installed the tree in the living room and made sure it fit in the corner.

The small room was going to be very full. But after all, it was Christmas. The more the merrier.

The tree needed to "relax" after coming inside, so although Aunt Nettie looked expectantly at the boxes of ornaments and lights Will brought downstairs, she handed Maggie a list of what they'd need from the grocery store for her party, and agreed to lie down while Will and Maggie did errands.

Maggie left her soaking boots inside to dry and wore her sneakers on this trip, assured that the parking lots would be plowed. "I'm glad Aunt Nettie is going to have her party. She seems so excited about it."

"I don't mind her inviting her friends to the house. I only wish she'd talked to me about it before you got here. I'd made plans for us, and now we're planning around her."

"Doreen Strait seemed excited about the party, too. I guess it really is a tradition with them."

"Tradition or not. She should have talked to me before you got here." Will sighed. "But I should try to get Aunt Nettie out more to see her friends. She hasn't socialized much since I've been here."

"I suspect you haven't done much of that either. It's tough on both of you."

Will glanced at her. "Not easy. But it's the way life is now. This fall I've kept busy getting the house set up. Now that's done, I'm hoping to have new projects to keep me amused."

"Oh?"

"For one thing, I'm going to try selling my antiques on-line. Maybe eBay. That's what I'm setting up in Aunt Nettie's old bedroom upstairs."

"Really? We've talked about that before," said Maggie. "We didn't think it would work well for either of our specialties. Prints, because they don't show well on-line, and kitchen and fireplace tools because of their shipping weight."

"True. But neither of us has actually tried it, and my situation is different now. I can't travel to shows, and there's a limit to how much I can sell locally. So I decided I'd test our assumptions; see if on-line could work. I have the inventory. I have the time. Might as well give it a try."

Maggie nodded. "Why not?"

"I've got a camera and tripod set up, and basic mailing supplies. I'm going to let people on my customer list know where to find me on-line, and then begin listing my smaller, less expensive pieces, after the first of the year. Start slowly. Give it six months. Maybe a year. If it doesn't work, I should know by then. If it does work, great. The best part is, I can do it on my own time, while Aunt Nettie is napping, or late at night." The car in front of them pulled over to check out the wreaths and kissing balls being sold by a vendor on the side of the road, the way blueberries were sold in late July. "In today's world we have to keep trying new ways to reach customers. Like your putting your antique prints in Gussie's new shop on Cape Cod."

"I'm still excited about that. The shop looks wonderful. I took a lot of prints there Thanksgiving week. Gussie's already sold a couple of thousand dollars' worth. Of course, she gets a percentage. But those are prints I wouldn't have sold otherwise. We're both pleased."

"How often will you have to go to the Cape to change inventory?"

"We haven't decided yet. She and Jim are taking a delayed

honeymoon cruise in January and then plan to relax and organize their new house, so after Christmas she's going to close the shop until March. I'm planning to take a couple of days during spring break at the college to drive up to visit and add more botanicals and other spring prints."

"Here we are." Will turned into the busy Hannaford Supermarket parking lot, and for the next hour the most serious discussion they had was deciding which cheeses would be best for the fondue Maggie suggested she make for dinner (a combination of Swiss and Gruyere) and how many loaves of thin-sliced bread they'd need for Aunt Nettie's tea sandwiches.

Maggie had a sudden memory of having tea at Lord & Taylor's Bird Cage Room as a child and eating tea sandwiches filled with colored cream cheese and chopped olives. And egg salad. And liver pâté. Will watched with amusement as she got more and more excited about the party, looking at Aunt Nettie's list, calling on her memory, and filling the cart.

"Maybe we could have crabmeat sandwiches, too. Or shrimp?" she said, lingering over the seafood section. "How wonderful to be able to get fresh fish at the local grocery."

"Why don't we just have a bowl of shrimp?" Will asked. "Not everything has to be a sandwich, does it? It doesn't matter if we have too much. We can eat the leftovers."

Maggie agreed. "A bowl of shrimp, then. And maybe four or five kinds of sandwiches. Oh—and one of them has to be cucumber, of course!"

"Of course," said Will, trying to keep a straight face. "I am now seeing a side of Maggie Summer I never dreamed of. Cucumber sandwiches?"

"With a touch of red onion," she added, ignoring his gibe. "And black pepper, of course. And mayonnaise."

The cart load was growing higher.

"You realize I'm an unemployed man," teased Will.

"Oh, let me do this. My house gift for Aunt Nettie," said Maggie.

"Don't worry. It's not a problem," said Will. "Although don't plan on doing this every day."

"Of course not. We'll be eating oatmeal three times a day from now on." She reached up and kissed him. "With blueberries. I remember. You said Aunt Nettie liked that." Several people walking by smiled, wheeling their carts around them.

"Maggie! This is a supermarket." Will blushed slightly behind his beard.

"Really? I hadn't noticed."

Maggie checked Aunt Nettie's list one more time. "I think that's it. All we have to do is decorate the tree and the house, and make the sandwiches right before the party, put Christmas music on in the background, and we'll be set."

Will checked the time. "Aunt Nettie will be waking up, and I can get the lights on the tree while you cut up the bread and grate the cheese. I'm looking forward to your fondue. As I remember, the tradition is that if you drop a piece of bread in the fondue you get a kiss. Right?"

"You won't even have to drop the bread," Maggie assured him, and gave him a preview.

6 | **The Christmas-Tree.** Wood engraving by Winslow Homer for *Harper's Weekly*, December 25, 1858. (Companion to print at beginning of Chapter 5.) Scene in an elegant home where a dozen children are playing around the Christmas tree with a drum, doll, and bugle. Father holds up more gifts for them. Seven adults watch and smile, enjoying the scene. 5.75 x 9.15 inches. Price: $225.

DECORATING the tree took longer than Maggie had anticipated. Each ornament had to be placed in the best spot, and almost every ornament had its own history to be recalled and shared. But by noon the next day Aunt Nettie declared it "Perfect!"

And it was. Maggie admitted to herself that she hadn't cared as much about a tree since she'd been a child. That caring made the tree, and the holiday itself, special.

The extra pine branches they'd brought back from the woods were now on the tops of cabinets and around the banister to the second floor; candy canes filled glasses on the tables; and red candles stood festively in silver candlesticks on the living room mantel. The fireplace was newly stacked with wood, ready to light. All was ready for Aunt Nettie's party except the food, and they had twenty-four hours to prepare that.

"For lunch we can heat the rest of the fondue and serve it like Welsh rarebit, on toast," suggested Maggie. The fondue had been delicious, but it would be good to finish what was left before they started cooking again.

"Today while you're taking your nap, Aunt Nettie, Maggie and I are going out for a drive. Just to get a little fresh air. We won't be gone long."

"Take your time. I'm a little weary from decorating the tree," Aunt Nettie agreed. "Why don't you stop and get those good fried scallops and haddock we like so much for dinner."

"Good idea. And when I get home I'll make a salad to go with them," Will promised. "Take it easy until we get back. Save your strength for your party tomorrow."

After Aunt Nettie was safely nestled beneath her quilts, Maggie and Will were off.

"To get fresh air?" Maggie asked quizzically.

"Actually, I wanted to show you something. Get your opinion about an idea I have."

"You know I seldom keep my opinions to myself." Whatever he was going to show her, Maggie had the feeling it was important. She braced herself a little. Should she bring up her adoption plans? Or wait until he asked about them? Everything was going well so far. True, they hadn't discussed any sort of mutual future. But they had plenty of time. And every day they spent together was a gift.

Will turned toward Waymouth's harbor and began slowing down.

"I remember this street," Maggie said. "The first summer I came to Maine you brought me here, to Walter English's Antiques Mall."

She'd been both intrigued and amused by the three-story Victorian house crammed with a motley collection of antiques. The local auctioneer also did appraisals there and met prospective clients for his auction house.

"I thought you'd remember it." He stopped the car in front of the house. "We didn't go here last summer because Walter'd closed it down. The roof leaked, and the dealers who'd rented space there weren't making enough sales. A lot of them hadn't renewed their contracts. Walter decided to concentrate on his auction business."

"Which explains the FOR SALE sign in front now."

"Exactly."

They sat for a couple of minutes.

"And you brought me here because..."

He turned toward her. "I'm thinking of buying the place."

Thoughts whirled through Maggie's head. Was he thinking of living here someday? Was this part of the marriage proposal he'd made in October? Or was he thinking of running an antiques mall himself? Did he want her business advice, or her personal thoughts? How should she react? How serious was he?

"Why? What would you do with it?" she asked cautiously.

"Obviously it needs a lot of work. But I think it could be turned into an upscale antiques mall."

An antiques mall. Not a home. Half of her felt relieved, and yet somehow, the other half was disappointed. It was a grand old house. Fixed up, it would be a wonderful place to raise a family. But realistically, it was too big. Hadn't there been about eight bedrooms on the second floor alone? And she remembered the dark, cluttered hallways and high ceilings. "You're thinking of running an antiques mall? Being a landlord?" Maggie said quietly.

"It needs a new roof, new wiring, and new paint, and most of the windows need to be replaced. It was too hot in the summer, as you may remember, and to make it a year-'round business it would need to be heated better in the winter."

Maggie watched Will as he talked. He was excited about the idea, and wanted her approval. But why should her approval matter?

"I don't want to be a downer. And I don't know how much Walter English is asking. But those improvements will cost a lot," she pointed out. "The last antiques mall failed. Plus, you've said you have to spend most of your time with Aunt Nettie. You can't be here, too."

"All that's true. But I want to reinvest the money I got from selling my house in Buffalo. And the mall I have in mind isn't like Walter's. I'm thinking early American furniture and fine art and maybe a silver or jewelry dealer. Perhaps a place people could bring their antiques to be appraised or restored. Like a group of upscale shops. I could do a lot of the building myself, and you remember I have cousins in the construction business. I could probably work a deal with Rachel's husband to have his guys do the electrical work, and my cousin Giles and his son have already agreed to work for me evenings and weekends, off the books, if I buy the place."

"You're serious about this."

"I am. But I wanted to know what you thought before I made an offer."

Maggie hesitated. "It sounds exciting. You've thought it over, and you know the area and dealers and potential customers better than I do. But it's a huge investment, Will. Not only of money, but of time.

You already have so much to do. You're taking care of Aunt Nettie and her house. You're going to try on-line sales. And this place ..." Maggie looked at the old house towering over them. "It needs a lot of care. It could eat up all you have and leave you with nothing."

"Or it could give me something for myself, outside of Aunt Nettie's little house."

Maggie suddenly saw it through those eyes.

"And if the antiques mall didn't work out, you'd have fixed up a grand old house and would be able to turn it over."

"I suppose that's true," said Will. "But I'm not ready to give up on it before I've started." He put one of his hands on hers. "Unless you hate it. Unless you really think it's a waste of time and you don't like the idea at all."

Maggie felt pushed into a corner. "I've never exhibited in a mall, Will. You have. You know much more than I do about this. And you've already checked out the house and what needs to be done to it. I only saw it once, two years ago. It's your project. If this is what you want to do, then do it. Don't ask me to make your decision for you."

"I'd like you to see the inside of the house again. I was so excited at telling you about the place I've probably rushed you. Let me call the real estate agent and we can walk through together, after the party. Okay?"

"If you'd like me to." Maggie squeezed his hand. "I remember liking the house. But I'm no expert on Victorian home repairs."

"That's my world. I just want to know if you can imagine it transformed into the kind of mall I'm talking about. You have an eye for that sort of thing. You're better at setting up booths at antiques shows than I am, and here I'm thinking of setting up a whole house."

"I promise I'll look at the house and give you my opinion," Maggie said. "But only because you're right about one thing. I am better at setting up booths than you are!"

Will bent over and kissed her. And then kissed her again.

While Maggie wondered: what was it about this house Will wasn't telling her?

7 **Christmas Belles.** Winslow Homer black-and-white wood engraving published in *Harper's Weekly*, January 2, 1869. One of only three Homer engravings that included what is believed to be a self-portrait. Depicts mustached man (probably Homer) driving a sleigh in which five elegantly dressed women are riding; another sleigh pulled by three horses is in the background. The letters "WH" are on the side of the sleigh. 9 x 13.5 inches. Price: $300.

"DOREEN'S GOING to come with Ruth and Betty," Aunt Nettie announced, as she put down the phone an hour before her guests were due to arrive. "Ruth needs her help with Betty. And they'll want to use our ramp to the back door, Will, because Betty uses a wheelchair or walker. Could you move my car and Maggie's van out of the driveway?"

"Not a problem," he said, reaching to get his coat as Maggie finished cutting the tea sandwiches into triangles.

"Those look absolutely elegant, Maggie," said Aunt Nettie. She'd loved the idea of the red and green–colored cream cheese and the cucumber sandwiches. "And crabmeat! Oh, this is going to be so special! I'd always just made tuna and egg salad. And a whole bowl of shrimp! Plus your delicious cookies. You know, none of us girls do much baking anymore. Fruit pies in the summertime, of course, or muffins. But cookies take so much time and energy."

Maggie secretly agreed, but she loved to make them. And inventing the tea sandwiches had been fun, too, although she'd notice the chopped-liver pâté hadn't stirred any enthusiasm from Aunt Nettie.

"So, you said Ruth and Betty are sisters. Have they always lived together?"

"Not always. Ruth's husband died in a horrible car accident when they'd only been married about twelve years. Betty was living in Boston then. After that she moved back home to live with Ruth. They raised their children together."

"And Betty's the one who isn't well."

"I'm afraid she's been going downhill for a while now. She's got that awful Alzheimer's; some days her mind's with you, and other days not so much. Plus, she's had diabetes for years. She won't be eating any of your cookies, I'm afraid, but she'll enjoy the shrimp and Ruth will watch out for her."

"That must be hard on Ruth."

"It is. But for the past couple of years they've had Carrie Folk come in days to care for Betty. Carrie's a gentle soul who's done private nursing in town for years. She helps with the housekeeping, too, and keeps Betty company and makes sure she's on her diet and checks her sugar levels and on the bad days can give her a sedative, so Ruth can go to her church meetings and her garden club and book group and such. Ruth takes over when Carrie goes home. It seems to work for them all."

"I'm glad." Until now she'd never thought about how much was involved in assuring that older people had the care they needed.

Will came back in, brushing snowflakes off his beard and coat. "It's snowing again. Just a little, so I don't think it'll bother your friends, Aunt Nettie, but I'll make sure the path to the back ramp is clear." He reached over and before Aunt Nettie could bat his hand away he'd liberated two cookies from the platter she'd been arranging.

"Get out of here! Those are for my guests!"

He grinned and headed for the back door.

"I think we have everything set," Maggie said. "I'll take the platters of food into the living room. Water is heating for tea, coffee is made, and Will and I will stay out of your way."

"Everyone will want to meet you," Aunt Nettie said, "So don't you worry about hiding. You're part of the family now."

Maggie smiled tightly as she picked up a heaping plate of sandwiches and carried it into the living room. Part of the family? Not exactly. Not yet. Maybe not ever. But maybe for the purposes of this afternoon.

"Aunt Nettie! Your guests are here!" Will's voice and the back door opening signaled the start of the gathering.

Maggie didn't have to be introduced to figure out who the guests were, but Aunt Nettie explained she was "Will's special friend," before anyone sat down.

She'd already met Doreen Strait, the youngest of the three by at least twenty years. Today Doreen was wearing a red Christmas sweater decorated with a green Christmas tree with sequin lights. She had her arm around the waist of a frail woman with short, white hair who had to be the sickly Betty. Her skin was as pale and thin as the paper of Maggie's oldest prints, although, like the prints, her hands and face were marked by a few small brown age spots. Her long brown wool skirt and sweater were well made, but hung on her as though her slight body was gradually disappearing into their folds.

Her sister, Ruth, on the other hand, stood tall and straight. She held Betty's other arm comfortably, as though helping her sister was a natural function. Betty leaned slightly in her direction, and although physically the two women did not look alike (Ruth was not only taller but heavier, with darker hair, which she wore pinned up) it was clear their relationship was close.

"Which chair would Betty be most comfortable in?" Will asked.

"The higher one." Ruth pointed to the armchair with a padded seat cushion. "I'll sit next to her."

"High chairs are for toddlers," Betty declared. "I'm not a toddler."

"Of course you're not," her sister assured her, helping her down into the designated seat. "But it's easier for you to get up if the chair seat isn't too low."

Will hung up the ladies' coats while Maggie added a bowl of shrimp and plates and napkins next to the sandwiches and cookies already on the coffee table.

Aunt Nettie took over at that point. "Maggie's made all these delicious cookies and sandwiches. Will, maybe you can put folding tables next to our chairs."

"That would be lovely," said Ruth, and Will went to a closet by the back door to get the folding tables while Maggie listened to drink orders. To her surprise, everyone decided to have wine. She turned off the hot water and coffee in the kitchen.

"Is this a picnic?" asked Betty, looking around. "It smells like a picnic."

"The Christmas tree and all the pine boughs do smell like the woods," said Ruth, without missing a beat. "Your tree looks lovely, Nettie. We're planning to put ours up tomorrow, aren't we, Betty?"

"I love decorating the tree," said Betty. "Papa always lets me put the star on the top because I'm the youngest."

"I'm so glad your party was this afternoon," Ruth added. "Carrie asked for the day off to go to a doctor's appointment, so we would have been sitting at home. Instead we're seeing everyone, and meeting Maggie, whom we've heard so much about."

Will had put up the tray tables while Maggie was passing out glasses of wine.

"A toast. To us. To dear Susan. And to our other friends with us in memory," said Aunt Nettie, raising her glass. "May we remember the good times, forget the bad, and always be there for each other. Merry Christmas!"

"Merry Christmas!" echoed the other three.

Maggie watched from the kitchen doorway. This toast, or one very similar to it, had probably been made on many other Christmases. How would it feel to have the same friends for most of your life?

She didn't have much time for contemplation.

"Maggie, would you mind helping us? We're going to pretend we're lazy old women today since you and Will are here. Would you fill our plates for us?" Aunt Nettie asked.

"Of course," Maggie answered. "Shall I give you all a taste of everything?"

Nods all around assured her that, as Doreen added, "For our first plate!" that would be fine, and Maggie went to work.

"Are your children coming for the holidays?" Doreen asked Ruth.

"We're going to have a houseful," said Ruth. "Betty's daughter Miranda is coming with Joan, of course, but they're staying at the Inn, aren't they, Betty?"

Betty nodded. "They wouldn't let the baby Jesus be born at the inn, you know."

"My older children can't make it, but Brian and Jenny are flying in from Philadelphia with the new baby. I'm dying to see my newest grandson."

Doreen smiled. "How wonderful to have a baby coming for Christmas."

"It is, isn't it? They named him Jonas, you know." Ruth glanced at her left hand, where she wore a narrow wedding band.

Wasn't it Ruth that Aunt Nettie had said lost her husband in a car accident years ago?

"Jonas is very handsome. He should be here to see his baby," said Betty. "When will he be here?"

"You did a wonderful job with these sandwiches, Maggie. The cucumber ones are delicious," said Doreen, adding two more to her plate.

"Who's Maggie? Is she one of Jonas's friends?" said Betty.

"Maggie's Will's friend," said Ruth. "She made these sandwiches and cookies for us."

While Doreen and Ruth had already made major inroads on their plates of food, Betty had hardly taken a bite. She was still holding her glass of wine, looking at it as though she wasn't quite sure what to do with it. As Maggie watched, Ruth reached over, took the glass out of Betty's hand, and handed Betty a crabmeat sandwich.

"And aren't the cream cheese and olive sandwiches pretty?" added Aunt Nettie. "I've always liked the combination of cream cheese and olive but haven't had it in years. And I never thought of coloring the cream cheese. Maggie here is real creative. And what about you, Doreen? Any company for the holidays?"

"Not me. I'm just hoping no one will be murdered, so Nick'll be able to get the day off. Working the homicide unit, you never know. He's put in for extra shifts the week after Christmas, hoping he can get the day itself free. If he's home, maybe Zelda will stay to home, too, and not go running off with her friends the way she sometimes does. I'd like to have her home for a good last Christmas before she graduates."

"Before I forget, everyone, Betty and I are going to have a Christmas Eve party, aren't we, Betty?"

Betty looked up, as though seeing the tree for the first time. "It's Christmastime!"

"Exactly," Ruth continued. "We've decided that with little Jonas visiting, we'd like to be especially festive this year. So all of you are invited." Ruth raised her voice. "Will and Maggie, you two hiding in the kitchen, you're included. And when you get a chance, I could use a little more wine and a few more sandwiches. Doreen, you tell Nick if he can get free, he's welcome, and of course so is Zelda."

"Don't count on either of those two," said Doreen. "Nick'll most likely be working, and Zelda always finds some reason not to party with anyone over the age of twenty. But I'll tell 'em, of course. And you can count on me to come. What time?"

"I think about four-thirty. It'll be dark by then, so all the Christmas lights in town will be on, and it can be a late afternoon cocktail party, before the carol sing. What do you think?"

"Sounds perfect," said Aunt Nettie. "But will you really serve cocktails, Ruth? I haven't had one of those in years."

"I might just do that, Nettie. In fact, now that I think about it, I may even hire a bartender," she laughed. "I want to enjoy my own party."

"We used to have the best parties, didn't we?" said Betty. "We danced and sang and everyone we knew came. Even people we didn't know came."

"I remember those parties, too. We did have fun," said Aunt Nettie.

"Will we get that band from over to Bath to play? Davy Jones and His Boys? Mary and I like them the best."

"I don't think they'll be free this time, Betty," said Ruth, as she and Aunt Nettie exchanged glances.

Maggie had added sandwiches to Ruth's and Aunt Nettie's plates, while Will saw that Ruth's and Doreen's wineglasses had emptied more quickly than he'd anticipated and was opening another bottle of cabernet. Maggie whispered, "They're sweet. But Betty seems to be losing it."

"She seems to remember a lot, though. 'Davy Jones and His Boys'? I wonder what era that was."

"I have the feeling a lot of what she's talking about happened years ago," Maggie agreed, opening her tins of cookies to fill a new plate. The women were eating more than she'd anticipated. Doreen had helped herself and was now on her third plate of sandwiches and had checked out all Maggie's cookie varieties, too.

"Maybe," he acknowledged. "I haven't been listening that closely."

"Will? Where's that wine?" Aunt Nettie called out.

"Right here," he answered, taking the bottle he'd uncorked back with him to the living room.

Betty picked up her glass again and drank it all at once.

Will reached for it, to refill it. She looked at him and screamed. "No! Why is he here? Who let him in? Rule number-one! Rule number-one! We all promised!"

"Will, put the wine down on the table and go back to the kitchen," Aunt Nettie said calmly, as Ruth reached out and put her arms around Betty, who had scrunched down in her chair and was babbling. "We promised. We did."

"Betty, it's okay. It's okay. The man's gone. It's all over. No one's here." She helped Betty sit up straighter again, handed her the newly filled wineglass, and held it so she could sip a little. Then she opened her pocketbook, removed a bottle of pills, shook two out, and gave them to Betty, who swallowed them with more wine.

Ruth gestured to Maggie, who got her a wineglass filled with water. When Betty wasn't looking, Ruth quietly exchanged her sister's wineglass for the one with water.

"We used to go for such wonderful long walks, down by the harbor," said Aunt Nettie. "Do you remember?"

"And the movie nights. When you'd all get into two or three cars and go to the drive-in over to Brunswick," said Doreen. "Once in a while Mother'd take me with her. You all thought I was sleeping in the backseat, but I just pretended to sleep. I didn't want to miss anything you were talking about. Or that was happening on the screen."

"I'll bet what we were talking about was more interesting!" said Aunt Nettie.

"It surely was," agreed Doreen. "But I never told Mother that. She'd have sent me to my room for months if she'd known I was listening. I got half my education at those drive-in movies!"

"We'd eat popcorn and clam rolls and laugh," said Ruth, as calm as though nothing had happened a few minutes before. "I remember." She looked around the room. "There were more of us then."

"There were. And we did have fun," agreed Aunt Nettie. "I don't know what I would have done when Jonas died, if it hadn't been for our group."

"That was one of the hard times. But we pulled together and got through it. And the other times, too." Aunt Nettie looked around the room. "And now there are only four of us left. Four of us who remember."

Maggie stood at the door and listened, as the little girl Doreen had done years before in the backseat of a car at a drive-in.

She watched as they all looked at Betty, who was happily, obliviously, finishing the wineglass full of water.

8 | **Quatrain XX.** Edmund Dulac's 1930 lithograph in blues and greens of a mysterious Mideastern castle-like building. An illustration for the *Rubaiyat of Omar Khayyam*, translated by Edward Fitzgerald. New York: Doubleday. 7.5 x 9 inches. Price: $60.

"JO HEARTWOOD is going to meet Maggie and me at Walter English's old mall," explained Will the next morning. He kept glancing at the clock and was clearly rushing Aunt Nettie through her second cup of coffee. Even she had slept in a little. It was nearly nine o'clock.

But her party had been a success, and she was still reliving it. "Betty doesn't look at all well, does she," Aunt Nettie repeated for the third or fourth time. "She'll probably be the next of us to go. Although God works in mysterious ways. Gloria had a heart attack and died in her sleep when she was only sixty-two, and we thought she was the healthiest of us all at the time."

She didn't mention Betty's strange outburst when Will was in the room, and neither Will nor Maggie asked about it. Betty was confused. Sadly, her words didn't seem to warrant examination.

"Why don't I pour you another cup? You can sit in the living room and watch TV while we're out," suggested Will. "We won't be gone long."

"I don't see why Maggie has to see that old building. She saw it when it was a mall, as I remember. And my memory is fine, thank goodness. I know you've got it in your head that you might buy the place—you can't keep secrets like that from me—but if you want to start your own antiques mall, why don't you look at buildings on Route 1, where there's more traffic? A building there would be newer, and you'd have less upkeep. An old dowager Victorian like Walter's place will cost a fortune to fix up and maintain. That's why he's trying to get rid of it, Will."

"I know, Aunt Nettie. I've thought of all that. Now, where should I put your coffee?"

Will was not to be dissuaded by his aunt's logic.

Nettie settled on the living room couch with the remote control in her hand and a cup of coffee and a plate of Christmas cookies on the table in front of her. (Maggie was beginning to think she'd have to bake more if they were going to have any left on the actual holiday.)

Will handed Maggie her coat and headed her toward the door.

The snow wasn't drifting down gently, as it had most days. This morning the sky was low and gray and a curtain of snow shielded most of the river from view. Today's snow was going to accumulate more than just a cover for yesterday's two inches.

Will brushed the new snow from the car as Maggie hugged herself, wondering if the inside of the car would warm up before they got to see Will's dream house. It wasn't far. On a summer's day it might be a comfortable half hour's walk. But in this weather? No, thank you.

This time she paid closer attention to the neighborhood the house was in. The only Victorian in a block of sea captains' colonials, it was certainly visible. But it was two blocks off Route 1, and parking was limited to the street and the wide driveway, now covered with several feet of snow, leading to the barn. A local artist had an in-barn studio and gallery down the street, but other than that it was a residential block. Maggie noted a SCHOOL BUS STOP sign two houses away. It would be a nice place to raise a family. She wasn't as sure about its future as an antiques mall. It *had* failed once. Could Will afford to put most of his savings into a business with a questionable future?

It was Will's decision, she reminded herself. Not hers.

They'd talked about money before, but always in terms of her business and his business. Buying this house was the riskiest decision she'd ever seen him consider.

Will pulled up in back of a red Subaru wagon. "That's Jo's car. Let's go."

Jo Heartwood looked almost as young as one of Maggie's students. Blond, and very earnest, her smile for Will was sparkling. "I'm so glad you decided to take one more look." She turned to Maggie.

"And you must be his friend from New Jersey! Merry Christmas, and welcome to Maine. I'm Jo."

Maggie accepted her outstretched mittened hand. She'd imagined a real estate agent as someone in their forties. Or fifties. Someone with experience and know-how. How could this girl know anything about Victorian houses? And how many times *had* Will looked at this house before?

"Let's take a look, shall we? I'm afraid it's snowing hard enough that they may declare an early closing at school and I'll get a call to pick up my kids. I want you two to have as much time as possible inside."

"You have children?" Maggie blurted as she and Will followed Jo up onto the wide porch that circled two-thirds of the house. Jo looked about twenty-two. At most.

"Three, actually," said Jo. "Christa's ten, Joey's eight, and Sophie's five. Full house."

"Sounds like it," Maggie agreed, taking another look at Jo.

"Jo's husband was in the Army Reserves," said Will quietly. "He was deployed to the Middle East. Didn't make it back."

Maggie's guilt went into high gear. How could she suspect anything of an armed forces widow with three children? "I'm so sorry," she said. "I didn't know."

"No way you would," said Jo, glancing at Will. "You're here to see the house. Will shouldn't have bothered you with my problems." She punched the code in the lockbox and took out a key. The two front doors were paneled with beautiful nineteenth-century stained glass. "Will's been real nice to me the past couple of months, when I've had rough days. He's a good listener." She pulled the door open and led them inside.

"I'm glad to hear he's been helpful," said Maggie, wondering just how helpful Will had been. "I imagine with three children you have your hands full." He didn't want to be a father, but he was happy to be a good listener to someone with three young children?

"I do. But you're here to see this wonderful home. Or business," Jo added quickly. "I always think of this place as a home, but of course, it was set up as a business and that's what Will has in mind, too."

She hesitated. "The electricity is on, but the heat is turned just high enough so the pipes don't freeze. Will, you've been here so many times before. Would you like me to leave you here by yourselves for an hour or so? I could come back and lock up then."

"Thank you. I'd like that, Jo," said Will.

"Then I'll go and do my grocery shopping before they're all sold out of the kids' favorite cereal and popcorn. That always seems to happen when we get a snow day. And I have a couple of errands for Santa to do, too. See you in about an hour. If you finish before then, turn off the lights so I know you've left, and close the door." She touched him on the arm (does a businesslike realtor do that?) and left.

"She seems…nice," said Maggie.

"She is. She's a friend of my cousin Rachel's. And she's been very patient with me. I've been in and out of here for a couple of months now. Luckily, no other buyer has been as interested, so I haven't had pressure to make up my mind. But if I'm going to get any kind of business up and running by next summer I have to make an offer soon."

"You've done some serious thinking about this," Maggie said, resolving not to make any other comments about Jo unless she knew more. No matter how tempted she was. But the way Jo Heartwood had looked at Will definitely had put her on high alert.

She swallowed hard and walked into the room on the right. "I remember this place when it was crammed with antiques. It looks a lot bigger empty."

Will grinned. "Enormous, isn't it? Almost every room has a fireplace. None of them are lined so they're not safe to use now, but they'd be showcases for my fireplace and kitchen inventory. And come back to the main hall again." He pointed up. "The front staircase goes all the way to the third floor, and then a smaller staircase goes to the tower room above that."

"I remember that." Maggie smiled. "I loved that little room. Glass all around, and a great view of the harbor and the village. If I'd lived in this house that would have been my hideaway."

"All the rooms on the second and third floors on the south side have great harbor views. Walter English squeezed as many dealers as possible in here, so no one ever noticed. If each dealer had one room, we could emphasize the views."

Maggie walked down the hallway, peeking into what had been the dining room and the sitting room. "But the work these rooms will need, Will. Taking down the layers and layers of wallpaper. Removing the heavy paint on the wonderful old woodwork so you can really see it. And the size and numbers of windows are wonderful, but dealers would want even more light. The place might have to be totally rewired."

"It would. I'm thinking of starting on the first floor, and trying to get that, and the new roof, taken care of so I could open at least a few rooms by summer. The second floor could be worked on more gradually, and other dealers added later."

Maggie found herself getting more enthusiastic as they walked through the house, and Will pointed out details like the laundry chute and the dumbwaiter, both of which went all the way to the third floor. "Probably to serve the needs of a nursery," said Maggie, musing about why such things would have been installed. "I can't imagine servants being provided with a dumbwaiter."

"There are only a few closets, of course," Will pointed out. "But for a business, that isn't a problem. And I keep hoping to find a secret passageway. But so far I haven't pressed the right spot on the woodwork."

Maggie looked at him. "Of course, if the business doesn't do well…"

"If the business doesn't do well, I'll have to deal with the lack of bathrooms and closets," Will agreed. "But for now, adding shelves to meet the needs of specific dealers should be all that's necessary. Supply houses will rent display counters and cases."

"I assume you'll leave that up to the dealers you rent space to."

"Unless they pay me a premium to handle it." Will grinned.

He'd thought this out. On the third floor, Maggie went straight to the little staircase and climbed up to the crow's nest room high above Waymouth. Will followed her.

The falling snow blurred the view, making them feel as though they were inside a snow globe. Maggie turned slowly, seeing the harbor and town below her. She ended her turn in Will's arms. "I give up being practical. Buy this place if you can, Will. It's wonderful. Magical. It will be an incredible amount of work. It will eat up your time and your money. But it's a great project, and, I hope, will eventually bring in a good return. For whatever reason you want my approval, you have it."

He pulled her to him and kissed her. Softly, and deeply.

"I shall, of course, expect email and telephone updates, complete with pictures, as the work progresses," she added, as she moved out of his arms and took one last look down at the transformed town. Seen from this height, the snow cover was complete. It could have been the model for a large-folio Currier and Ives *New England Winter Scene* if it weren't for the lone lobster boat on the river strung with Christmas lights and a few cars moving on Main Street. And Currier and Ives would have added a skating pond, of course.

Waymouth, Maine. How could anything bad ever happen in a place as beautiful, as perfect, as this one?

9 **Christmas Post.** Black-and-white wood engraving by Thomas Nast (1840–1902) for cover of *Harper's Weekly*, January 4, 1879 showing a young boy with his dog in a snowstorm, putting an envelope addressed to "St. Claus, North Pole" into a United States post box. A toy store with a Christmas tree in front of it is in the background. Thomas Nast, often called "the man who invented Santa Claus," produced Christmas drawings for *Harper's* regularly from the 1860s until 1886. Although he based his "Santa" on Clement Moore's poem, he added details such as Santa's living at the North Pole and having a toy workshop, and children writing letters to Santa. Nast also popularized the Democratic donkey and created the Republican elephant, and his political cartoons helped take down Tammany Hall in New York City. 10 x 15 inches, including *Harper's Weekly: Journal of Civilization* masthead. Price: $225.

DESPITE THE SNOW, the U.S. postal carrier had made his or her appointed rounds. Aunt Nettie was opening mail at the kitchen table as Maggie and Will stomped back into the house, scattering clods of snow as they shook off their jackets and took off their boots.

"Glad you're home," she said, looking up from a pile of Christmas cards and letters. "I was beginning to worry about you two. It's really coming down out there."

"We noticed," said Will, giving Maggie a fast hug. "We were inside the house most of the time, though. I see we got a lot of cards today." He peeked over his aunt's shoulder at her collection of Christmas trees and angels and photographs of families posed with family dogs, cats, dead moose, and in one case, a newly purchased home in San Diego.

"From family, mostly," she said. "Quite a few were addressed to both of us. Do you want to look at those? I've separated them. I put your mail on the counter."

"I'll look at mine first. You go ahead and put the cards on the mantel. I'll look at them later."

"Do you need any help, Aunt Nettie?" Maggie asked.

"I'll be just fine, dear. Thank you." Aunt Nettie stood up and slowly walked with her cane toward the living room carrying a stack of cards, while Will started looking through his mail. Maggie poured herself a Diet Pepsi and then followed Aunt Nettie.

The elderly woman glanced through the cards, hesitated, and then slipped one envelope into her pocket before carefully arranging the others on the mantel among the pine boughs.

Maggie smiled to herself. Even Aunt Nettie had her secrets. Perhaps an old admirer? Or a special card she'd kept to put in her own room.

"The cards look very festive there," she commented. "You've gotten so many you'll need to find another place to put them soon."

"They do look nice, don't they," said Aunt Nettie, standing back a bit. "I always do enjoy getting Christmas cards. It's like seeing all your old friends and family at the holidays, even if they're not with you in person. Every name on a card brings back memories. At my age, what more can I ask for?"

"Now, that's not true!" said Maggie. "As long as you're still alive, you're still having experiences. Making new memories."

"You'll see, the older you get. At every age you experience life differently. When you're a child all you can think about is growing up. Every hour seems to last forever. Then you're a teenager, like Doreen's granddaughter, Zelda, full of horrible and wonderful emotions, all at the same time. You're sure no one else has ever felt the way you do. Then, all of a sudden, you're grown up. You still have hopes and dreams and all the crazy plans you had as a teenager, but now you also have responsibilities. Some people ignore the responsibilities and refuse to grow up. Some people ignore the dreams."

Maggie listened.

"Neither of those ways works in the long run. You're grown up a long time. You need those dreams to keep you focused. But the responsibilities you take on…they're what earn you your place in this world."

"Do you still have dreams, Aunt Nettie?"

"At my age, they're more like hopes. But, oh my, yes."

"What do you hope?"

Aunt Nettie paused. "I hope I'll live a bit longer, but not be in pain. I hope when my end comes it'll be quick, and I won't be a bother to anyone. And I hope I'll be around long enough to know what happens to people I care about. People who're making decisions that will make a difference to the rest of their lives."

Maggie grinned at her. "You know a lot, don't you?"

"I keep my eyes and ears open, young woman. Life would be pretty boring if I didn't. You'd be wise to do the same. And," she looked directly at Maggie, "if an old woman can be forgiven one bit of advice. Don't be foolish. You'll regret the things you didn't do, not the things you did. Now—what's that man in the kitchen going to suggest we have for lunch on this snowy day? Or is he going to leave that to us women?"

Lunch turned out to be grilled ham and Swiss sandwiches with potato chips. Will declared he'd become addicted to Cape Cod chips after his October trip to the Cape. Maggie grated carrots, cabbage, and a bit of red onion, and made coleslaw while he was grilling.

After lunch she cleaned up while Will helped Aunt Nettie settle in for her afternoon nap. She'd almost finished when she heard Will on the telephone.

Maggie couldn't hear every word, but she was pretty sure he was talking to Jo Heartwood, making an offer on the Walter English house. She crossed her fingers that it was the right thing for him to do, and that the emotions of the moment hadn't pushed her too far when she encouraged him. And that the only offer he was making to Jo was for the house.

It truly was a majestic house, full of possibilities. His possibilities.

"Offer made?"

Will had come back into the kitchen.

"I couldn't help hearing you on the phone."

"Offer made, to Jo, anyway. She'll call Walter's realtor. If the deal looks as though it'll go through I'll have to get a lawyer," Will said, almost as though he was talking to himself. "I don't want to use Aunt

Nettie's lawyer. He's a strange old guy, and at some point there might be a conflict of interest."

Maggie nodded. "I was thinking about making hot chocolate. You?"

"Coffee, I think."

A few minutes later Will had a fire burning in the fireplace, the Christmas tree lights were on, and Will and Maggie were snuggled on the couch, their cups almost forgotten on the coffee table in front of them.

Will was the first to speak, softly. They both knew Aunt Nettie's room was only a wall away. "I know I've done a lot of the talking since you've arrived. I wanted you to see what I've been doing. What I've been thinking about for the future, here in Waymouth. How Aunt Nettie was doing."

Maggie held his hand tightly and reached up and kissed his cheek. "I understand that. I didn't know what you were coping with. I'd imagined she was back the way she was before the stroke. And I hadn't realized you'd had to make as many changes in your life. I'm impressed, and frankly, a bit overwhelmed with everything you've had to do." She squeezed his hand. "I honestly don't think I could do what you're doing. Aunt Nettie's very lucky to have you in her life."

"I'm lucky, too. Since my mother and father died she's been a sort of surrogate parent to me. Someone who's known me all my life, and who's listened and given me sound advice when asked, and kept her mouth closed when I haven't asked."

Maggie felt a twinge of envy. There was no Aunt Nettie in her life. And, she thought, Will's aunt had been giving her advice, too. What advice had she been giving Will? "She's special, that's for sure."

"She's ninety-two, Maggie. Our family has good genes, but I won't have her in my life forever. I want to give back a little of the comfort and care she's given me over the years. Plus, of course, I've always wanted to live in Maine, so being here is not exactly a sacrifice. It will take time to figure out how everything's going to work. One of the big questions is the financial one. I don't want to make any commitments until I have that figured out."

Will needed to feel he could support himself. Maggie got that.

But in the meantime, her life was moving on. Her decision to adopt was a final one; one that would change the rest of her life.

"But all that's me. Remember what we said in October. No more holding back." Will squeezed her hand.

Maggie could feel her heart beating. Was this going to be a repeat of the scene they'd had on the Cape when she'd said what she wanted, and Will had walked out?

That time she'd talked him into coming back. They were still together. Here. In Maine. At least for now. This was another chance.

She could feel his arm around her tighten, very slightly.

"So—I want an honest answer."

She didn't let go of his hand. She thought of what Aunt Nettie had said. "I love you. I don't doubt that for a minute."

"I'm glad." Will bent down and kissed her. "In fact, I'm happier than that. I'm delighted and relieved. And I love you, too. But that's not the answer to my question."

She turned to look at him, steeling herself. He was going to ask about her adoption plans. This was it.

"Maggie, if I buy the Victorian house—would you exhibit your antique prints in it?"

"What?" The bubble of tension she'd built up collapsed. That was his big question?

"I know you've never exhibited in an antiques mall, but I think it would be a great venue for you. You could design one of the rooms, or the hallway, the way you wanted to. And I'd give you a special rate."

Maggie turned away from him and started laughing.

"What? You think that's such a crazy idea? If you do, I need to know why."

"No. It's nothing. I guess I'm tired." She turned back toward him. Maybe this was a message. A sign they were on very different wave lengths. "I agree. My prints would look wonderful in one of the rooms. Or in the hall, if the lighting were much better. Of course, I'd need to see your contract to make sure I could afford to be a tenant in such an upscale establishment," she teased. "But assuming all terms were to my liking, I think you have your first dealer."

She reached out her hand and they shook on it. Which might have led to further words…or interactions…if Will's telephone hadn't rung.

"Drat," he said, disentangling himself. "But it might be Jo."

It wasn't. It was Nick Strait.

"Nick gets off at four o'clock this afternoon. He wanted to know if we'd meet him at The Great Blue for a drink before dinner. I told him we would," said Will, returning to the couch.

"In this snow?"

Will shrugged. "It's Maine. The plows are out, and I can dig out the car. The Great Blue will be open. And I thought I'd make a light Alfredo sauce and throw the leftover shrimp from yesterday's party together with pasta for dinner tonight, so that will be easy. Aunt Nettie will be fine for an hour or two."

Conversation about adoption…postponed. "All right, then. I'd like to see Nick."

"Then I'll go and clear away the snow that's fallen since we came in."

"I have Christmas wrapping to do, so I'll finish that while you're shoveling," replied Maggie, looking wistfully at the fire and cozy couch.

Will kissed her forehead. "We'll only be gone for a while. The evening and night are still ahead." He winked at her. "Partner."

The snow wasn't falling as persistently as it had been earlier. Streets and parking lots were plowed, stores were open, and the weather didn't seem to have slowed commerce in any major way. About a dozen customers were at The Great Blue, at the bar or at tables near the welcoming fireplace, ablaze with warmth.

Maggie walked over to the windows overlooking the Madoc River. "In the summer I've looked out these windows and seen sailboats and lobster boats and cormorants drying themselves on the pilings and herons on the mud flats at low tide. Seeing the flats covered with snow and crackled ice is like being in an entirely different place." She turned to Will. "Through the flurries the weathered gray pilings from the old wharves are like a veiled forest of bones sticking out of the mud flats. But it's still beautiful, isn't it?"

"And when the sun comes out tomorrow and all that ice sparkles, it'll be spectacular. Not that I'm prejudiced or anything."

"Trying to sell Maggie on Maine winters?" Nick had come up behind them. "Welcome to Maine, Maggie."

"Good to see you again, Nick. If he's trying to sell me on Maine, he's doing a pretty good job," Maggie admitted. "Although tramping through your field to get to the woods to cut a Christmas tree wasn't my favorite part of the week."

"Her boots weren't high enough," Will explained.

"Ah. Feet got a bit soggy, then," Nick said. "But you found a right good tree?"

"We did," Maggie agreed. "It's up and decorated, in the living room. You should come and take a look."

Nick shrugged. "I've seen a few Christmas trees. But glad you found a good 'un. Bar or table, Will?"

"Since Maggie's with us, why not table? It's easier for three to talk there."

Maggie ordered a Sam Adams, Nick a Shipyard, and Will a Gritty McDuff's, and three bottles quickly appeared on the table.

"So, how's the crime business, Nick?" Will took a long slug of his beer.

"Luckily, Homicide's pretty quiet now. Around holidays it can pick up fast, though, so I'm on call pretty much twenty-four/seven. People drinking too much. Families finding reunions aren't all they're cracked up to be in the movies. Old quarrels being revived. The usual."

"What made you decide to be a state trooper, Nick? I've always been curious about what would draw someone to a profession like that," Maggie asked.

"You mean a job dealing with the rotten sides of people?" Nick asked. He paused. "Funny. I don't think anyone's ever asked me that. My grandpa farmed; my dad lobstered. Mainers through and through, both of 'em, though one took to the land and one to the sea. When I was growing up they each tried recruiting me. Telling me why his way was best." He smiled and drank. "Guess I was more like 'em both than they wanted to know, 'cause I chose my own way. Decided to be a cop, or a trooper—whoever solved murders—when I was about eight or nine. That's when a girl, maybe seventeen or eighteen years old, was found dead a few blocks from here, in the cellar of an old building that'd burned down years before."

Maggie stared at him. "The 'hidden garden'?" She'd visited that peaceful place. In summer chipmunks chirruped and raced along and between the old granite stones in the walls. Stone chairs and benches had been set along paths so visitors could relax and enjoy the perennials and thick plantings several feet, and a world away, from the street.

"Ayuh. That's what they call the place now. The Waymouth Garden Club claimed it and planted it real nice some years back. But when I was a kid it was a wild, dirty place where teenagers went to smoke and hang out. Other things happened there, too, I suspect. I was only a kid, but I heard stories. Ghost stories, mostly, but still. And then a girl's body was found there. People talked about it for weeks. But no one ever found out who she was, or where she came from."

Nick paused. "I used to go and look at that cellar. Imagine her body there. Thought if I were a cop, I'd be the hero who'd figure out who she was. And get the guy who killed her."

"Did they ever identify her?" Will asked.

"Nope. First thing I did, once I was a state trooper, was read her case files. She's still a Maine State cold case. All these years later." He paused. "When I have extra time, between cases, I still go over that file. I've read it hundreds of times. Maybe thousands. I've fed the information we have, such as it is, into every new state and federal database that comes on-line. Talked to everyone around at the time. Zip. Nada. I always figured someone in Waymouth knew something. That eventually it would come out." He shook his head. "The town buried her, but we still don't know who she was, or where she came from. Or who killed her. Or why."

"Wow," said Maggie. "There must be a family who's missed her for, what—thirty years or more?"

Nick shrugged. "You'd think so. But she never matched any reported missing persons. That might be the saddest part."

"But you're still investigating," said Maggie. "You haven't given up."

"I'm still looking," said Nick. "I'll admit, after all this time, I may never close the case. But at least I'll know I tried. And I've solved a few other murders along the way. So I'm still glad I chose this profession. I'm just too stubborn to give up on that one case."

"I'm glad," said Maggie. "And glad you told us."

Nick took a long drink. "Hey, Maggie, you're a girl. Here's a question for you. What would a teenage girl want for high school graduation? My Zelda's a senior, and her mom wants to buy her a piece of fancy jewelry."

"Jewelry's a lovely idea," said Maggie. "It would be something for her to remember the occasion by. Maybe to pass down to her own daughter someday."

"Don't mention her having kids any time soon. That's not going to happen if I have anything to do with it." Nick raised his fist. His eyes didn't smile. Then he seemed to relax. "That heirloom idea? Could work for some girls. But Emily—that's my ex—she sent Zelda a real pearl necklace for her sixteenth birthday last year. And you know what my kid did with it?"

Maggie shook her head.

"Pawned it. Gave it to a friend who was over twenty-one and he pawned it. I don't know what she did with the money. Maybe new clothes." Nick looked at Will. "I don't pay attention to what jewelry she's wearing. I wouldn't even know what she'd done if the pawnbroker hadn't called to tell me he'd had her in his place and figured the necklace didn't belong to the guy who pawned it."

"What did you do?"

"I got it back, and put it in my safe deposit box. There could come a time when she'd want it. And I skinned her alive for what she'd done."

"But it was hers," said Will.

"Yeah. It was," said Nick.

"Is she going to college next year?" asked Maggie.

"She's smart enough. But I don't know about college. I don't want her to go far away, you understand. I don't want her getting in any trouble." He leaned over. "I don't think she's applied anywhere, and that's fine with me. Biggest reason I'd have to tell her to apply is this boy, Jon Snow, she thinks she likes. She needs to get away from him."

"What kind of a boy is he?"

"Just a kid. No one she should be planning her life around," said Nick. "So what should I tell Emily about the jewelry?"

"Is Emily in touch with Zelda? Do they see each other?" asked Maggie.

"Nah. Not for a few years. When Zelda was eleven or twelve Emily came up to Maine for a weekend and bought her a fancy lunch and a pile of clothes she didn't need. Now she sends her cards and money for her birthday when she remembers. Not close."

"Why don't you suggest she invite Zelda to go and visit her for a week or so? As a graduation present. Maybe it's time they got to know each other better," Maggie suggested.

"I don't think you understand. I let Zelda go, she might never come home. Speaking of which," he stood up, "I should be getting home now. I'm expected. We're decorating our tree tonight. Maybe I'll see you both tomorrow night at the Westons' party."

Maggie looked at Will as Nick left. "That was abrupt."

Will shrugged his shoulders. "You were telling him what to do about Zelda. He's a little touchy about her."

"He asked me!"

"No difference. It's just his way. Don't worry. Next time we see him he won't even remember. We need to be getting back home anyway."

Maggie finished her beer. "Nick makes me curious to meet Zelda, though."

"Better not tell him that," said Will. "He'll think you're trying to recruit her for your college in New Jersey and planning to take her away."

"You're joking?" said Maggie, as Will helped her on with her jacket.

"I'm not sure, actually," said Will. "Nick's a little protective about Zelda. I've found it's better to keep your peace when it comes to her."

10

'Twas The Night Before Christmas—A Chance to Test Santa's Generosity. 1876 black-and-white wood engraving by Thomas Nast from *Harper's Weekly*. Nast, a German immigrant, began working as an artist for *Harper's* when he was fifteen. Later, using his own five children and his home in Morristown, New Jersey, as subjects, each year he drew at least one Christmas illustration for *Harper's*. He based his ideas on Clement Moore's poem "The Night Before Christmas," but his drawings give us the vision of Santa we have today. In this engraving one of his young sons is in pajamas, hanging a stocking almost as long as he is from the mantel of Nast's home. Santa's face and a circle of holly are pictured on the fireplace screen. 10 x 14 inches. Price: $225.

BY MIDMORNING on Christmas Eve wrapped packages were appearing under the Christmas tree. Maggie added several boxes of her own to the pile, resisting peeking at the tags, but feeling like a child. She hadn't had a tree with unknown gifts under it since she'd been a little girl.

Christmas was for children. Next year. Next year …

Will's telephone rang several times about the offer he'd made on the Victorian house, but he didn't volunteer what was happening, and she didn't ask.

Aunt Nettie's suggestion that it was a perfect day to make gingerbread people solved the problem of what she was to do, and soon they were cutting out and decorating gingerbread boys and girls with a vengeance, focusing on lining up silver buttons and raisin eyes.

Aunt Nettie was looking forward to the party at her friends' house, no matter the weather. "Did you bring a nice dress, Maggie? Ruth and Betty will expect us to dress up a bit. You'll see."

Maggie bent over the last tray of gingerbread children. "I have a dress," she answered. She'd brought a silky red dress with a fitted top and swirly skirt she'd seen in a boutique window in Flemington and couldn't resist. It wasn't her usual style, but it fit perfectly, and she'd hoped she and Will might go to a nice restaurant for dinner, maybe in Portland. Or even go out New Year's Eve. But it looked as though the party at Ruth's and Betty's house would be the dress-up occasion for this trip.

"Wow!" Four hours later, the look on Will's face was more than worth the dress's price. "We should get dressed up more often."

Aunt Nettie nodded wisely. "You look very nice, dear. Will, you don't look half-bad yourself. I'd forgotten you owned a tie." Will was dressed in navy pants and a pale blue dress shirt (the color Maggie always thought reflected his eyes) and a red tie, topped by a tan wool sweater. For Maine, that was about as dressy as a man would get, short of his own wedding or funeral. Aunt Nettie was wearing a gray wool skirt with a red sweater set and pearls.

"Very elegant," Maggie announced, checking them all out. "And festive."

"It's fun to have a party to go to Christmas Eve," Aunt Nettie agreed.

Will and Maggie each took one of her arms and helped guide her down the now-icy ramp.

Their drive through Waymouth was as beautiful as it had been the night Maggie had arrived. Maine marked Christmas with thousands of tiny sparkling white lights woven in wreaths, trees and lamp posts, and through pine garlands and wide red ribbons bedecking bridge railings. In New Jersey most decorations were multi-colored flickering lights. Not to mention the grotesque inflated vinyl Santas and Rudolphs and Frostys that appeared on too many suburban lawns.

Somewhere in Maine there was no doubt a totally tacky lawn scene, including roof lights, complete with Santa and all eight (or nine) reindeer. But wherever that was, it wasn't in Waymouth.

The large house where Ruth and Betty lived was on Hill Street, the highest elevation in town, lined with colonial homes built in the era when ships' captains and owners wanted to look out over the harbor, survey their property, and watch for arrivals of schooners from distant lands and coasters from New York, Boston, and Portland.

In those days there'd been few trees in towns; the Victorians' value of trees as landscaping had yet to be established. Trees had been cut down for use in construction or as fuel. Today's residents of those same houses found their harbor views blocked by large maples, oaks, and pines, and by taller houses, like the one Will might buy. But the stately captains' colonial or Federal style homes still stood, grandly looking down at a town that had grown up to them in space, but not in elegance, over the past two centuries.

Tonight Ruth's home shone brightly, all rooms lit, electric candles centered in the wreaths hung in every window, and real candles set in the snow to mark the path to the door.

In New Jersey the path would have been marked by paper bags filled with sand to support the candles inside. Here, with little wind and ample snow, there was no need for bags to hold the candles.

"Quite a house," Maggie commented.

"Ruth always had more money than the rest of us," said Aunt Nettie. "Although she never acted like it made a difference. Ruth's and Betty's father owned Waymouth Hardware, back before everyone shopped at chain stores. And then Ruth married Jonas Weston. His father had an automobile franchise outside Portland. Jonas inherited it. Lots of money there, too. This is Ruth's house. Betty inherited money from her parents, but she never had as much as Ruth. Ruth's always looked out for her."

"You said they'd lived together for years?" said Maggie, as they got out of the car and Will lifted Aunt Nettie over the snow bank onto the sidewalk.

"Since Ruth's husband died. Their children grew up together."

Will rang the doorbell.

A middle-aged man with a thick gray mustache and frameless glasses answered. "Welcome! Merry Christmas! I'm Ruth's son, Brian. Ms. Brewer, I recognize you, of course. Come on in."

"Thank you, Brian," said Aunt Nettie. "This is my nephew, Will, and his friend, Maggie."

A piercing cry came from deep in the house. "And that's my unhappy son. He's probably wet again. You'll excuse me." Brian headed up the stairs toward the second floor.

"Aunt Nettie, give me your coat," said Will. "And Maggie? Yours? I assume there's somewhere to put these."

Ruth appeared from the room to the right. "So glad you're here. We're a bit less organized than I'd hoped. Will, could you take the coats up the stairs and put them on the bed in the first bedroom? That's my room. No one should be in there." She smiled at Maggie and Aunt Nettie. "I hope." She bent over and whispered as Will headed up the wide staircase, "Little Jonas is a bit colicky and Jenny and Brian are nervous parents. No one's getting much sleep, and I'm afraid everyone's blaming everyone else." She grimaced a bit. "I'm so glad we'd planned this party. I can use a little relief."

A short, heavy man wearing a Red Sox hat and a Patriots sweatshirt came out of the living room. He had two cookies in one hand and a glass of soda in the other. "Mrs. Weston? How many cookies can I have?"

"It's a party, Billy," she answered, patiently. "I told you. Have as many cookies as you want."

"Can I have all of them? Can I take them home with me?"

"Oh, no! I didn't mean that. Where's your mother, Billy?"

"She's with Ms. Hoskins. She's giving her a shot. She told me to talk to you."

"I see. Well, why don't you eat those two cookies, and drink your soda, and then come back and talk with me again. Or maybe your mother will be free by then."

"All right, Mrs. Weston." The man wandered off down the hall, dripping cookie crumbs on the Oriental carpet as he went.

"I haven't seen Billy in years," said Aunt Nettie. "He's gotten... even bigger."

"Fatter is the word you're looking for," said Ruth without hesitating. "Carrie lets him do and eat whatever he wants. And you haven't seen him because he's always with her. He follows her around and copies whatever she does. I'm surprised he isn't with her now. I guess the desserts and drinks were too tempting. Usually we don't have those in the house, with Betty being diabetic, and Billy eating like a whale." She glanced down the hall. "I'm sorry. That wasn't kind. It's a sad situation. I should go and check on Betty. It shouldn't take this long for Carrie to test her levels and give her that insulin. Betty's exhausted, like the rest of us, because of the baby's screaming all night, but she should be out here with our guests, and Carrie should be keeping her eye on Billy. You both go on in and get something to drink. I'll be right back." Ruth hurried off down the hallway.

"Tell me about Carrie and Billy," Maggie whispered as she and Aunt Nettie went into the living room. "Before Ruth comes back."

"Let's sit on the couch over there." Aunt Nettie pointed. "Carrie Folk used to nurse at Rocky Shores Hospital, but after Billy was born she started working with private patients at their homes. She's been taking care of Betty for over a year. Maybe two. You could see Billy's what I think they're now calling 'intellectually challenged.' One of the conditions Carrie has in her contract is that if you hire her you get Billy, too. He's with her all the time. Always has been, ever since he was born."

"What about when he was in school?" Maggie's friend Gussie's nephew, Ben, had Down Syndrome, but had graduated from high school. Not the college track, but he'd been in school until he was eighteen. He was in Special Olympics, helped Gussie with her antique doll and toy business, and did odd jobs for others in their Cape Cod community. He certainly didn't need someone with him all the time.

"Billy never went to school. I don't know the whole story. I do know Carrie's husband left her a year or two after Billy was born. He wanted to put Billy in an institution. Carrie refused to consider that. I don't know what Billy's capabilities are. Once years ago I asked Carrie if he could read, and she said he couldn't. That he didn't need to. She read to him. That when he was born the doctor told her Billy'd never be able to take care of himself, so it was her job to do that."

"Sad," said Maggie.

"What's sad?" said Will, joining them. "Sad that two such lovely ladies are sitting by themselves and don't even have glasses of wine?"

"There is that," Maggie agreed.

"I like a problem I can solve," Will said. "Red or white? Or a cocktail?"

"I'd like an Old Fashioned," requested Aunt Nettie. "I haven't had one of those in years."

"Red wine for me," said Maggie. "In honor of Christmas."

"And it'll match your dress," Will approved. He headed for the corner, where, as Ruth had promised, a complete bar was set up.

If this was the house where Ruth had brought up her children, they must have had a less formal room for playing, or she'd redecorated when they'd grown. The room they were in was handsomely paneled in Federal style, with tall period windows equipped with folding inside shutters to shield occupants from winter winds. The fireplace, now glowing with a warm fire, would have been the only heat in the room when the house was built.

Maggie admired the mahogany Queen Anne card table and chairs arranged as though someone was about to begin a game of chess, and the portraits on the wall. "Ruth's family?" she asked Aunt Nettie.

"I don't know," Aunt Nettie answered. "But I doubt it. Money only came into both sides of Ruth's family two generations ago. Those paintings look older than that."

Maggie nodded. "Mid-nineteenth century or earlier." Probably, she thought to herself, what antiques dealers called "instant ancestors." Portraits that came out of estates and were bought by people who didn't care who the subjects of the paintings were. They just liked the look of oil portraits on their walls. Or wanted people to think they'd come from a family wealthy enough to commission oil portraits several generations before.

"Ruth made a lot of changes in the house after her children left home," Aunt Nettie said. "Hired a decorator I think. I remember her saying she paid a lot for the hunting prints in the dining room."

"I'll look when I get there," Maggie said. There were no well-known American hunting prints unless you counted twentieth-century prints of hunters shooting deer and partridge. She suspected those would not fit with this décor. On the other hand, it wouldn't be unusual to see Chinese prints on a New England wall, as so many captains had been involved in the China trade.

Will hadn't returned, and smells from the buffet table in the dining room were wafting her way. "Would you like me to fill a plate for you?" she asked Aunt Nettie.

"Why don't we wait until we've had a drink?" Aunt Nettie looked across the room where Will had stopped for a few minutes, filled glasses in hand, to chat with Nick Strait. Nick must have gotten the evening off.

Maggie was tempted to go and greet him, but she didn't want to leave Aunt Nettie alone.

"That's Nicky over there with Will, isn't it, Maggie," said Aunt Nettie, following her gaze. "I'm guessing Doreen must be here, then, too. I wonder if they convinced Zelda to stop in as well." Just then a young woman with bouffant blond hair wearing a gold lamé sheath and holding a small baby walked in and immediately became the center of attention.

"That must be Brian's new wife, Jenny, with baby Jonas," said Aunt Nettie. "You go and admire the baby with the others. No reason for you to be stuck here with me."

Excused for the moment, Maggie went and looked over several sets of shoulders at the youngest Mr. Weston. He was two or three months old, and his clearly doting mother had dressed him in a tiny red sweater and pants for his first Christmas and wrapped him in a red blanket, no doubt for both warmth and for protection of his mother's rather dramatic (at least for Maine) outfit. His recent screams had reddened his cheeks to match his clothing, but now he'd settled in with a bottle.

Maggie left the admiring throng and headed for Will and Nick. Babies. Children. It seemed no matter where she was they surrounded her. More reminders that next year she, too, would be a mother, although her child or children would be far beyond the bottle stage.

Her eyes filled. Where were her daughter, or daughters, this year? Were they happy? Were they safe? Were there gifts under a tree somewhere for them?

She stopped in front of the wide-boughed Christmas tree to blink away a couple of tears. The tree was decorated with colored lights, tinsel, and ornaments of all sorts. Some were delicate Victorian blown glass, the sort collectors looked for at auctions or in antiques shops. Of course, when this house had been built Waymouth would not have celebrated Christmas with a tree. Christmas in early nineteenth-century Maine would only have meant a special church service on Sunday. A few gifts might have been exchanged on New Year's Day.

No trees would have been decorated in this home until at least the

1850s. Queen Victoria's Prince Albert had brought that custom with him from Germany, and it had spread rapidly throughout England and then to the States.

But the ornaments Maggie found herself drawn to weren't the Victorian ones. They were the clumsy ones made with uncooked macaroni and papier-mâché and clam and mussel shells and construction paper; the ones Ruth's and Betty's children had made. They'd been treasured and saved, and although some were now faded and torn, they'd been hung here, next to the valuable Victorian ornaments, in an elegant, formal room. She looked for the crayoned signatures. Brian, she'd just met. Stacy. That must be another of Ruth's children. Miranda, whose ornament was covered with glitter. And Noah, the third of Ruth's children. Did the two who weren't here tonight have children of their own? Were they remembering Christmases spent in this house?

Would her children come home for Christmas when they were adults, bringing their families, as Brian and Miranda had? Or would they, like Stacy and Noah, have reasons to stay away?

As a child she'd dreamed of living in a house like this, with a Christmas tree like this one.

With parents who'd treasure her awkwardly pasted snowmen and Santas instead of consigning them to the kitchen bulletin board for a day or two before they ended up in the trash.

For a moment Maggie grieved for the child she'd been. The child who'd been fed and clothed, but who'd longed to be cherished.

She shook her head slightly, trying to banish her thoughts. The past couldn't be changed. Hers wasn't a fraction as bad as that of millions of children in the world. Or even as bad as Will's had been, with a father whose temper and drinking had convinced Will he could never be a good father himself.

No life was perfect. And now was not a time to feel sorry for herself. Now was the time to live the life she'd chosen. Which meant, tonight, that she'd better retrieve the drinks Will had promised her and Aunt Nettie.

"Merry Christmas, Nick!" she said, joining the two of them. "What are you two handsome men doing talking to each other and not to us ladies?"

Will grinned. Nick blushed from his cheeks up to the top of his thinning hair. "You look nice tonight, Maggie."

"'Nice!' How're you going to get a girl with words like that, Nick," Maggie teased, as Nick's face got redder. "I'd toast you if I had a drink." She looked pointedly at the glasses Will was holding.

"Sorry. We got to talking." Will handed her the glass of red wine and looked guiltily toward Aunt Nettie.

"And yes, I'll take Aunt Nettie's glass to her. No problem. You guys have fun." She turned and walked back to the couch, where Doreen had taken her place, and handed Aunt Nettie her Old Fashioned. "Will got a little involved."

"I saw. Thank you, Maggie."

"You look wonderful, Maggie," said Doreen. "I'm surprised Will even took the time to say hello to Nick."

"I'm afraid I just embarrassed Nick. I was teasing him about having a girlfriend. Is there a special friend in his life?"

"My Nick? Heavens, no. I don't think he's had a date since his divorce was final, sixteen years ago." Doreen shook her head. "A few women have been interested. But he's always busy with his job, and with taking care of Zelda and me." She leaned toward Maggie. "Truth be told, I think he's a bit shy. Once burned, you know."

"Is Zelda here tonight?" Maggie glanced around, but didn't see any teenagers in the room. "I'd love to meet her."

"No; she was going to come, but she had to be over at the church, practicing."

"Practicing?"

"She's in the choir. They're part of the community carol sing on the Green at seven, and then singing at the Christmas Eve candlelight service at eleven. It's lovely. You should come."

"I'll see what Will wants to do. I haven't been to a candlelight service in years."

Her thought was interrupted as a slight gray-haired woman Maggie assumed was Carrie Folk wheeled Betty in and placed her chair next to the couch. Billy was following them, still holding one of his cookies. Or maybe by now it was another one.

Carrie bent down and said something to Betty. Then she took Billy by the hand and went toward the buffet table in the next room.

"Who are you?" asked Betty, looking up at Maggie.

"I'm Maggie," she answered.

"Oh," said Betty. "That's a nice name. Where is this? It's a lovely room. It looks like Christmas."

"This is your living room," said Maggie. "And it's Christmas Eve." She turned as Ruth joined them. "I saw Jonas. You have a handsome young grandson. And what a cute Christmas outfit."

"Jonas? You saw Jonas?" said Betty. "He should be here to see his baby, you know. He has a beautiful baby."

"Yes, Betty," Ruth moved a step away from Betty before she answered Maggie. "The baby is cute, isn't he? I bought that outfit for him. Jenny and I don't always see eye-to-eye. I'll admit I preferred wife number-one. But I was real pleased to see she'd put that red suit on him this afternoon." She turned to the others. "Have you all tasted the buffet? I think I overdid it a bit with the food, and I don't want any wasted."

"Why don't I go and get you a plate now, Aunt Nettie," said Maggie, putting her glass down.

The buffet table was as generous as Ruth promised, although not many people were taking advantage of it yet. Maggie had almost filled a plate with bites of shrimp, mussels, sausage, stuffed mushrooms, oysters, pasta salad, deviled eggs topped with caviar, and a few slices of different cheeses when she sensed Will at her shoulder. "Is that for Aunt Nettie?" he asked. "Make sure you add some of the crabmeat. She loves that."

He was topping his own plate off generously and didn't seem to be skipping anything. "Then be sure to come back and get enough for yourself."

"I will," she promised, keeping an eye on the lavish tray of Damariscotta and Pemaquid oysters. "By the way, do you know who the two women in the corner are? They're not mixing with anyone else."

Will glanced in their direction. "The taller one, wearing the patchwork-quilt skirt, is Betty's daughter, Miranda, and the other one is her spouse, Joan. They've been together for years. Live in Portland. They got married as soon as it was legal here."

"I remember hearing Betty's daughter lived in Portland. And I think that 'patchwork-quilt skirt' is made of hand-embroidered silks and satins. Gorgeous. I've been admiring it. They're the ones I think Ruth said would be staying at an inn instead of here at the house."

"Portland isn't far, but I guess because of the holiday they're staying in town overnight. Aunt Nettie once mentioned that Miranda and Ruth had a falling out about how Betty was being cared for. That could be another reason they're not staying at the house."

"Families!" said Maggie. She picked up a napkin and fork and headed back to deliver Aunt Nettie's plate.

Her second trip to the buffet was for her, and since Aunt Nettie seemed settled with friends, she and Will walked and peeked at the downstairs of the large house as they nibbled.

In the back of the living and dining rooms (the hunting prints turned out to be Henry Alkens, as Maggie had suspected), were a large kitchen and pantry. On the other side of the first floor were a more formal parlor and an area that had been turned into two rooms; one for Betty, and an adjoining one seemingly designed for her caretaker. It included two single beds, a small television, and a shelf of trucks and picture books, perhaps for Billy.

Betty's room was equipped with a hospital bed, a larger television set, and an adjacent handicapped bathroom. A tall bookcase held shelves of DVDs, and the walls were covered with framed photographs of family and friends. Near Betty's bed a large chalkboard read TODAY IS DECEMBER 24. CHRISTMAS EVE. WEATHER IS COLD AND SNOWY. An infant-sized baby doll sat in a chair near the bookcase.

Everything in the room—every picture, every wall and light switch—had an attached yellow sticky note identifying it. The names of the people in the pictures. TV. LAMP. BED. CEILING. REMOTE CONTROL. WINDOW. REFRIGERATOR was on a small refrigerator in the corner. Perhaps it held Betty's medications.

At first neither of them spoke. The reality of dementia was very close in that room.

Maggie shuddered. "Two other beds. It must be hard enough to have a nurse with you at all times. But to have Billy as well… It would drive me crazy to have no privacy."

"But how much does she still understand? I assume Betty wants to stay at home, and needs someone close at hand. But I don't think

Carrie and Billy are here all the time. Ruth takes care of her most nights, and when Carrie has time off."

Maggie nodded.

"Taking care of a loved one doesn't have to be horrible, you know."

Maggie leaned against Will for a moment. "I know." That was what he was doing. But somehow here, with Betty in her wheelchair, not sure of where she was or who she was talking to, caretaking seemed much worse than helping Aunt Nettie, who could still do a lot for herself, and knew exactly what was happening.

Back in the living room, Ruth was feeding Betty.

Aunt Nettie had disappeared.

"Will? Maybe I should go and look for Aunt Nettie. Make sure she's okay, in case she needed to use the bathroom or felt a little weak." She handed her empty plate to him.

She paused outside the parlor that had been empty a few minutes before. Aunt Nettie's voice was coming clearly from inside. Maggie didn't want to interrupt.

"I've known you since you were a child. This isn't like you. I don't know what's wrong, but this isn't going to help. It's going to get you into trouble. Tell me what you need. If I can help you, I will," Aunt Nettie was saying.

"You don't understand! You've always had everything you wanted and needed. You've never been in my situation. I don't have any choice." That was another woman's voice.

"We've all had times when it didn't seem as though there were any good choices. But there are always options. If you don't want to talk to me, have you thought of talking to someone else you trust? A minister? Or doctor? A counselor?"

"I don't want to talk to anyone. There's no time for that nonsense. I know what I have to do. Clearly you don't want to help me. If you did, you'd give me what I asked for."

"I can't do that, Carrie. I don't have it."

"I don't believe you. Rich folks think they can get away with anything. But they can't. Not always. It's time for payback. You think about it. You think hard."

"Are you sure there's nothing else —"

"I told you. There's nothing. So, all of you, stop acting like you know better than me. Because you don't know nothing. What I know, I know, and I'm not keeping my peace any longer."

Maggie pretended to be studying a group of hand-colored Bartlett steel engravings of Boston in the hallway.

Carrie Folk hadn't met her. She hoped she wasn't even noticed as Carrie left the parlor and walked quickly down the hall and into the dining room.

She'd overheard a strange, but clearly private, conversation.

A minute or so later Aunt Nettie came out of the parlor. "Maggie! What are you doing out here in the hall?"

"Looking at the engravings," Maggie lied.

"Hmm," said Aunt Nettie. "Well, why don't we go back and get another drink from that bar instead of standing around by ourselves? We're at a party."

Carrie had taken over the task of feeding Betty by the time they reached the living room. "Is Betty all right?" Maggie asked Aunt Nettie softly. "She didn't need that much help to eat the other day at your house."

"Ruth said she's very tired today. The baby cried most of the night and a lot today, too, and it upset Betty. She wasn't able to sleep. When she's tired, she loses muscle control. They thought it would be best if Carrie helped her."

Maggie looked around for Billy. She found him in a corner of the dining room with a plate of food, pushing it into his mouth with his fingers. "Billy!" she said. "Does your mother let you eat like that?"

"This food is really, really good."

"Yes, it is," said Maggie. "Why don't you take the rest of your plate into the other room where your mother is and eat your food there."

"Okay," he said.

"Here," she said, handing him a napkin and a fork. "Wipe your hands and mouth first. And then take another napkin. You don't want your mother to see you like that."

"No. Then maybe Santa Claus wouldn't come." Billy wiped his fingers carefully and handed the dirty napkin back to Maggie. "You won't tell him, will you?"

"I won't. But I don't want to see you eating with your fingers again."

Billy nodded. Then he picked up his plate and left.

"Well done, Maggie," said Ruth, who'd come into the room in back of her. "Not many people can cope with Billy. You did that just right."

"I hope I wasn't interfering. But his mother looked so tired sitting there and feeding Betty, and I was sure she wouldn't have approved of the way he was eating."

"Sometimes I wonder," said Ruth. "It's hard sometimes to watch Billy. Carrie doesn't discipline him the way...well, the way I disciplined my children. I know he's different. But, still. I try not to interfere. Carrie's so good with Betty, and we've known them both for so long. Betty's comfortable with her. It's hard to find a competent and caring nurse you can trust in your home."

"You have a beautiful home."

"Thank you. I'm so glad you could come this afternoon."

The baby's screams interrupted them. "There Jonas goes again. I swear, if any of my children had cried like that I wouldn't have had three." Ruth smiled. "But here I am, telling you how I'd discipline Carrie's son, or my grandson. Poor Jonas has colic. I think he just needs to be burped a little more, and perhaps he shouldn't have been put on the bottle so early. But he's not my child. Do you have children, Maggie?"

Maggie swallowed. Hard. "Not yet."

"Well, once you do, you'll know. You want to raise your children your way, even if you know you're not doing a perfect job. It hurts when anyone gives you advice. So I try not to. With Brian and Jenny, I keep reminding myself I'm just the grandmother. Last night I think his mother was crying more than little Jonas was. And when she's tense and upset, Jonas senses that and cries more. Brian left and went out walking in the middle of the night. If I hadn't had to look after Betty I would've been tempted to join him, even in the snow and at my age."

"How long are they staying?" Maggie asked.

"Until New Year's," Ruth answered. She lowered her voice. "I love my family dearly, but I really hope that baby stops crying. For all our sakes."

At about 6:30 people began to leave the party, many saying they were going to the community sing.

"It's not far," said Will to Maggie. "Would you like to go?"

"What about Aunt Nettie?" Maggie said, quietly.

"Aunt Nettie is going to stay right here if you young folks want to go along," Aunt Nettie put in. "Ruth's invited me to stay and chat while she has a little to eat and starts to clean up. Go ahead, you two. Brian and Jenny are taking the baby to the carol sing, and Carrie's going to put Betty to bed. I'll be fine here."

"You're sure?"

"I'm sure. Just don't have such a good time you forget to come back for me."

"I haven't been to one of these in years," Will admitted, as they pulled their coats on. "But why not? It's part of small-town Christmas."

"Oh good! It's snowing, too," Maggie said as they joined others walking down the street toward the center of town. A few people carried candles or flashlights, but most houses had turned their outside lights on, so the whole town seemed bright in the snow.

Maggie and Will held hands as they walked through the night toward the Green. "It's perfect."

Will squeezed her hand. "It is."

The high school band had assembled in front of the Congregational church and choirs from several churches in town were gathering, their long robes flapping over their heavy sweaters and boots. Townspeople as young as baby Jonas were there, bundled up warmly. One wizened man wrapped in blankets in a wheelchair on one of the shoveled walkways around the Green was smiling and chatting, ignoring the cold and snow.

"Can we get a little closer?" asked Maggie. "I'm curious. Which of the girls in the choir is Zelda?"

Will guided her around the center crowd until they found a place where they could see the sopranos assembling, checking music and looking around for friends and family.

He peered through the snow, which had begun to fall more heavily again. "See the second girl from the end? She's wearing a red turtleneck under her robe. I think that's Zelda."

Maggie stood on her toes. "You mean the girl talking to the blonde with really short hair? The one who just waved to the tall, skinny young man over near the pine tree."

"That's the one. And the boy she waved at is Jon Snow, the one Nick doesn't want her to see."

"Clearly she isn't paying too much attention to that rule," said Maggie.

"Obviously. And she has a lot of makeup on for a choir girl. No wonder Nick gets upset with her," added Will.

"Will, are you sure that's Zelda?" As they'd moved closer to the singer, Maggie could see more clearly. "Because I don't think that's all makeup. That girl has a black eye."

11

Filled All the Stockings. Red-and-black lithograph by Arthur Rackham (1867–1939) of elf-like Santa with a stocking, surrounded by toys—dolls, trains, animals—some of which are strange and possibly scary, especially with their black shadows behind them. One of four color illustrations Rackham did for a 1931 edition of Clement Moore's *The Night Before Christmas*. The verse this illustration accompanies is, "He spoke not a word, but went straight to his work, And filled all the stockings; then turned with a jerk." In Rackham's vision, not all children could count on receiving happy gifts at Christmas. 4 x 5 inch picture on 8 x 5.5 inch page. Price: $65.

CHRISTMAS MORNING dawned sunny, bright—and frigid. Maggie heard Will in the kitchen below and hid her head under the quilt for a few last, luxurious moments before opening her eyes. It wasn't quite seven, but the bedroom was filled with light despite the frosted patterns on the windows, and the smell of coffee perking had reached the second floor.

Next Christmas I'll be the first one up, she thought. I'll have the tree lit, the stockings filled, and presents from Santa will be waiting to be unwrapped. It will be our first Christmas together.

Whoever "we" would be.

She stretched her toes under the covers once more and smiled to herself. She could hardly wait.

Except…Will wouldn't be there. She'd visualized a scene at her home in New Jersey. He'd be here in Waymouth, fixing coffee for Aunt Nettie.

They hadn't had "that" talk yet. In fact, she had the feeling Will was avoiding it. But clearly he was settling into Maine life. Her life was in New Jersey. They were both moving on. Separately.

Life wasn't a fairy tale.

She allowed herself a fleeting thought about Nick's daughter,

Zelda. How was she this Christmas morning? At first she'd thought Nick was being overprotective, and Doreen had implied that, too. But if Zelda's boyfriend—Jon, his name was Jon Snow—had given her a black eye, maybe Nick was doing what a father should do. Protecting his daughter. Will had certainly thought so when she'd pointed Zelda's injury out to him.

But maybe Zelda slipped on the ice or had another minor accident embarrassing to anyone, but especially to a teenaged girl. There might be nothing to worry about but her bruised ego.

Maggie allowed herself one or two more thoughts about what she'd do if Zelda were her daughter. Then she scrambled out of bed and headed for the bathroom. It was Christmas morning. Much better to be here than alone in New Jersey.

Will met her at the bottom of the stairs with a hug, a gentle kiss, and a glass of champagne.

"Really?" she asked, accepting it.

"Really. Longtime Brewer family Christmas morning tradition," he assured her. "Did I forget to tell you?"

She raised her glass. "Then—Merry Christmas!"

"Merry Christmas, Maggie!" called Aunt Nettie, who was sitting in the kitchen with a similar flute of champagne alongside her coffee. "After the party last night I decided I needed a caffeine jump start, too."

"Would you like hot chocolate or Diet Pepsi with your champagne?" asked Will.

Maggie frowned in pretend contemplation. "I think I'll stick with champagne."

"Good choice," he nodded. "I'm going with champagne, too. And not to worry. I have three bottles chilled."

"One for each of us!" Aunt Nettie almost crowed. "Merry Christmas!"

Maggie wondered how long she and Will had been up, and how much Aunt Nettie'd had to drink already. Besides her coffee.

"The next Brewer tradition is a special Christmas breakfast," Will explained. "Sit down, relax, drink up. I'm in charge. Blueberry muffins are already in the oven."

"I thought I smelled something good." Maggie sniffed. "You didn't make blueberry muffins this morning, did you?"

"He certainly didn't," said Aunt Nettie. "They're muffins I made last summer and froze. But we decided they'd make a good holiday bread for today."

"Excellent decision," Maggie agreed.

"The plan, you see, is that we have a big breakfast and keep sipping champagne. Then we'll open our gifts, and take the rest of the day off. Or," Will raised his eyebrows and leered at Maggie behind Aunt Nettie's back, "take naps."

"I see," said Maggie, trying not to burst into laughter. "And this is a years-long tradition?"

"Absolutely," said Will. "My parents celebrated Christmas morning this way, and my father said his parents had inherited the tradition. Right, Aunt Nettie?"

"In some variation. When I was a girl the meat was moose steak and the bread was apple pie. And my father liked his cider—not the kind you buy at the grocery today. But the idea was basically the same."

"So, instead of moose steak, what are we having with our blueberry muffins, Chef Will?"

"Filet mignon, covered with sautéed mushrooms and onions in a brandy sauce."

Maggie swallowed. "Okay. You got me. I am totally flabbergasted."

Will bowed. "Happy to hear that, my dear."

"And totally starving. So, demonstration time. Please!"

While Will pulled out ingredients and pans he'd managed to keep in places Maggie hadn't noticed, Aunt Nettie leaned across the table. "Don't worry, dear. He's been practicing."

She had no need to worry. Will did a fantastic job.

"Are you sure you want to open an antiques mall, and not a restaurant?" Maggie half groaned, as she ate the last few pieces of her filet. "This was spectacular. Really spectacular."

"I found a great butcher, asked for advice, and tweaked a recipe. And I have two women I love to cook for. What more does a man need?" replied Will, clearly pleased breakfast had gone the way he'd hoped.

"Now I understand why collapsing after breakfast is a part of the Brewer Christmas morning tradition," said Maggie, patting her stomach. "I don't think I've ever eaten this much so early in the day." She raised her flute in his direction. "Or had this much champagne."

"It isn't time for naps yet," said Will. "Presents first. Let's adjourn to the living room. We can clean up later. Today is a holiday."

"I think I might need a bit of help," said Aunt Nettie. "I've had a little more champagne than I'd planned."

Will helped her to her feet as they laughed and Maggie gathered up their champagne glasses and the most recent bottle they'd been pouring from.

The telephone rang when they were halfway to the living room.

"You get that, Maggie. It's probably someone wishing us 'Merry Christmas,'" said Will, who was helping Aunt Nettie to her chair.

"Merry Christmas!" she answered, picking up the phone in the kitchen. "Yes, of course. I'll get him." She put her hand over the receiver. "Will, it's Nick. He sounds serious. I don't think he's calling to say hello."

She joined Aunt Nettie in the living room. "The tree looks so lovely with all the lights and ornaments and the packages under it. I hate to open them. Then Christmas will be over. It's been such a perfect day so far."

Will was back in a moment. "This is rotten news to have to deliver on Christmas. Nick was calling to tell us that Carrie Folk died late last night or early this morning."

Billy's mother. That little woman who took care of Betty. And who'd been arguing with Aunt Nettie yesterday at the party.

"Was there an accident?" Aunt Nettie asked. "She seemed well last night."

"No. Worse than that. She was murdered. Nick's calling everyone who was at Ruth's party yesterday, in case someone noticed anything he should know about. Anything unusual."

Aunt Nettie nodded slowly. "Will, would you call Nicky back? I know it's Christmas Day, but I think he should come over here. I have something he needs to see."

12 **Untitled.** Lithograph of seated female angel, naked, with large blue-tinged wings, holding a sleeping infant. Above angel are tan vines covered with white and brown flowers, birds, and a squirrel; at her feet are rabbits and mice. Illustration by Arthur Rackham for *The Springtide of Life: Poems of Childhood* by Algernon Charles Swinburne, edited by Edmund Gosse, Garden City, New York: Doubleday, Page & Co., 1926. British illustrator Rackham's tipped-in (attached to pages of books) illustrations of fanciful creatures were extremely popular throughout the first quarter of the twentieth century. 7 x 10 inches. Price: $65.

WILL AND MAGGIE looked at each other questioningly, but neither said anything. What did Aunt Nettie have to show Nick? Will went back to the telephone and delivered Aunt Nettie's message.

"Nick'll be here in half an hour," he said when he returned. He glanced around at the champagne bottle and glasses. "I guess we should clean up a little."

"We're not driving anywhere, and I didn't murder Carrie, in case you're wondering," said Aunt Nettie. "What's important is that Carrie's dead, not that we've been drinking champagne." Aunt Nettie, who a few minutes ago had been tipsy enough to need Will's help to walk safely into the living room, now sounded totally sober. Deadly sober. "Will, sit down. We have to talk. And before Nicky gets here I want Maggie to open one of her presents."

"We could wait for the gifts until later," said Maggie. "There's no hurry."

"I'm afraid there is, now." Aunt Nettie turned to her, pointing to the pile of packages. "It's the one in the corner there, on the left side of the tree. Wrapped in red-and-white striped paper."

For whatever reason, Aunt Nettie was now in charge. Maggie wasn't going to question her.

The package was heavy. "Shall I read the tag out loud?"

"Please."

"'For Maggie and her future child. Don't give up your dreams. With love, Aunt Nettie.'" The handwriting was shaky, but clear.

"Just open it, dear. As it's turned out, we don't have all day."

Why didn't we have all day? Why was it important that she open this gift now? Maggie wondered, as she tore the wrapping paper back and opened the box.

Inside were six children's books, all with Maine connections. *Counting Our Way to Maine* was on top. Below it were familiar classics: *Charlotte's Web*, *Blueberries for Sal*, *Miss Rumphius*, *Island Boy*, and *Sarah, Plain and Tall*.

"Aunt Nettie!" Maggie's eyes filled with tears. "How did you know I've been hoping to adopt a child? Did Will tell you?" For a moment she wondered if... She turned to Will. "Was this your idea?"

One look at Will's face and it was clear he knew nothing about the gift. But he was smiling.

Before he could say anything, Aunt Nettie answered her question. "I know it's none of my business. But I've been silently cheering you on, Maggie. I think you'd be a wonderful mother. And if you don't adopt, if you don't do something you've so set your heart on, you're always going to regret it." She stopped for a moment. "Rachel helped me choose the books. They were a few of her daughter's favorites. And she's the one who ordered them for me, since I don't get out too much anymore."

Rachel's daughter had been murdered two years ago. Since then Rachel had remarried and begun a new life. Maggie looked through the titles again. "You and Rachel did a perfect job. They'll be the first books in the bookcase I'm going to buy for my daughter's room." *My daughter's room.* Maggie smiled just saying it, but she had to wipe a couple of tears off the book jackets. She put the books carefully on the floor and went over and hugged Aunt Nettie and whispered, "Thank you, thank you. You're the first person who's really been on my side in all this."

Before she could say anything more, to Aunt Nettie or to Will, Aunt Nettie nodded and pushed her gently back. "Will, now I think I'd like a little more of that champagne."

"Are you sure you want more to drink, Aunt Nettie? Hearing about Carrie's death has been upsetting to all of us, and you're looking a little pale."

"I'm fine. At my age a little champagne can't make any difference." He filled her glass and handed it to her.

"Now, both of you sit down and listen. I'm going to tell you something I'd hoped you'd never have to hear. Everyone has secrets. Some people manage to take theirs to their graves. But —"

They heard pounding on the front door.

"That must be Nicky. Go let him in, Will."

"Not such a Merry Christmas, Nick," said Will as he opened the door.

Nick was wearing his Maine State Trooper's uniform. He was on duty. "No, it isn't," said Nick. "The state assigns us to investigate murders near our homes, thinking we'll have insights into the cases. But knowing those involved doesn't make it easy." He stepped into the living room and removed his trooper's hat. "Good morning, Maggie. Ms. Brewer."

"Can you tell us what happened, Nick?" said Maggie, gesturing that Nick should sit down.

He sat on the edge of the chair next to Aunt Nettie. "In general, yes. In detail, no. I can't tell you anything everyone in Waymouth won't have heard by noon anyway." He half smiled, but his eyes didn't change. "The joys of working a case in a small town. Okay. Owen Trask at the Waymouth Sheriff's Department called me early this morning. He's been working with me ever since."

"We know Owen," said Aunt Nettie.

"He and I are checking, but so far as we know, the last people to see Carrie Folk alive, other than her son and the killer, were the guests at the Westons' party last night. You were all there, which is why I called."

"You were there, too, Nicky. The guest list isn't a secret. And there weren't that many people there."

"No. And so far, everyone who didn't sleep at the Westons' home last night says they left the party, went to the carol sing or to their own homes, and stayed there, except for a couple of people who went to midnight services. We're checking on all that, of course."

"What about Carrie? Did she go straight home?" Maggie asked.

"That's what her son Billy says, although he's upset, and I don't know how reliable a witness he is. He says he and his mother put out cookies for Santa Claus and then she read him *The Night Before Christmas* and put him to bed. When he fell asleep she was in the living room listening to the news on television, the way she does every night."

"Probably waiting for him to go to sleep so she could play Santa," said Aunt Nettie. "If Billy still believes in Santa, that's what a mother would do, I suspect."

"Oh, he definitely believes in Santa," Nick said, dryly. "He told us he was so excited about Santa coming he kept waking up. He even thought he heard Santa in the house later, but didn't get out of bed because he wasn't allowed to look at the tree until morning. It was a rule. When it was light he got up and went into the living room and saw Carrie on the floor next to the tree." Nick shook his head. "One of his rules for Christmas morning was that he couldn't open his presents until after he'd finished breakfast. He really wanted to open his presents, so when he couldn't wake his mother he went next door, to the Lodges' house, and asked them for breakfast. They went back with him to his house. They're the ones who found Carrie's body and called 911."

The room was silent.

Maggie spoke first. "Where's Billy now?"

"Still with the Lodges. They're a nice young couple, and they've been very good with him. He doesn't seem to understand about his mother. He's most upset that we haven't let him open his Christmas presents yet. But his house is a crime scene and we don't want to take anything out of there that might have fingerprints on it." Nick looked at Aunt Nettie. "You asked me to come here. You said you had something to show me."

"First, I have to tell you all a story." She took a breath, put down the empty champagne glass she'd been holding, and clasped her hands tightly in her lap. "This isn't easy, but in a minute you'll all understand why I have to tell you. Many years ago, during the war, the Second World War, when I was engaged to be married, I got pregnant."

Maggie and Will exchanged glances. Their Aunt Nettie?

"I would have loved to have had the child of the man I loved. But ..." Aunt Nettie hesitated. "It was a difficult situation. The child wasn't his. He was overseas. After I got over the shock of knowing what condition I was in, I panicked. I wanted more than anything to have a baby. I thought about leaving Waymouth; starting life somewhere else." Aunt Nettie's voice broke a little as she continued. "But I wasn't brave enough to have a child when I wasn't married. And I was sure I'd lose the man I loved. He wouldn't have understood what had happened. Instead, even in those days when it was illegal and dangerous, I knew someone who knew someone. I went to Boston, and had an abortion."

She looked at Maggie. "The butcher who did what he called surgery hurt me so badly I was lucky to survive. I could never have another child. And then my fiancé was killed, and I lost him, too." Even after so many years, or maybe because of them, Aunt Nettie's eyes filled with tears. "I've regretted my decision not to have that child every day of my life since."

Nick shuffled his feet a little and looked down at his notes. "Ms. Brewer? I'm sorry for your pain. But that happened a very long time ago. You made a mistake. Why are you telling us now?"

"Will, would you get the white envelope in the top drawer of my bedside table?"

Will returned in a moment and handed it to her. It was the same envelope Maggie had seen Aunt Nettie putting in her pocket instead of adding it to the other Christmas cards on the mantel.

Aunt Nettie gave the envelope to Nick. "This arrived in the mail a couple of days ago. It's from Carrie Folk. She threatened to tell my family and friends the story I just told you if I didn't give her money."

"Carrie Folk was trying to blackmail you?" said Nick, holding the envelope by its edges. "About something that happened over seventy years ago?"

"Exactly," said Aunt Nettie. "Last night I told her I planned to tell Will and Maggie myself what had happened, and anyone else, too, if need be. I couldn't think many people would be interested. What happened then is ancient history."

"But Carrie's dead," said Maggie. "You didn't have to tell us after all."

"But I did," said Aunt Nettie. "Because maybe I wasn't the only one to get a letter from Carrie Folk this week. And maybe someone else decided to stop her blackmailing another way."

13

Family Party Playing at Fox and Geese. Wood engraving by nineteenth-century American artist Winslow Homer published in *Ballou's Pictorial* on November 28, 1857, when Homer was only 21 years old. Shows adults playing a circle game during which a man is pursuing an attractive young woman. Although "Fox and Geese" was a well-known board game (one of Queen Victoria's favorites) during this period, this game appears to be closer to an outdoor children's tag game of the same period and name in which children pursue each other by racing through patterns in the snow. (Or Homer may be making fun of such a game!) 5.5 x 9.5 inches. Price: $195.

NICK HELD the envelope by the edges, as though it contained ricin. "I appreciate your sharing this with me, Ms. Brewer. If you don't mind I'd like to keep it, as evidence."

"Keep it. Burn it. I never want to see it again," said Aunt Nettie. "I've known Carrie Folk most of her life. I don't know why she sent that. She must have been desperate for money. Writing that letter was a cruel and spiteful thing to do, and I've never thought Carrie was a cruel or spiteful person."

"Not to mention that blackmail's illegal," Nick said, almost to himself. He pulled an evidence bag out of his jacket pocket and slipped the letter and envelope into it.

"But no matter what she did, she didn't deserve to die." Aunt Nettie was adamant.

"How would Carrie Folk have known what you did so long ago?" asked Maggie. "She's younger than you are. If she was even alive then, she was a baby during World War Two."

"Carrie wasn't even sixty," said Nick.

"I've been thinking about that," said Aunt Nettie. "Most people, I'd guess, have a few secrets in their lives. Some people's are bigger than others'. But not everyone has a secret worth blackmailing them with.

Mine, for example. For years I've held close what happened to me back then, but I'm ninety-two now. Telling you won't change my life, or anyone else's for that matter." She held her hands tightly together. "But that's not the case with every secret folks in this town hold. It's your job to find out who's responsible for Carrie Folk's death. Not to dig up every secret hidden in a Waymouth flower bed or graveyard."

Nick stared back at her. "That's being a little dramatic, don't you think? Especially coming from someone who knows more than most about what's happened in Waymouth in the past seventy years."

"Things I know because they were told me in confidence will stay in confidence. I'm no—what do they say on those police programs on the television? Snitch. I'm no snitch." She sat back in satisfaction.

"But if you're right about Carrie, that she sent other letters like yours, then she likely sent them to people we both know. And one of them went to the person who killed her," said Will.

"Exactly," agreed Aunt Nettie, turning from Nick to Will. "That's what I figure. That's why I wanted Nicky to stop over this morning. I gave him the envelope so he'd know what to look for. It's his job to find out who killed her."

"Sure. But there are times I need the help of concerned citizens, like you," said Nick. "If you hadn't given me this letter, I might not have known Carrie Folk was trying to blackmail anyone."

Aunt Nettie nodded slightly, in acknowledgment.

"Ms. Brewer, will you help me with this? You know people who knew Carrie Folk well. She's spent the past year working for one of your closest friends. And as you just said, you know secrets that other people don't know."

"I've always said you were a bright boy, Nicky."

"I can't go up to people in town and say, 'Excuse me, but do you have a wicked deep dark secret that Carrie Folk was trying to blackmail you about?'" Nick leaned over and looked Aunt Nettie in the eye. "Doesn't sound as though folks would cooperate too well, does it?"

"Not likely," she agreed. "They'd have to admit they were hiding something before they talked to you. And by doing that, which might put them in trouble, it would also make them murder suspects."

"Exactly. So I need someone who understands that. Who's a friend, a close friend. Who can find out, quietly, who Carrie might have been blackmailing. Or trying to blackmail. Find out who might be suspects in her murder." He leaned back in his chair. "I'll take it from there."

"Are you asking me to do your detective work for you?" asked Aunt Nettie.

"I'm asking an old friend to make inquiries of her friends. Do a little kitchen-table gossiping about the death of someone they all knew," said Nick. "In the meantime, I'm going to find out why Carrie Folk needed money so desperately she resorted to blackmail."

"What's going to happen to Billy?" asked Maggie.

"Owen Trask's going to work on that. That's not the job of Homicide. Owen will see if we can locate Billy's father, or any other relatives, and then check to see what state agencies might be able to help. Billy's too old for Child Protective Services to get involved, but there is a unit that's in charge of developmentally delayed adults in need of protection." He turned to Aunt Nettie. "What do you say? Will you help me out?"

"Detective Jeannette Brewer. I like the sound of it," she said. "I don't know what I'll be able to find out. But Maggie's had experience with these things before. Maybe she can help me."

Nick hesitated. "I guess so. Just don't either of you tell anyone you're doing it for me. You're a confidential informant, Ms. Brewer. Make sure all three of you keep this under your hats." He hesitated, and looked directly at Maggie. "And don't do anything dangerous. Anything which might be even remotely hazardous to anyone else's health. All right?"

"I'd be happy to help out, Nicky," said Aunt Nettie, her eyes twinkling. Or maybe bright with champagne.

"Okay. That's settled, then." Nick got up. "Sorry to disrupt your Christmas. We'll stay in touch." He and Will walked to the door. Maggie could hear them talking softly.

Aunt Nettie reached over and touched her hand. "Maggie, my dear, it looks as though we're in for some interesting days ahead. But now I'm feeling a bit weary. Since Will's still chatting with Nicky, would you mind helping me to my bed? I think I'd like a bit of a lie-down. That champagne is making me woozy after all. And I need time to think."

A few minutes later Maggie found Will sitting on the living room couch pouring the last of the champagne into their two glasses.

"What a Christmas!" she said, accepting hers.

"And we haven't even opened the gifts," he said.

"Plenty of time for that. What were you and Nick talking about so seriously before he left?"

"He repeated that I shouldn't let Aunt Nettie get too carried away with this detective thing. To keep an eye on her. And you. And to remember that she got a letter."

"Yes?" said Maggie.

"That means that, officially, she's a suspect. Along with you and me, since Nick has no proof we heard her story for the first time today. Maybe we saw the letter before this morning and wanted to protect her. And we're each other's witnesses about where we all were last night."

Maggie put down her drink. "Seriously? Aunt Nettie's a suspect?"

"If he has a list, we're all on it."

"He never said how Carrie died."

"I guess that's part of the police-only information for now."

"And Aunt Nettie didn't tell us all of her story, either."

"What do you mean?"

"Who was the father of her child? Who performed the illegal abortion? Who else knew what happened? And how did Carrie know about it?"

Will shook his head. "Aunt Nettie. An affair and an abortion. I never would have thought."

"Which? The affair? Or the abortion?"

"The affair, I think."

Maggie smiled. "Sadly, me, too. I wish she'd had legions of admirers. And a dozen children if she'd wanted them. No wonder she gave me those books. She never had a chance to buy books for her own child."

"Don't get all maudlin on me, Maggie. It was years ago. In those days single women didn't keep babies when they got pregnant."

"But abortions were so awful in those days. Not just illegal, but dangerous. Women died."

"Well, she didn't. And it was years ago. No one really cares anymore."

"Aunt Nettie cared," Maggie said softly. "I wonder if the father of the baby knew, or cared."

"I know Aunt Nettie was upset. But the important fact now is that Carrie Folk was killed, and chances are it's because she was blackmailing people. Or trying to. If Aunt Nettie's letter was an example, she was doing a pretty incompetent job of it. We need to find out how Carrie knew so much about a part of Aunt Nettie's life she never told anyone."

"And what else Carrie knew about other people in town."

"You've been involved in murder investigations before, Maggie. You've managed to help the police. Nick appreciates that. But you know I've never liked your getting mixed up in dangerous situations. And I have to tell you, I am not at all enthused about my ninety-two-year-old aunt getting involved when a killer is wandering around town."

Maggie shook her head. "She said she'd be his 'confidential informant.' I liked that."

"I'm afraid she did, too. We've got to keep a close watch on her, so she doesn't get herself in trouble."

"She doesn't go anywhere by herself now, does she?"

"No."

"So you or I will be with her, wherever she wants to go." Maggie snuggled next to Will. "After she wakes up, why don't we talk to her about where she'd like to start. Whom she'd like to talk to."

"And we still need to open our Christmas gifts," Will pointed out.

"And that, too," Maggie agreed. She reached up and kissed him. "Merry Christmas, Will. So far this Brewer family Christmas has been one I'll never forget."

14 Christmas Presents. Black-and-white wood engraving from December 30, 1865 issue of *Harper's Weekly.* Drawn by Solomon Eytinge (1833–1905), it shows a father and mother holding a baby with a rattle, seven other children with their gifts (a watch for the oldest boy, for the others a book, an easel and paints, a box of tools, a doll carriage, a sword.) Grandparents admire a doll the little girl is showing them, and in the background, by the decorated tree, a black woman, perhaps a servant, admires her new bonnet. A sword hangs over the fireplace, symbolizing the end of the Civil War. Eytinge is an American illustrator most remembered today for his illustrations of Charles Dickens's work. 11 x 15 inches. Price: $50.

WILL'S GIFT to Maggie was a gold necklace with a green tourmaline pendant to go with the earrings he'd given her during her first trip to Maine. ("They reflect your eyes. And tourmaline's the Maine state gem.")

She gave him three framed pages of hand-colored engravings from Diderot's *Encyclopedia* ("I love the full title: *Encyclopedia, or a Systematic Dictionary of the Sciences, Arts and Crafts*") from 1772 illustrating carpentry tools, trunk making, and fishnet making in eighteenth-century France. ("Perfect for my office upstairs," he pronounced. "And you didn't even know I had an office here!") She gave Aunt Nettie two large engraved and hand-colored seabirds by the Reverend F.O. Morris to go with the ones that had been hanging in her bedroom upstairs. ("How thoughtful of you to remember that I love Morris prints, Maggie. I've moved my others to my downstairs bedroom, so these will be wonderful additions. I'll think of you every time I see them.")

Will's big gifts to his aunt were a red (her favorite color) comforter for her bed and a brown-and-white alpaca shawl. "Wonderfully warm and soft," Maggie said, admiringly fingering the shawl. "I didn't know there were alpacas in Maine."

"Quite a few actually," said Will. "Majestic-looking creatures from a distance. But mean up close. When I was at the farm where I picked out the shawl one of them spat at me."

He helped her fasten her new necklace around her neck, and insisted on hanging his new prints in his office that afternoon.

Maggie helped him find the perfect spot on his office wall. The room was already full of all the supplies he'd need for on-line selling. But he'd added personal touches. She smiled at seeing a shelf of structures made with Tinkertoys in his bookcase. ("My old favorites. I couldn't throw them out," he explained.) They were next to a small photograph of his wife.

He'd hung the "adults only" Advent calendar Maggie'd sent him six weeks before on the bulletin board above his desk. "I guess I'll have to take it down now," he said regretfully. "Every night before I went to bed I opened one of the little windows and thought of you. It was as though you'd left a gift on my pillow."

She gave him a quick hug. "I'm glad you enjoyed the brandy-filled Swiss chocolates. I hoped you wouldn't think the whole idea was silly."

"Not silly. Sweet," he answered. "And I don't just mean the chocolates."

"It's been a memorable Christmas," declared Aunt Nettie when they'd returned downstairs. "And not all for bad reasons, either."

Daylight ended by four in the afternoon. Winter days were shorter in Maine even though they were only four hundred miles north of New Jersey.

They'd cleaned up the morning's food and drink, and wrappings and ribbons from the afternoon's gift opening, added wood to the fireplace, and settled in the living room. Lights and ornaments were still glittering on the tree and the house smelled of pine, but Christmas morning already seemed long past.

"Have you thought about where you want to begin on your detective mission?" Maggie asked Aunt Nettie as they snacked on crackers and locally made cheeses and a few carrot sticks with Will's homemade hummus. No one wanted wine after the morning's champagne, and as planned, they were still too full from breakfast to crave heavier food.

"Since I got that awful letter, what's bothered me most is how Carrie could have known about what I did so long ago. I thought only two, or maybe three, people still alive knew even part of that story. And I can't believe any of them would tell Carrie. They'd have no reason to betray my trust."

"Sounds simple to me," said Will. "Despite what you thought, someone you know can't be trusted. One of them told Carrie."

"It's more complicated than that," said Aunt Nettie. "I wish it were simple."

Maggie reached out and touched Aunt Nettie's hand. "It's Betty, isn't it?"

Aunt Nettie bit her lip and was silent for a minute. "I hope, for now anyway, that you're brighter than the state police."

Will looked from one of the women to the other. "Betty Hoskins? She's not coherent enough to tell anyone a story."

Aunt Nettie shook her head. "That's the problem. Carrie's spent hours and hours with Betty for the past year. And yes, Betty's thoughts and words are confused. Alzheimer's does that. But most of what she gets confused is what's happening now. She has much better recollections of what happened in the past."

"When she was here, at your party, she was remembering events from years ago, wasn't she?" Maggie said. "She got confused when Ruth mentioned her new grandson, Jonas. She got him confused with Ruth's husband, Jonas, who died years ago."

"I remember that," said Will. "So you're thinking Betty may have told Carrie about events that happened when she was young."

"Sometimes what she says doesn't make sense unless you know her well. Unless you understand the context of what she's trying to say. But Carrie's been with her so many months, she may have been able to put the stories together."

"How sad," said Maggie. "Sad that Betty doesn't know she told your secret, and even sadder that Carrie took the time and effort to try to blackmail you about an event so painful. It hurt you, and forced you to talk about something you wanted to forget."

Aunt Nettie waved her hand dismissively.

"No," Maggie continued. "I'm sorry, Aunt Nettie, but that's the truth. It was cruel. Will and I don't think any less of you for knowing your secret." She looked over at Will for confirmation, and Will nodded slightly. "It was a different time, and you were in a horrible situation. But to have someone force you to relive it again, now, was barbaric!"

Aunt Nettie smiled a little. "'Barbaric' is a little strong, Maggie. But thank you for understanding, both of you, and for being on my side. It's funny. I got the letter several days ago. I had time to think about it. And I decided I really didn't care anymore. Secrets hurt those who keep them, too. I'm glad mine is out in the open now."

"But knowing how Carrie found out about you doesn't tell us who killed her. Maybe her being killed had nothing to do with blackmail," said Will.

"Carrie had a decent job," said Aunt Nettie. "I'm sure Ruth paid her whatever she asked for, and nursing help doesn't come cheap. Nicky is going to figure out what she needed the money for. For some reason, she was desperate. That's why I can't believe I'm the only one she was trying to blackmail."

"How much did she ask for?" Will asked.

"She wanted twenty-five thousand dollars."

"That's not an amount most people in Waymouth could easily get hold of," he said. "Although maybe your friend Ruth has that much easily available. But, on the other hand, twenty-five thousand dollars wouldn't be enough to change anyone's life."

"Or to risk going to jail for," added Maggie.

"Which is why, you see, she must have sent letters to other people, too. And Betty wouldn't have chatted just about me. My life's been pretty boring compared to most other people's."

"That's why Nick asked for your help," Maggie pointed out. "He didn't think of Betty's being the source of the information. But he knew you'd guess who else might be vulnerable to blackmail."

"He has no idea what he's asked me to do. Betty knew everything," said Aunt Nettie, softly. "We all knew each other's secrets. Or most of them. And many had more consequences than mine."

"Who is 'we'?" said Will. "'The girls'? You and Ruth and Betty and Doreen?"

"Those are 'the girls' today. In the past there were more of us. Gloria and Susan and Doreen's mother, Mary, of course, who was Nicky's grandmother. They're gone now. Betty might confuse stories about all of us, and our families, and maybe about other people in town, too."

"But if the only ones of the original group who're left are you and Ruth and Betty," said Maggie, "then it's simple. Carrie couldn't have tried to blackmail Betty. And you can ask Ruth whether she got one of the letters."

Aunt Nettie shook her head. "What she wrote in my letter only affected me. But most events weren't isolated. They have causes and effects that have gone on for years. Even in families, different people know parts of the whole. What Betty might have said could involve a lot of people in Waymouth. And who knows what Carrie was able to put together…whether it was the truth, or some combination of partial truths that Betty dreamed or remembered or imagined." She paused. "Knowing part of a story doesn't mean you know everything. It might mean you really know nothing." She clasped her hands and held them tightly. "I wish I knew exactly what Betty told her."

"I'm not following you," said Will.

"I can't be any clearer now," said Aunt Nettie. "I'll talk to people. I'll ask questions. But I'm not going to be like Carrie or Betty. I am not going to tell what I know about other people unless it's a matter of life or death."

"But it might be," said Maggie. "How long will it be before other people figure out Betty was the one opening the bag of past secrets? Whoever killed Carrie could kill again."

"It took Carrie a year or more to take bits and pieces of Betty's words and fit them together. And Betty's making less sense now than she was even three months ago. No, I don't think we have to worry too much about Betty. Anyone who knows her will understand she can't reveal much more now. We'll tell Nick when we need to, or he'll figure it out on his own. She won't be able to help him."

Will and Maggie exchanged glances.

Aunt Nettie was making a serious decision about what to tell the police and what not. But on the other hand, she was probably right. Betty couldn't be questioned with any hope of getting clear information. And she certainly wasn't the murderer. Even if she'd understood what Carrie was doing, she couldn't have gotten to Carrie's house, much less been able to focus on why she was there, or been able to kill her.

"You're right, Maggie. I have to talk with Ruth," Aunt Nettie continued. "She's the only one who needs to know what Betty did. She'll understand, and she'll be able to keep an eye on anyone who wants to talk to her. Will you go with me to see her tomorrow morning? You can help me get over the snow and ice, and I should have a witness. You've helped Nicky before, and he trusts you."

"I'd be happy to, Aunt Nettie. But what about Will?"

"Will's a Brewer. He's part of my family, and he's living in Waymouth now. You're from away, and Ruth doesn't know anything about you. Sometimes people feel safer talking to someone they may not run into at the town wharf or see at The Gull's Cry or The Great Blue when they stop for a sandwich. Plus, you're a woman. It's easier for a woman to talk with other women."

Aunt Nettie had planned this out.

"We'll call first, of course, but with Carrie gone, Ruth will be home. She has to look after Betty. I don't think that daughter-in-law of hers, that Jenny, will be helping her a lot."

"What about Betty's daughter, Miranda?"

"She may be there," agreed Aunt Nettie. "But her business is in Portland. She doesn't stay around here long. She loves her mother, but she's not big on nursing."

"I'll go with you tomorrow," said Maggie. "Maybe Betty's family will be more help than you think."

"Family? It all depends," said Aunt Nettie. "Do you have family, Maggie? You never talk about your family."

"My mother and father were killed in a car crash about eleven years ago. I do have an older brother, Joe, twelve years older than I am. But he left home when I was six and I haven't seen him since my parents' funeral. Last time I heard from him was a Christmas card about five years ago, postmarked in Arizona."

"So you're not close."

"Not exactly," said Maggie. Where was Joe today? Was he married or single? Was he a father? She couldn't begin to know, although she often wondered. She sent him silent good wishes, hoping his decision not to be part of her life was the right one. She would have liked having a big brother to confide in; a caring uncle for her child. But maybe, for his own reasons, Joe couldn't be either of those people.

"The best of families can be blessings. Like Will, moving from Buffalo to come and keep an eye on me," Aunt Nettie said. "The worst of families can be nightmares. Or emotional or financial drains. But we all crave those ties that bind. And most of the time, for better or for worse, they give back what we put into them."

Come to think of it, Maggie thought, hadn't she read that most murder victims were killed by close friends? Or family.

15

What Shall We Do Next? Winslow Homer wood engraving published in *Harper's Weekly* July 31, 1869. Pictures six elegantly dressed young women playing croquet on a summer's day. Two younger girls watch from a porch with another woman who is sewing and looks bored. 13.75 x 9 inches. Price: $350.

AFTER A QUICK breakfast the next morning Will went upstairs to his office to make phone calls while Aunt Nettie used the house telephone to call Ruth.

Maggie cleaned up the kitchen, keeping out of both their ways, and then pulled on her heaviest sweater and her jacket and boots and headed outside to clear the driveway after the night's snowfall. In the morning sun the snow glistened as though tiny pieces of mica had been sprinkled on top, like sugar on Christmas cookies.

Mica had been mined nearby in the nineteenth century, she remembered. It was used instead of glass as window panels in Franklin stoves and small oil lamps. She threw shovelfuls of snow onto the piles lining the driveway that were already over four feet high. Her shoulders and back would ache tonight.

If Will bought that other house he could move his RV and everything in Aunt Nettie's barn into the barn there, put Aunt Nettie's car in her barn, and plow this drive. Digging out two vehicles with shovels every day would drive anyone south in winter.

Ready for a little sitting-down time, she went back in the house. Aunt Nettie and Will were glaring at each other.

"Maggie. There you are," said Aunt Nettie, turning to her. "I wondered where you were hiding."

Hiding? "I was shoveling the driveway."

"Good. Because I'd like you to take me to see Ruth now. In my car."

Maggie glanced at Will. "Yesterday I said I'd go with you to see Ruth. But it all depends on Ruth's schedule. And Will's."

"Ruth can see us now. She's invited us. And I don't want to try to climb into your high van. My car will be easier. I can drive it, or you can." Aunt Nettie shot a look at Will. Had she been threatening to drive herself? She probably still had a license. Only last summer she'd been driving.

"I'd be glad to drive." Maggie looked over at Will, who was frowning and shaking his head. "But what about Will?"

"Will isn't coming with us. If he needs to go out he can take your van."

Ah. That was it. Will had made other plans that involved using a car.

"Will, that's all right with me. You can use my van."

"It would be nice to be consulted before people make plans around here." He stalked off, muttering about "not being needed" and "grocery shopping" and "lawyer," but Maggie didn't have time to follow him. Aunt Nettie was already trying to put her coat on. "Ruth's expecting us, Maggie. I knew you'd be on my side."

Maggie reached around Aunt Nettie's back and helped her on with her coat. "I didn't realize we were choosing sides. But I guess we'll be off. Mustn't keep Ruth waiting." She held the back door to the ramp open and called upstairs, "Will, Aunt Nettie and I are leaving. We'll be back as soon as we can."

"Don't hurry. You're busy, so I'm having lunch with Jo," he answered.

Maggie ground her teeth as she helped Aunt Nettie down the back ramp.

Today the inside of Ruth's house didn't resemble the elegant home that had been decked for a party two days before.

Nor did Ruth herself resemble the refined hostess she'd been then. She met them at the door, cashmere sweater wet with baby spit-up, designer jeans sagging, and hair straggling. The dark shadows under her eyes were not makeup.

She started to hug Aunt Nettie, but then glanced down at her damp sweater and shrugged. "You'll excuse the general chaos."

"We've both seen worse," said Aunt Nettie, patting her arm. "How's Betty holding up?"

"She's totally confused. She depends on her schedule, and now there's no schedule." Ruth shook her head. "She doesn't understand why Carrie isn't here during the day, or why the baby's crying so much, or why 'other people' are in the house. Come back to the kitchen. I can hear her more easily there."

Maggie glanced into the living room as they walked past. The bar was gone, but the furniture that had been moved to allow it to fit in the corner had not been replaced. Christmas wrapping paper, boxes, toys, and baby clothes littered the floor. Dirty dishes and glasses were on several tables, along with an open bag of potato chips and an empty bottle of Dewar's.

The door to Betty's room was closed.

"I'm hoping she can sleep a little," said Ruth. "The baby's napping, and so are his parents. The house hasn't been so quiet in days. That's why when you said you could come right over, I said you should."

"Maybe you should be sleeping yourself," said Aunt Nettie. "Ruth dear, excuse me, but you look dreadful."

"And feel worse. Between the baby's crying and watching Betty, I've hardly slept in days now."

"Have you called that home health aide agency here in town? Maybe they could find a temporary person to help you with Betty until you can hire someone full time."

"I called. But it's the holidays, and they have no one available until January at the earliest. And most of their people aren't trained nurses, the way Carrie was. With Betty's diabetes, I need to trust that someone knows what he or she is doing."

"Oh, Ruth."

"Doreen's volunteered to come and sit with her tonight. I'm looking forward to getting a good night's sleep then."

"Thank goodness," said Aunt Nettie. "You can depend on Doreen."

"She hasn't been an active nurse since Zelda was little, but I'm sure she can deal with Betty's diabetes and she knows how to lift her. And Betty knows Doreen as well as she knows anyone now, so even one night will be an enormous help."

"I understand."

"The one blessing's been that I've been so involved with coping here, I haven't had time to focus on what happened to Carrie. I still can't believe anyone would kill her."

"Ruth, I brought Maggie with me because she's been involved with murder investigations before. You remember, when Rachel's daughter was murdered a couple of years ago?"

"Horrible situation. Yes, of course I remember. How could any of us forget?"

"Maggie was the one who found her killer. Maggie can be trusted."

Ruth looked Maggie up and down, as though she were buying a horse. "What do you mean, Nettie?"

"I think we have a problem, Ruth. Tell me the truth, now. Did you get a letter from Carrie? Or did she ask you for extra money recently?"

Ruth stopped short and lowered her voice. "How did you know that?"

"She sent me a letter last week, asking for twenty-five thousand dollars."

"You? But why?"

Aunt Nettie leaned toward Ruth and spoke very carefully. "You remember...the abortion...I had years ago?"

Ruth glanced at Maggie and then swallowed hard. "She knew about...that?"

"She did. I won't ask what she knew about you."

"No, no."

Clearly they were talking in circles and avoiding actual topics because Maggie was there. But it didn't matter. Ruth had a secret. Carrie had known what it was.

"She was trying to blackmail you?"

"She asked for a hundred thousand dollars."

Aunt Nettie nodded. "She knew you had more money than I did."

"I gave her ten thousand. I told her I'd give her more in January. And of course I asked if she was in trouble. I asked what she needed the money for."

"And?"

"She wouldn't tell me. She just said she had to have the rest of the hundred thousand by the end of January. That she couldn't wait around."

"That doesn't sound like Carrie."

"I didn't think so either. I was worried about her. I kept wondering what she'd gotten herself into that she needed that sort of cash. She didn't spend money on clothes or jewelry. She's lived in that little house of hers for years. Her car is ten years old. Billy's with her all the time, so she doesn't eat out, or travel. I thought of on-line gambling, although she doesn't seem the type. But then, I'm not sure there is a type for gambling." Ruth hesitated. "I wondered if Billy might be ill. She's taken time off for doctors' appointments several times recently. But she said he wasn't, and he hasn't seemed ill to me. Of course, with Betty having a weak immune system, I'm very conscious of anyone being near her who might be carrying germs."

Aunt Nettie nodded sagely. "Who else do you think she might have tried to blackmail?"

Ruth thought. "I don't know. I haven't thought about that. I thought it was just me. Honestly, I didn't even think of it as blackmail. She worked here, and somehow she'd found out…things. I was afraid she'd tell my children, or the police, or …" She looked over at Maggie. "I was afraid she'd blab about things that were none of her business. You understand. I thought I could manage. That I could keep her quiet."

"And now someone else has," said Aunt Nettie. "Permanently. And I'm afraid you and I are both suspects."

"Suspects!" said Ruth. "You mean the police think we might have killed Carrie?"

"Nicky Strait talked to me yesterday. I told him about the letter Carrie'd sent to me. He said anyone she'd been threatening would be a possible suspect."

"He can't think you or I …"

"That's why I'm here. We have to figure out what Carrie knew, and who might have killed her."

"I don't want anyone investigating my family." Ruth glanced at Maggie. "You understand, Nettie. Not even at this late date."

"That's why we're in a pickle, don't you see?" Aunt Nettie said, reaching over and touching Ruth's trembling hand. "That's why we have to get this taken care of before Nicky does."

"I'm too old for all of this. It's too much to cope with at my age, Nettie. Too much."

"Ruth," Maggie interrupted softly, "how did you think Carrie found out about your secret?"

"I've been pretty sure she heard parts of it here in this house. Betty's tongue meanders some days. What she says isn't clear. But Carrie sat with her for over a year, and Carrie grew up in Waymouth. She probably put Betty's words together with old rumors or stories she'd heard."

"I agree. That's how I thought she learned what she wrote in her letter to me," said Aunt Nettie. "Even if what Carrie understood wasn't exactly the truth, her version could still be dangerous. Most of what we're thinking of," she looked at Ruth, who nodded, as though they were communicating in a secret language, "happened a long time ago. Few of us are still alive to explain or give our versions anymore."

"Who else might Betty have talked about?" asked Maggie.

"Anyone in town, I suppose," said Ruth. "Most likely herself, of course. And she was close to Mary and Susan. And Gloria, I suppose. But they're all gone now."

The two elderly women looked at each other, perhaps seeing the past, and the friends they'd shared it with.

"Carrie was a good woman," said Aunt Nettie finally. "She had a hard life, coping with Billy and all. No one should have killed her."

"If she'd needed money she could have just asked me," agreed Ruth. "If she had a good reason for needing it, I would have helped her. She went about it in the wrong way. Why, for heaven's sake, did she have to cause all this trouble?"

"She's the one who's dead," Maggie pointed out.

"True enough," Ruth agreed. "She used up her life taking care of Billy, and now Billy has no one. Who knows what will become of him now?"

"So you can't think of anyone else Carrie might have tried to blackmail?" said Maggie. "Anyone at all?"

The two women shook their heads.

"This may sound paranoid," said Maggie. "But I'd keep a close eye on Betty. Someone killed Carrie. And if that someone was another person she tried to blackmail, then he or she is going to want to stop whoever gave Carrie the information. And you both agree Betty was most likely that source."

"I don't think you need to worry, Maggie. I can't find anyone else to watch Betty. Not even her own daughter will look after her. Miranda wants Betty in a nursing home. So unless you think I'm a danger to Betty, or I die of exhaustion, she's safe." Ruth tried to smile, but her expression was more of a grimace.

"Good. Now, will you excuse me?" Maggie asked. "Ruth, would you mind if I used your bathroom?"

"Use the one off my bedroom, upstairs," Ruth answered. "Go up the front stairs. My bedroom is the first on the right. The bathroom's just inside. Brian and Jenny have taken over the other one."

Maggie had felt like an interloper in the kitchen. Ruth and Aunt Nettie might be talking in front of her, but they weren't saying all they wanted to. Perhaps if she left them alone Aunt Nettie would learn more. If there was anything more to learn.

On her way upstairs she noted the hand-colored Curtis botanical engravings on the staircase wall. Their elaborate French matting and frames probably cost more than the mid-nineteenth-century prints themselves, but the selection was excellent, and the progression of colored flowers from brightly colored reds on the first floor to pinks and then to yellows and finally to blues on the second floor worked well. She glanced down the hallway to see if the progression of prints was continued there, but instead the colors were picked up in the wallpaper.

Ruth's bedroom wasn't empty.

A man with his back to the door was rifling through the contents of the top drawer of a mahogany desk. She stood for a moment, certain he didn't know she was there, before she spoke. "Excuse me, but is this Ruth's bedroom?"

Brian almost jumped as he turned toward her. "Ah, yes."

"I'm Maggie Summer. We met at the party Christmas Eve? Sorry to disturb you. Ruth said I could use her bathroom."

"Of course. It's over there." He pointed to his left. He stuck a couple of papers in his pocket as she passed him.

When she left the bathroom he was gone. Ruth's checkbook was on top of the desk.

Downstairs, Maggie helped Aunt Nettie into her coat. "By the way, what does Brian do for a living?" she asked as they were walking to the front door.

"He's a lawyer," said Ruth. "Works for a bank in Philadelphia. He just bought a big new house. He's the most successful of my children."

"You must be very proud of him," said Maggie.

"I am," said Ruth. "Everything turned out well for him."

"Does he know you gave ten thousand dollars to Carrie?"

"I didn't tell him, if that's what you're asking," Ruth answered. "I hadn't told anyone until now, when I told both of you. Why?"

"I just wondered who else knew about Carrie's attempts to get money," said Maggie.

"It wasn't anyone's business but mine and Carrie's. Did you tell anyone about her contacting you, Nettie?"

"Not until Christmas morning, after we heard what happened to her. Then I told Will and Maggie. And Nicky Strait, since he's heading the investigation."

"We appreciate your taking the time to talk to us," said Maggie.

"You'll let me know if you find out anything more?" Ruth asked.

"We will," Aunt Nettie assured her. "And you'll call if you think of anything else that might help?"

"We've always been here for each other," agreed Ruth. "Always. No matter what."

The two old friends clung to each other for a moment in more than a hug. It was a moment of solidarity.

16

Trapping in the Adirondacks. Winslow Homer wood engraving of two trappers in a canoe. The man paddling the craft, probably a guide, is roughly dressed. Ahead of him in the canoe is a younger, better-dressed man, holding up a trap from which a dead beaver is hanging. Published in *Every Saturday*, one of the smaller-circulation papers Homer worked for, on December 24, 1870. From 1870 until 1902 Homer often visited the Adirondacks, usually the North Woods Club in Minerva, New York, and painted there. 9 x 12 inches. Price: $450.

FOR THEIR LUNCH Maggie heated turkey noodle soup Will had made (under Aunt Nettie's direction) and frozen after Thanksgiving. Will was still out. ("Having lunch with that Jo Heartwood again, I see," said Aunt Nettie.) Again?

"How many children does Ruth have?" Maggie asked, she hoped, casually. She wanted to know more about Brian. And didn't want to think about Jo.

"Three. Noah, her oldest boy, he's a carpenter up to Caribou. Followed a girl up there years ago and stayed. They have two grown children. Stacy, she's next. Lives out in California. Thought she could be a movie star. Ruth paid for acting lessons for a while, but then Stacy got a job doing something technical for one of the television companies. Hasn't been home in a while. You met Brian, her youngest. He got into a little trouble when he was a teenager, and changed colleges a couple of times, but finally got his law degree. Ruth was partial to his first wife, but hasn't taken to Jenny, this new one. They've been married a couple of years now. Little Jonas is his first child, and I don't recall Brian's coming home for Christmas in a while. So maybe the new baby will bring Ruth and Brian closer together." Aunt Nettie yawned. "I think it's time for my nap. I don't usually have as busy a morning."

After Aunt Nettie was curled up under her new Christmas comforter, Maggie decided it was time to check in with Nick. It had been over twenty-four hours since Carrie's murder. Maybe Nick's team had found evidence at the murder scene that yielded more information than she and Aunt Nettie had heard at Ruth Weston's home. The call went to Nick's voice mail. But a few minutes later Maggie's cell phone rang.

"Hello, Maggie Summer? This is Waymouth Deputy Owen Trask. I believe we've met before."

"Yes; I remember," answered Maggie. Owen Trask was Nick's local Waymouth Sheriff's Department contact on murder cases. She remembered him as young, determined, and in Nick's shadow.

"Detective Strait asked me to return your call. How can I help you?"

Maggie hesitated. Nick had cautioned Aunt Nettie not to talk to anyone but him.

"I'd rather speak directly with Nick."

"Wouldn't we all?" Deputy Trask sighed audibly. "He isn't here now. He's up to Augusta, with the medical examiner. He told me you or Ms. Brewer might call. That you were checking sources for him."

Then it wasn't a tightly held secret, at least not from Owen Trask. "I was calling to update him," said Maggie. "This morning Nettie Brewer and I talked with Ruth Weston. Carrie Folk *had* tried to blackmail her. She'd asked Ruth for one hundred thousand dollars. It was similar to what she tried with Nettie, but in Ruth's case it worked. Ruth gave Carrie ten thousand dollars and promised her more in the new year. Carrie was insistent she needed the rest within the next month, but refused to say why."

"Did Ruth tell anyone else about this?"

"She says she didn't."

"Did she have any ideas about anyone else Carrie Folk might have approached for money?"

"She and Nettie both think Carrie was basing her threats on rambling things Betty Hoskins, Ruth's sister, said while Carrie was taking care of her. Betty's in her eighties and has Alzheimer's. She gets the past and the present confused."

"So based on the confused thinking of a senile old woman Carrie Folk managed to patch together what she felt was enough incriminating information to ask Ruth Weston for one hundred thousand dollars—and Ruth started to pay it?" asked Deputy Trask.

"That's right. Carrie's probably the source of her information about Nettie Brewer, too."

"I've seen the letter Nettie gave Nick. I'm sorry she had to go through that. Clearly it was embarrassing for her, but what was in the letter was hardly serious enough to warrant blackmail. Even Carrie must have known that. She only asked for twenty-five thousand. One hundred thousand is a lot more."

"Nettie and Ruth seemed to think the difference in the amounts asked was because Carrie knew Ruth was better off financially."

"Maybe so. What was she threatening to reveal about Ruth?"

Maggie'd been waiting for that question. "I don't know. Nettie and Ruth both seemed to know what it was, but they didn't say it out loud, so I have no idea."

"Okay. So Ruth's now on our list. She's a suspect. She was being blackmailed for some dark past secret."

"I guess she has to be on your list for now. But she's almost as old as Nettie," Maggie reluctantly agreed. "And her son and daughter-in-law, Brian and Jenny Weston, and their baby were in the house that night, too, along with her sister, Betty. Ruth would have been up, or dozing, most of the night, watching Betty. And the baby has colic, so Brian and Jenny didn't sleep well. If Ruth had left the house someone in the family would have noticed." Although, Maggie thought to herself, Ruth and Betty would have been on the first floor, and the young couple on the second floor, unless they'd gone down to the kitchen to heat formula or to the living room to play Santa Claus.

"Good point," said Deputy Trask. "I was planning to talk to the Westons' neighbors to see if anyone'd seen a member of the family leaving their house late that night or early Christmas morning. I've just moved that item up on my priority list."

"One more thing," Maggie added. "Do you know anything about Brian Weston? I mean, personally?"

"Brian Weston?" Deputy Trask paused. "He grew up here in Waymouth, of course. He's about ten years older than I am, so I didn't know him well. He was sort of a dork. The kind of kid who tries to be cool but gets caught every time he scores a smoke or a six-pack. I remember hearing once he'd been caught in the high school cafeteria sharing liquor from a thermos he'd filled from his family's liquor cabinet. That sort of thing. Why?"

"Ruth Weston said he was a successful lawyer at a Philadelphia bank; that he'd recently bought a new house. He has a young blond wife, and a new baby."

"Good for him. Guess he's not a dork anymore."

"While I was at their house this morning I walked in on him. He was in his mother's room, rummaging through her desk as though he was looking for something. He took several papers before he left."

"Interesting. And you're wondering?"

"I'm wondering whether he found out about the blackmail. Maybe he found the letter from Carrie. Or, if Ruth paid her the ten thousand dollars by check, maybe he found the receipt. Or he overheard them talking. I don't know. But if he thought his mother was being blackmailed, that might give him a motive."

"Good thought. Although I'd think a blackmailer would want cash, there might be evidence that Ruth withdrew the money from somewhere. Nick has all the papers and the computer the crime scene crew removed from Carrie Folk's house. I'll follow up with him and see whether she deposited the money Ruth says she gave her. I'll also make a note to see what I can find out about Brian Weston. We hadn't gotten to the possibility of anyone else finding out about the blackmailing yet." Maggie could hear paper rustling at the other end of the line. Deputy Trask was not working in an all-electronic environment. "And you're sure neither Ruth nor Nettie thought of anyone else Betty Hoskins could have mentioned when her mind was wandering? Any random thoughts? Carrie Folk's done home nursing for families in Waymouth for years. She probably knew more about folks around here than most people. It seems strange she'd choose two old ladies to blackmail."

"Maybe they're not the only ones. Or maybe she thought of them because they're the ones she's been with most recently. I have no idea. But I agree. Nettie's incident happened in the 1940s, and I have a feeling that whatever Ruth's secret was, it's been hidden for a long time, too. They mentioned that Betty had secrets of her own, but of course, she has no money, and Ruth would know if Carrie were attempting blackmail on her behalf. They did mention three other names—Susan, who I assumed was Susan Newall, and Mary, Doreen Strait's mother. And a Gloria. I don't know anything about her. But all three women are dead, so they're not prime candidates for blackmail either."

"I wouldn't think so." Deputy Trask sighed. "What about Betty's daughter, Miranda? If we're considering Ruth's son, seems to me we should think about Betty's daughter."

"Why? If Betty wasn't being blackmailed, that doesn't make sense. Although Miranda was in Waymouth at the party Christmas Eve with her spouse, Joan. I think they were spending the night here in town, but not at Ruth's house."

More rustling of papers. "That's somewhere in my notes. They live in Portland, but stayed over at the Captain's Quarters on Christmas Eve and came back to the Westons' house to open gifts Christmas morning. They're back in Portland now." Trask cleared his throat.

"If Carrie had a nasty story about Miranda's mother, maybe she tried to get money out of Miranda."

"I suppose it's possible," said Maggie. That sounded a little far-fetched. At this point Betty couldn't care what was said about her.

"Could you see what you can find out about Miranda Hoskins? You being a woman and all."

That would qualify me, Maggie thought. Along with fifty percent of the population. "I'll see what I can do," she promised, a bit tartly. "But I only have a few more days here. Isn't that your job?"

Pause. Deputy Trask's voice dropped. "I know Nick's Will's friend. So you probably know Nick has family issues right now. I'm helping him out here. Waymouth's Sheriff's Department doesn't report directly to the Maine State Police, so I've got my own job, too, and this time of year there's a lot going on. I'd really appreciate your help. As I remember, you're good at this, Maggie. As a favor?"

Weird. Was Nick having that many problems with Zelda?

"Okay, Owen. I'll find out what I can about Miranda. But fair is fair. You let me know if you find anything that heads you in another direction. Because I came to Maine for a vacation. And so far I haven't had much of one."

"Deal. And I owe you a beer. And maybe a batch of Christmas cookies. My wife makes terrific Christmas cookies."

Just what she needed. Maggie looked down at the tight waistband of her jeans. More Christmas cookies.

"SO, how was your morning playing detective?" Will hung his L.L. Bean barn jacket on a hook inside the kitchen door.

"Added a couple of possible suspects to the list," Maggie answered.

"How was your lunch with Jo?"

"Lunch was fine. Jo wasn't the only one there. She'd brought Art Krieger along, the lawyer she's suggesting I use to look at the contract, if we go to one. He's new to town, and hungry for clients. Seems nice enough. We talked about several things I'd like negotiated, and he agreed to work on them. Plus, he'll give me a special rate for doing the house plus a new will, power of attorney, and medical directive. All things I need to take care of anyway."

"So you're negotiating for the house?"

"Work in progress." He bent over and kissed her. "Aunt Nettie napping?"

"I think talking with Ruth this morning exhausted her."

"Did Ruth receive one of those blackmail letters, too?"

"Hers asked for a hundred thousand dollars. She gave Carrie ten thousand, with the promise of more after the first of the year."

Will whistled. "Ruth must have a serious secret."

"I guess. She didn't share it with me. I'm hoping Nick's able to figure out why Carrie needed the money. That would help explain why she was doing this."

"I ran into him at the restaurant. He said Carrie'd been researching cancer treatments on the Web, and high-end facilities for people like Billy."

Then Nick wasn't in Augusta with the medical examiner. Or maybe he'd gotten back and hadn't checked in with Owen.

"Ruth mentioned Carrie'd taken days off for doctors' appointments. Maybe either she or Billy had cancer. That could explain why she needed money. Treatments can be expensive."

Will shrugged. "When they get the medical examiner's report

back they'll know if it was Carrie. If it was Billy, that would be important to know before they find him a place to live."

"They haven't heard from the medical examiner yet, then?"

"Didn't sound that way. But I just saw Nick in passing. Why?"

"I talked with Owen Trask about an hour ago. He said Nick was in Augusta, with the medical examiner."

Will shook his head. "Owen must have gotten mixed up. An hour ago Nick was at The Great Blue. Maybe he was going to Augusta after that."

"Maybe."

"Why were you talking to Owen?"

"I called Nick. Owen returned my call. He's helping out with the investigation. He's going to check out Ruth's son Brian, on the chance that Brian found out about the blackmail. He's asked me to talk to Betty's daughter, Miranda. Do you know anything about her?"

Maggie knew she was sharing more information about the investigation than she should. But Aunt Nettie had promised not to tell anyone what she found out. Maggie hadn't promised. And Nick was Will's friend. She didn't think he'd mind Will's knowing.

"Not a thing. I haven't seen or heard from her in years. Other than seeing her across the room at the party the other night, of course."

"But you did know her?"

"She and Brian are both about the same age as Nick and I, so they were around town when we were young. But I was only here summers, so I didn't know the local kids the way Nick did. I just remember Miranda lived in that big house and hung out at the library. Not a party type. Brian was sort of a hanger-on. He tried to be one of the crowd, but never quite got it right. You know; the kind of kid who wears a buttoned shirt when everyone else wears a T-shirt. I knew who he was, but didn't know much about him. Nick would know his whole story. I think they were in the same class at school."

"Brian was a lost soul who kept getting in trouble because he wanted so hard to be liked. He'd be the one who'd buy beer for under-age parties, and then his 'friends' would tell the police he'd done it… and keep most of the beer he'd bought for themselves." Aunt Nettie had appeared in the doorway of her room leaning on her cane. "Miranda was the smart one. She's never been in any kind of trouble.

She lives in Portland, and thinks her mother should be in a nursing home for people with Alzheimer's, not at home with Ruth. To give her the benefit of the doubt, I believe she thinks it would be best for Ruth, too, if Ruth would let go, and trust other people to care for poor Betty. But Ruth refuses to consider that."

"With Carrie gone, it's going to be especially hard for Ruth," said Maggie. "I can see Miranda's point."

"But Ruth won't let go. They've been together too long. Miranda wants to have a say in the care of her mother, and Ruth won't listen to her. Then she complains when Miranda doesn't come to visit Betty more often, even though Betty doesn't always recognize her."

"What does Miranda do for a living?"

"She owns a fancy clothing boutique in the Old Port. What we used to call cocktail dresses and prom dresses and elegant gowns for garden parties. Lord knows who buys them nowadays. Maybe there are benefits for the Portland Museum or other galas. I understand Portland is more high-style than it used to be."

"And her partner?"

"Joan's a dentist. So the two of them are set for fancy dresses and white teeth." Aunt Nettie shook her head. "Owen Trask thinks you should investigate Miranda? I'll leave that up to you. I can't see Miranda in her finery murdering anyone, and Portland's a mite far for me to journey. Maybe Will would go with you."

Maggie looked at him. "Will? I've never made it to the Portland Museum of Art. They have several Winslow Homers I'd love to see. Do you think tomorrow we could make a field trip?"

"Actually, I'd hoped we could take at least one day in Portland." He hesitated, and then tapped his pocket. "As long as I keep my cell phone turned on, I don't see why it shouldn't be tomorrow. Aunt Nettie, if I make up a sandwich for your lunch, and we get back by the middle of the afternoon, will you promise to take it easy? I could see if Cousin Rachel could come to visit you."

"Don't you go bothering Rachel for those few hours," Aunt Nettie said. "I'll be fine. You two go have fun. I may be old, but I'm not doddering or senile."

Thank goodness, Maggie thought. Although who would guess that anyone's losing their memory would lead to murder?

17 **City of Portland, Maine.** Map of city, black-and-white (slightly off-white with age) with surrounding water (and parks and cemetery inside city) blue. Detailed; shows and names streets and wharves. Also shows a little of Deering, Cape Elizabeth, Back Cove, Fore River, and adjoining Portland Harbor (not Casco Bay). 1880 or 1890. Map outer dimensions 9.5 x 12 inches; on paper 11.5 x 14 inches. From an atlas of the period. Price: $70.

AS WILL headed the car out of Waymouth and down Route 1, Maggie reached over and touched his knee. "An adventure! We haven't been out of Waymouth since I arrived."

"And it's time. I do love Aunt Nettie and that town. And I love living in Maine, Maggie. I do. But there are days I feel a bit strangled." He looked over at her. "After having lived in Buffalo, and spending years traveling to do antiques shows in Boston, New York, Philadelphia...well, I need to at least get to Portland more often. Portland's growing up, and it's growing in the right direction. In the past few years it's become an exciting place to visit."

"We have the day. We don't need to get back until late afternoon. That meatloaf you made last night won't take long to heat for dinner. I'm assuming Miranda will be at her boutique after Christmas, and talking to her shouldn't take long."

"I hope not. But after all, it's your talking with her that's giving us an excuse to go to Portland to begin with. Last night I was thinking we could spend all day down in the Old Port, near the harbor, exploring the little stores and galleries and restaurants there."

"But those Homers..."

"I know. You want to see the Homers, but they don't have a special exhibit of them up now, and seeing their regular exhibit won't take all day. There are so many places I'd love to show you in Portland." Will glanced at her. "You've never visited the Victoria Mansion, and this is the best time of year to see it, when it's decorated for Christmas. And I know we can't stay long enough to see the harbor lights or even the city Christmas trees lit, but we have to go to the Ice Bar."

"What?"

"The Ice Bar. In fact, I'm not going to tell you what it is. I have it all planned out. I'm going to drop you off at Elegant Attire, and then, while you're interviewing Miranda Hoskins, I'll pick up fantastic pastries at the best bakery in town. I'll meet you at the boutique, and we'll do a little Old Port exploring, and then visit the Victoria Mansion, and finish up at the Portland Museum of Art."

Maggie laughed. "It sounds complicated. And busy."

"But possible. Portland's a small city. We can hit a few highlights in a day." Will looked delighted that he'd figured out what they would be doing. "Food, drink, old, new, and my very favorite lady. I can't imagine a better day."

He switched on the radio and twisted the dial until carols filled the car.

Elegant Attire's windows were lined with tiny white lights. Inside were a Christmas tree shaped from a tower of white poinsettia plants, and a mannequin dressed in a dark green silk gown cut high in the front, and draped low—very low—in back. Wide green ribbons matching the gown were artfully strewn on the floor.

Maggie wondered for a moment if she should have called first. This didn't look like Maine. This looked like a Madison Avenue boutique. Maybe she should have dressed up. But, too late. She hadn't. Her jeans and jacket would have to do.

"May I help you?" A slim redhead wearing a gray sheath and pearls approached her. Definitely not Miranda. She'd been a little older, a little heavier, and not a redhead.

Maggie had planned to glance at the clothing, merge with the crowds, pretend to be shopping, and then ask for Miranda. But no other customers were in sight, no SALE signs, and it was apparent this was not the sort of shop where one rummaged through racks. It was more a "what may I bring you from the back, if you really think you can afford us," establishment.

"I'm Maggie Summer. I met Miranda Hoskins on Christmas Eve, in Waymouth. I wondered if I might speak with her briefly."

The redhead seemed doubtful, but glanced toward the back of the store. "May I ask what about?"

"It's personal. A family matter."

The redhead checked Maggie out, from head to toe. The look clearly said, You? Miranda's family? "I'll see if Ms. Hoskins is free."

While she was gone Maggie walked over to a rack of short silk dresses in different rainbow shades. The sort a confident business executive might wear to a meeting or conference. One had a price tag: $3,500.

Not in a college professor's or antique print dealer's league.

"Ms. Hoskins can see you for a few minutes." The redhead led Maggie down a mirrored hallway past a series of dressing rooms and a raised platform partially surrounded by additional mirrors to an office in the back corner. She knocked on the closed door, and left.

"Come in!" said a voice from inside.

Miranda Hoskins was dressed for her role. Her brown hair, streaked (professionally?) with white was short and she wore long gray slacks and a matching sweater; not so unusual in itself. But the sweater was beautifully cut with wide sleeves (there was a name for those sleeves, Maggie thought, but she couldn't remember it) and accessorized with a long hand-painted scarf in shades of blue and green and gray. Gold bracelets and earrings completed the ensemble.

Maggie doubted Miranda had shopped at Reny's or L.L. Bean recently. She was clearly a representative of one of the "other" Maines. The Maine that had money.

"Suzanne said I'd met you Christmas Eve. I'm sorry. I don't remember you."

"I was at Ruth Weston's party. I came with Nettie and Will Brewer."

"Oh, yes."

Clearly Miranda had no clue who she was.

"And you're here now, because?"

"I assume you heard about Carrie Folk's death."

"Nick Strait called Christmas morning to let us know. We'd wondered why she hadn't shown up for work."

So Carrie had been expected to come and take care of Betty Christmas morning.

"It must have been very upsetting."

"For my Aunt Ruth, certainly. She's been depending on Carrie to help with my mother for over a year now. As far as I'm concerned, it may be a blessing."

"A blessing? Why?"

"I don't mean it's a good thing the woman was murdered, of course. That's dreadful. But I've been wanting Aunt Ruth to put Mother in a nursing home with an Alzheimer's unit; a place they have trained staff to take care of her twenty-four hours a day. It would be better for Mother, and better for Aunt Ruth, too. They're wearing each other out; they both look worse every time I see them. I'd like Mother to be in a good, safe facility, maybe halfway between Portland and Waymouth, so I could visit her more often, and Aunt Ruth could see her, too. Mother doesn't know either of us on more days than Aunt Ruth wants to admit. She won't miss being at home. Maybe now, with Carrie Folk gone, Aunt Ruth will come to her senses. I've given her information about a couple of good places. I've told her I'd cover the cost. There's no reason she shouldn't agree now."

"I see."

"But what do you have to do with any of this?"

Maggie suspected this woman was not to be trifled with, or told some story. "You know Carrie Folk was murdered. Because I've had experience in similar situations, Nick Strait, the state trooper in charge of this case, asked me to talk to a few of the people involved."

"So? Why me? Certainly I'm not involved."

"Carrie Folk was blackmailing people in Waymouth. Your Aunt Ruth was one of them."

"Aunt Ruth? Are you sure?"

"She's said so. She gave Carrie money." Maggie watched Miranda's face. "So, you didn't know anything about that."

"No! I hadn't even seen Aunt Ruth or talked to her for the past couple of weeks, except to plan Christmas. What was she blackmailing Ruth about?"

"Can't you guess?"

Miranda leaned back in her chair. "Why would you ask that? How should I know?"

"The assumption is that Carrie got her information from shreds of memories, images, maybe parts of stories, that your mother told her."

"My mother? My mother doesn't even know who I am or where she is most of the time. How could she tell secrets or confidences from the past?"

"That's part of the problem. Most likely she wasn't totally coherent. Carrie may have confused random events she heard about that weren't connected. Misunderstood what she heard. Things that would be embarrassing to people, or to families."

"I don't know anything about that." Miranda hesitated, and then leaned forward. "Has she said anything about my father?"

"What about your father?"

"I don't know. That's the problem. She's never told me anything about him. I wondered, if she was saying things about the past, whether she's said anything about me. Or him."

Maggie shook her head. "You'd have to try to ask her. Or your aunt."

"As though I've never done that before." Miranda got up suddenly and looked at a small oil portrait of a mother and daughter hung behind her desk. Mothers and daughters. Relationships that were seldom simple.

"You didn't stay at the house after the party Christmas Eve," Maggie said.

"No. I didn't want to cope with Brian's pain-in-the-ass trophy wife. We made reservations at the Captain's Quarters Inn. After we left the party we went to the carol sing, and then The Great Blue and had a couple of drinks before going back to the Quarters. We were there until about eleven o'clock, when we walked up to the church for the candlelight service. After the service we walked back to the inn and went to bed, where we stayed until we went back to the house for breakfast at about eight Christmas morning." Miranda looked straight at her. "Does that adequately cover my alibi for the time Carrie Folk was killed?"

18

Portland, from Peak's Island. Circular wood engraving from *Picturesque America*, 1876, foreground picturing boy and girl playing with dog and pulling smaller child in a wooden wagon. Behind them, and framed by trees, a view of Portland Harbor, with the city of Portland in the distance. Several boats and one ship are in the harbor, including one sailing vessel. A charming black-and-white Victorian illustration. 7 x 7 inches. Price: $50.

TRUE TO his word, and clearly aggravating to the Elegant Attire's "hostess," Will was standing in the middle of the shop, holding a bakery bag whose fragrance was wafting through the front of the boutique. "Here she is," sniffed Suzanne. "Her brief meeting took a little longer than anticipated."

"Thank you for your help," Maggie said sweetly to her, taking Will's arm. "And thank *you* for waiting."

They joined the crowds outside, and Will reached in the bag and handed her a croissant. "I bought cinnamon rolls, too, but if we ate them on the street we'd end up needing to wash off half our outside clothes, they're so sticky," he admitted. "So they'll be for later. Maybe at home. I left them in the car."

"Why not for dessert tonight?" agreed Maggie. "And these croissants are fantastic! I didn't know Portland had a bakery that produced good pastries."

"Several, actually," Will said. "It's become a real foodie destination. How was your talk with Miranda?"

"She's interesting. Definitely runs a high-end shop. I won't be one of her customers unless I win the lottery and my lifestyle changes big-time. She didn't seem to know anything about the blackmail, and didn't guess what it might be about. She did ask whether I'd heard anything about her father."

"Her father?" Will had stopped and was looking in a home design shop window. "Sure you wouldn't be interested in a couch covered with fabric featuring life-sized green and red lobsters? There are lampshades to match."

"Not in the market," she answered. "Not today. Not ever. Anyway, Miranda wanted to know about her father. When I told her Betty was telling old stories, she wondered whether maybe she'd said anything she, Miranda, was trying to find out."

"Interesting. But makes sense," said Will, reaching into the bag. "Another croissant?"

"Not for me. One was plenty." Maggie brushed flakes of her croissant off the front of her jacket. "Miranda didn't seem too disturbed about the murder. With Carrie gone, she thought Ruth might consider moving Betty to a nursing home. She's already picked out several possibilities."

"Hardly a motive."

"I agree."

Most of the stores were selling decorative items or souvenirs neither Will nor Maggie were interested in. Neither of them needed clothing ("I'll get anything I need at Reny's, thank you," said Will, mentioning the Maine chain store that discounted name brands) and jewelry wasn't in the cards for this occasion. The galleries and bookstores were tempting, but today they were more in the mood to people watch.

"Next stop is the Ice Bar," said Will. "We won't stay long, but you're not allowed to order a Diet Pepsi there. This is a *Maine experience.*"

"Yes, sir," said Maggie. "Order received."

"We're headed to the Casco Bay Hotel," he added.

"A hotel?"

"To the bar at the Casco Bay Hotel," he clarified, with a slight leer. "Although if you insist," he glanced at his watch, "we do have a few free hours...."

"Never mind," laughed Maggie. "I'm having too much fun."

And there it was. On the patio of the Casco Bay Hotel ("carved from twenty thousand pounds of ice," the bartender informed them) was a bar made of ice, surrounded by ice sculptures of fish and lobsters. And wine bottles, of course. Chairs and barstools, also carved from ice, were covered by (pseudo) animal skins. Even the shot glasses were made of ice. The sign above listed "ice-tastic" special cocktails, with a percentage of sales going to charity.

"Only in Maine!" said Maggie. "Choose a drink for me. I don't care which one. This is an adventure." They stood on the snowy patio sipping their cocktails and watching post-Christmas shoppers go by laden with shopping bags.

"Ice bars are a new fad. They appear in several places in Maine in winter, usually for a couple of weeks," Will said. "I checked before we came today to see if there was one in Portland now. Cool, right?"

"Downright frozen, actually," said Maggie. "Which is definitely more than cool. What happens if there's a heat wave and temperatures go above thirty-two degrees?"

"Unlikely. But I assume they have ice sculptors and refrigeration units on retainer," said Will. "Now, finish your drink, because our next course is down the street."

"Oh? You mean after croissants and cocktails there's another course?"

"Absolutely," he said seriously. "We're going to have Belgian French fries."

It must have been whatever was in that icy cocktail. Because Maggie started to giggle. "No snow cones?"

"Not today," said Will, putting their empty glasses back on the bar. "Belgian fries."

The restaurant's name was simply Duckfat, which was what the potatoes were fried in. They arrived in cone-shaped containers with a tempting choice of dipping sauces such as "truffle ketchup" and "lemon–herb mayonnaise."

Maggie picked up the menu. "There's nothing here I wouldn't like. Even the milkshakes sound great, although I don't think I want one after that cocktail. And they have poutine. I haven't had that in years."

Will shook his head. "Don't even look. Believe me. We're here for the Belgian fries. Another time we'll order from the menu."

"Got it." And she did. And was grateful for the advice. They even requested second orders of fries, with different dipping sauces.

"Now," he said, "we drive to the Victoria Mansion."

"Now I've gained ten pounds and could use a nap," said Maggie.

"Not allowed. We have promises to keep. And miles to go ..."

"Got it," said Maggie. "Victoria Mansion. Are you playing tour guide?"

"Yup. Showing my girl the joys of my new home state. Got an agenda here."

So far that day they'd seen what Maggie considered high fashion, eaten French croissants, had a drink at the kind of establishment Maggie had thought only existed in Iceland or Norway, eaten Belgian fries, and soon they were touring an amazing home built between 1858 and 1860 for a man who'd made his money building hotels in New Orleans, but who wanted a summer home where it was cool. He chose Portland. Unfortunately (by Maggie's standards) he and his wife had no children, but their four-story home, complete with tower, allowed plenty of space for guests and their servants.

The elaborate home was now a museum, and decorated lavishly for the holidays. Maggie could see why many Mainers made a visit there an annual part of their Christmas celebration.

"Inspired?" she asked Will. "Is that how you picture the Victorian you're bidding on? Because this house started out more elaborate and better built than the one in Waymouth."

"I'll admit that," said Will. "And it is one story higher. And a bit larger ..."

"A bit!" said Maggie. "Twice as big."

"Maybe," said Will. "And although I'd love to restore my house—if it is my house someday—to its Victorian splendor, I'd also modernize parts of it. They've kept the Victoria Mansion the way it was. I wouldn't want to own a museum." He paused and looked up at it as they got in the car. "It is a beauty, though, isn't it?"

"It is," Maggie agreed. "But no one lives there, or sells antiques there. Drive on, friend. I might just have enough energy and," she glanced at the clock in the car, "we might have enough time to see those Homers at the art museum."

The Portland Museum of Art was small compared to the New York City museums Maggie knew well, but she loved it immediately. Floors of Maine-related art and special exhibits. She glanced at the floor plan and wanted to see everything. She lingered at the small bookstore and gift shop, looking at the tempting selection they had for children. And the Winslow Homer souvenirs. Postcards and note-cards and books of prints, including books about his wood engravings, she was pleased to note, since she featured those in her business. But who bought Winslow Homer soap? Winslow Homer mustaches? Or, perhaps strangest of all, a Winslow Homer mustache bottle-stopper? The genteel artist, who so valued his privacy that he escaped cities to the Adirondacks of New York or the coast of Maine or the islands of Cuba or the Bahamas to paint, must either be laughing or shuddering in his grave.

She proudly noted that the museum displayed several of Homer's wood engravings, all of which she had. But it was the Homer paint-ings she'd come to see. Will was right. Compared to collections in one of the major museums, there weren't many. But they were worth a visit. Maggie paused for several minutes looking at *Weatherbeaten,* his masterpiece of surf pounding the rocks at Prouts Neck, Maine, where she'd visited the summer before. And she gazed at Homer's watercolor box in the display case nearby, half-used, as though he'd put it down while taking a nooning break.

She could have spent much more time there. But Will tapped his watch.

Time to go.

"We'll come back?"

"Maine will be here."

Aunt Nettie was fine. The meatloaf was savory. They devoured the cinnamon rolls for dessert. Bedtime came early.

It wasn't until the next morning that Aunt Nettie remembered to give them two messages.

19

Winter Has Come (Godey's Paris Fashions Americanized). Hand-colored steel fashion engraving for *Godey's Lady's Book*, engraved by J.I. Pease, c.1860. An example of French fashions simplified and designed for American women or their dressmakers to replicate, typical of *Godey's*. Two women standing on stark ground, in front of bare trees and a towered Gothic building. Both women are wearing bonnets tied under their chins and knee-length capes (one green and one black), and one is carrying a fur muff. Their sleeves and the part of their skirts showing are blue in one case; mauve in the other. (The woman in black and mauve is clearly in mourning.) 6.4 x 9 inches. Price: $60.

"LAST NIGHT it was so much fun hearing about what you did in Portland I plain forgot to tell you," Aunt Nettie apologized the next morning. "Nicky called. He wanted to know what we'd found out from Ruth. I told him, and said you'd already talked with Owen, Maggie, and you were in Portland to talk with Miranda. Nicky wants to talk with both of us again as soon as possible. I told him you'd call him when you got home. I guess you'd better call him this morning."

"I'm sure you told him everything we found out, which wasn't much," said Maggie. "But I'll call him."

"Good. I don't want him thinking I'm getting forgetful, or like Betty. And, Will? A Mr. Krieger called for you. Something about the building inspection."

"That could be important. Why didn't he call on my cell phone?" Will muttered. He headed toward his office, calling back over his shoulder, "My paperwork is upstairs. I'll be back after I talk with him."

"I assume Will's going ahead with trying to buy that house from Walter English," said Aunt Nettie.

"Sounds that way," said Maggie. "He hasn't told me much. I guess he'll tell us when the deal does or doesn't go through."

Aunt Nettie shook her head doubtfully. "I've said my piece about that place. He'll do as he pleases. Doesn't make much sense to me. But he's got to have something to do other than take care of an old lady, and there are a lot worse things a man could do than fix up an old house."

Put that way, it was hard to disagree.

"I'd better call Nick," said Maggie.

This time he answered immediately. "Maggie! I was trying to reach you yesterday, but Nettie Brewer didn't have your cell phone number. She said you were in Portland talking to Miranda Hoskins. How did that go? Did she say anything helpful?"

"We spent maybe fifteen minutes together. She seemed very open. She didn't know anything about the blackmailing, or have any idea about what was being kept quiet."

"Really. I'd like to get together with you and Nettie today, and maybe pull Owen in, too, and see what we have so far. Would you be free?"

Maggie turned to Aunt Nettie. "Could we meet with Nick and Owen today?"

"I'd have to check to see if Queen Elizabeth would mind moving our date for tea to another day, but…of course, Maggie. You go on and tell him, yes."

Maggie hesitated. What if Will had plans? But he was still upstairs. "Nick? Nettie and I could meet with you and Owen. Perhaps this morning? If you could come here it would be easiest."

Aunt Nettie was nodding her approval.

"Eleven o'clock, then. We'll have coffee ready."

"So, they'll be coming?" Aunt Nettie confirmed.

"I don't think they'll be here long. We haven't found out a lot. But the sooner we let them know we've done all we can, the sooner they can get on with finding the murderer." She'd uncovered killers in the past. It had been exciting. But it had also been dangerous. Will had been right. It was definitely not anything ninety-two-year-old Aunt Nettie should be involved with.

Not to mention how Will felt about her amateur sleuthing. Although solving murders wasn't exactly a hobby she went looking for.

In the past couple of years several people near her had met horrible ends. She'd been lucky enough to figure out why, and who was responsible.

All she was doing this morning was brewing a large pot of coffee. And wondering how long Will would be upstairs on the telephone.

It must have been a complicated conversation. Will hadn't come back downstairs before a rap on the front door announced that Deputy Owen Trask and Detective Nick Strait had arrived, a little before 11:00.

Maggie sent them into the living room while she followed with two large mugs of coffee, one black and one white.

"So can you tell us what that medical person up to Augusta said about Carrie?" Aunt Nettie asked. "What killed her?"

Nick and Owen exchanged looks.

"I guess it'll get around soon enough. Carrie Folk died from blunt force trauma. That's a fancy way of saying someone crushed her skull, probably with one of the logs waiting to be burned in her fireplace. Sorry to be so direct, Ms. Brewer," said Owen. "There'd been a fire in the fireplace, so we suspect the log in question was burned."

"We also know now it was Carrie who was sick. She had pancreatic cancer. Stage four. The medical examiner said she didn't have long to live." Nick sipped his coffee. "Which probably explains why she needed the money, and needed it quickly. Part perhaps for medical expenses. But we also found brochures in her home for a couple of expensive private facilities for developmentally disabled adults."

"She was blackmailing people so she'd have enough money to provide for Billy, then," said Maggie.

"Looks that way," said Owen.

"What will happen to him now?"

"So far we haven't found any trace of his father. He hasn't provided support for Billy in over thirty years, and Billy doesn't seem to know anything about him. He may have died, or left the country. And no other relative is known, or has come forward. Billy's used to being cared for, and doesn't have many skills. He'll probably be placed with a foster family that specializes in working with special needs adults. When they feel he can manage living semi-independently he could move to one of the group homes in the state for developmentally challenged adults."

"So there are options for him," said Maggie. "I'm glad."

"Absolutely," Owen answered. "He'll have an adjustment period, of course. But if Carrie was worried about Billy being locked up in an institution, she was thirty years too late. We don't have places like that in Maine anymore. She didn't have to leave a lot of money with him. The best thing she could have done for Billy was help him develop as many day-to-day living experiences as possible, so perhaps he could hold down a job, under supervision."

"So all her worry about Billy wasn't necessary."

"He won't be cared for the way she catered to him," said Owen. "But Billy will be all right. Maybe better than all right. He's going to meet with a case worker this afternoon who'll write up an evaluation and develop a placement plan for him."

"Billy isn't the reason we're here." Nick inserted, impatiently. "I want to thank you for the help you've been. Especially for talking with Ruth Weston. You won't be surprised to hear that we don't consider her a serious suspect. But we haven't ruled out everyone in her household, and there might be other people we haven't thought of yet. Our investigation is far from over."

"Other people in her household?" asked Aunt Nettie.

"I assume anything we say here is strictly confidential," said Nick. "You're Ruth's friend, and I have to know that nothing I say to you will get back to her, or to anyone else."

"Certainly," said Aunt Nettie. "I'm no gossip."

"I don't think Betty's daughter, Miranda, knows anything helpful," said Maggie. "She didn't know about the blackmail, and didn't seem to have any idea of what it could be about."

Nick nodded. "That fits what we suspect. We're checking out Ruth's son, Brian. Nothing definite so far. Just a few questions. But Owen talked to a neighbor who says he saw Brian leaving the Weston home at about two o'clock on Christmas morning."

"I remember Ruth's saying he went for a walk the night before. The baby was crying, and he needed to get away for a while. Maybe he makes a habit of late-night walks," Maggie suggested.

"That may be his story," Nick said. "But he left the Weston home at about the time the medical examiner thinks Carrie Folk was murdered. And we checked the bank he works for in Philadelphia. He's employed there, but although he's a lawyer, his salary isn't a large one. And that new house he's bought is a small pre-fab, and it's eighty percent mortgaged. For a newly married man, at his age, with a new baby, I'd say he's struggling. Especially since, based on their credit card bills, his wife seems to have expensive tastes."

"Not being wealthy doesn't make the man a murderer," Aunt Nettie pointed out.

Owen shrugged. "We didn't find any money in Carrie's house. No cash at all. Ruth Weston said she'd given her ten thousand dollars a few days before. So the cash may have been in the house when she was killed."

"If she was robbed, maybe Carrie was killed by a burglar? Maybe her murder had nothing at all to do with the blackmail," Maggie suggested. "Someone could have known she'd recently cashed a large check and gone looking for the money. They might not have expected to confront her."

"If so, it was a pretty smart burglar. We've found no fingerprints; everything was wiped clean."

"And why would all of this lead you to suspect Brian Weston?"

Nick started to count on his fingers. "He wasn't at the Weston home at the time of the murder. He needed money. Maybe he thought he could take the money his mother had given to Carrie and no one would know. I don't know exactly what he had in mind, but we're checking all possibilities."

"It's not an airtight case. Not yet. We're just saying Brian's on our radar," added Owen.

"Is there anything else you'd like me to do?" asked Aunt Nettie.

"I think we have all the information we need that you can help us with," said Nick. "If I think of anything else, I'll let you know."

"We appreciate your talking to Ruth and Miranda." Owen stood up.

"You're quite welcome," said Aunt Nettie. "We're glad to have helped out."

Maggie walked with the two men toward the back door. "How is Zelda?" she asked Nick. "I saw her at the concert Christmas Eve, and I've been thinking about her."

"She's fine," he said. "Why would you ask?"

"She had a black eye."

"There's nothing wrong with Zelda. She and the Christmas tree ran into each other. Then she insisted on covering her face with make-up, making herself look even more ludicrous." He shook his head. "Zelda's fine."

Owen looked at Maggie. "You'll be here a few more days?"

"Through New Year's."

"Enjoy your vacation." He tipped his hat, and both men headed out.

"What were they here for? I heard voices." Will had finally come downstairs.

"Nick and Owen Trask were here." Maggie looked over at Aunt Nettie, who nodded slightly. They'd promised not to tell anyone what they'd been told, and Will qualified as "anyone." "How'd your phone call go?"

"I've got problems with the building inspection. I'm going to have to spend part of the afternoon at the house with the inspector going over the details. I need to make sure we agree about what needs to be done to make the place livable." Will ran his hand through his hair, clearly vexed. "This isn't at all what I'd planned to do. I'd hoped all this would be over before Christmas. I'm sorry, Maggie. I'd much rather be spending time with you. But this is critical."

"I understand. I'm sure Aunt Nettie and I can amuse ourselves."

"We certainly can. You go ahead. Maggie and I'll be fine," agreed Aunt Nettie.

"Thank you, both. I'm going to pull together the papers I need and head over to Art Krieger's office, then." Will went back upstairs, as Maggie sat down near Aunt Nettie.

"What do you think of the idea that Brian Weston killed Carrie Folk?" Maggie asked.

"It's rubbish. Doesn't make sense. That boy hasn't got enough energy to kill anyone. He might steal her money. I could see that. But kill her? Not Brian." Aunt Nettie frowned. "And it sounded to me like Nicky wants us to stop asking questions."

"I thought so, too," agreed Maggie. "So? What do we do now?"

"We ignore Nicky. We need to talk to Betty," Aunt Nettie said. "She's the center of all this."

"Betty? But she doesn't always make sense."

"She may not to you. But she might to me. And besides, Maggie. I haven't seen her room in a long while. But as I remember Ruth had hung pictures on the walls there."

"Will and I saw them there. We looked in when we were at her house Christmas Eve."

"Did the pictures have names on them? Labels that said who the people were?"

"I think so. We didn't go inside the room. But there were signs on everything."

"Then Carrie would have known who was in all the pictures. We definitely need to pay another call on Ruth."

20 | **Girl in a Hood.** Lithograph of young brunette woman wearing a warm brown corduroy hood whose ends tie under her chin. Part of illustrator and painter Harrison Fisher's (1875–1934) 1909 *American Beauties* portfolio. Fisher drew popular covers for *Cosmopolitan*, and had a talent for drawing beautiful women. Gibson's successor, his "Fisher Girls" helped define style for a generation of American women in the early twentieth century. 8.5 x 11 inches. Price: $75.

A FEW MINUTES after Will left the house Maggie and Aunt Nettie were on their way. This time they hadn't called ahead.

"Ruth will be there," Aunt Nettie said. "Where else would she be? You don't think Jenny or Brian would know how to check Betty's sugars or help her use the commode, do you?"

But it was Miranda who answered the door. "You again!" she said, looking at Maggie. "Oh, and hello, Ms. Brewer."

"Good day, Miranda. We've come to pay a call on your mother and your aunt Ruth. Would you invite us in?"

"I'm sorry. Of course, you're welcome," she said, moving back and allowing space for Aunt Nettie and Maggie to move past her into the hallway. "They're both in Mother's room. I'll tell them you're here."

"No need. We'll join them there," said Aunt Nettie, her cane briskly leading the way.

"Are Brian and Jenny still here?" Maggie asked Miranda.

"Oh, yes," said Miranda. "The gang's all here. But Brian decided to show Jenny the coast, so they drove to Camden for lunch. It's been blessedly quiet for an hour now."

"Nettie, what a surprise. Look, Betty, Nettie and Maggie've come to visit us." Ruth looked less than thrilled at their appearance. "First Miranda stopped in, and now we have more company."

Betty was in her wheelchair in the corner of her room. She smiled uncertainly. "Who are these people? Is this a party?"

"It feels a little like one, doesn't it, Betty," agreed Ruth.

Miranda stepped in front of Betty. "Mother gets confused when more than one or two people are here. I know you're an old friend, Nettie, but you really should have called before you came."

"Old friends are the best friends," said Betty, clearly. "Are you one of my old friends, dear?"

"I'm Miranda, your daughter? Remember, Mother? We've been talking about when I was a little girl. When I was a baby."

"Miranda, I don't think you should be bothering your mother about that anymore," said Ruth. "I told you before. It was years ago. She's already confused. You know anything she says now can't be taken seriously."

"But she was so close," said Miranda. "She said my father was tall, and had dark hair, like I do. She's never said that before."

"Lots of men are tall and have dark hair. That doesn't mean anything," said Ruth. "Maybe she doesn't know. Maybe she never did."

Miranda looked at her. "You're telling me my mother never knew who my father was? I can't believe that of her. And then who was Robert Hoskins? His name is listed on my birth certificate."

Aunt Nettie took a step further into the room. "We've come at a bad time then."

"Where is my baby? I want my baby now," said Betty, looking around the room.

"I'm here," said Miranda, kneeling down by her mother's wheelchair. "I'm here, with you, right here."

"You're not my baby. You're a grown woman. I want my baby."

Ruth picked up a lifelike baby doll dressed in pink pajamas from the floor near the bed and put it in Betty's lap. "Here's your baby."

"My baby." Betty gently held the doll and started rocking it back and forth, as though it were a real baby. "She's been crying again. She needs her mother."

Miranda just stared.

Ruth touched her gently on the shoulder. "About a month ago she started asking for her baby. She must be remembering when you were born, Miranda. She loved you so much. Nothing would console her. So I went and bought her that doll. It seems to help."

Miranda stood up and backed away, not taking her eyes off her mother. "Thank you, Aunt Ruth. I'm sorry for pushing her about my father. But for years I've tried to find out more about him, and she'd never tell me." She glanced back at Maggie, who was near the door. "When Maggie said she was talking about the past, I hoped, maybe, she'd say something about him. Who he was, or where he came from. Anything. I didn't mean to cause her pain."

Ruth shook her head. "I don't think you caused her any pain, Miranda. She can't help you. She's buried parts of her life so deeply that now they're gone. But the parts about you, about having you, are memories she relives with happiness. She loves you very much."

Miranda watched her mother rocking the doll that might be her. "I don't know how you deal with this day after day."

Ruth reached over and hugged her. "One day and then another day. Some are easier than others."

Miranda broke away and looked at Nettie and Maggie. "I'm so sorry this happened when you were here. I'm embarrassed. I kept thinking, Maggie, after you left the store yesterday, that maybe this was my chance. I could find out more about my father than his name. I guess I was wrong."

"You've searched for him?" Maggie asked.

"I started looking years ago. I was born in Boston, so I checked Massachusetts newspapers and directories and Social Security and on-line sources. I haven't found anyone with that name with a connection to New England who sounds remotely the right age to be my father. It's like Robert Hoskins is a ghost." Miranda pulled a tissue from her pocket and dabbed at her eyes. "My head says it doesn't make any real difference. But it's like having an empty spot in my life, not to know."

Maggie looked past Miranda. Ruth was pursing her lips, looking from Miranda to Betty.

Ruth knew Robert Hoskins, Maggie suddenly thought. Ruth knew. And she knew why Betty hadn't told Miranda anything about him. Whatever the reason was, it must be important.

While they'd been talking Aunt Nettie was looking at pictures on the walls. "Ruth, you did a wonderful job with these. I haven't thought of these people and places in years."

"Since Betty was living so much in the past I wanted to put things in her room that would help her remember. Especially the good times."

"I love these pictures of all of us in elementary school." Aunt Nettie pointed at several photographs on the wall near the bathroom door. "I'd forgotten. Betty played the flute, and you played the violin."

"Viola, actually," Ruth said, joining her. "Father thought all girls should play instruments. He had the mistaken idea we were musically talented!" They both laughed. "All those hours practicing. We hated it! That's why we never asked our children to take music lessons."

"And here are you and Mary and I in the high school play. I can't even remember the name of it."

"I can't either. All I remember is that Betty wanted a part, and they made her an understudy because she was a freshman. She didn't speak to me for at least a month."

They moved to another corner of the room. Aunt Nettie bit her lip. "You put this up."

"It was a big part of our lives, Nettie."

"True enough. I don't have any pictures taken there."

The photograph showed four smiling young women wearing overalls and holding soldering irons, standing beside a large piece of metal. "What is that picture of?" Maggie asked. The names on the attached yellow label were familiar, but she couldn't place the setting.

Ruth answered. "That's Nettie and I and our friends Mary and Susan, working at Bath Iron Works. Remember, Nettie? 'Bath Built is Best Built.' They hired thousands of us young women during the war. In 1944 there were over eight thousand workers, around the clock. We launched a new destroyer every seventeen days."

"Wow. I didn't know you were a Rosie-the-Riveter, Aunt Nettie," said Maggie. "I've read about those days. I even talk about them in my American Civilization classes. But you're the first two people I've met who really did it."

"Oh, we did it," said Aunt Nettie. "We didn't just do riveting, either. We did everything. Wiring, operating the stamping machine and drill press. Whatever needed doing."

"A family in Bath opened their home for a few of us who needed places to stay. We were crowded in like sardines, but we worked long hours, and kept the equipment running around the clock," said Ruth. "They called us 'production soldiers.' We did everything we could for our men at sea. Waymouth's year-'round population was only about eleven hundred in those days. But two hundred of them served in the armed forces. And about three hundred of us worked in defense jobs. It was a frightening time. We were warned that Bath Iron Works could be a German target because it was a defense plant. But we tried not to worry. We all knew dozens of men, and some women, who were serving overseas. They were in constant danger. We wanted to do our part."

"And then the war was over, and the men came home and your jobs went away," said Maggie. "But your generation broke down so many walls for women in the workplace."

"It wasn't quite like that," said Aunt Nettie. "Not all of us worked until the end, to begin with. And the navy didn't need as many destroyers after the war. Plus, when their men came back, most of the girls were happy to go home. Start their lives together. Or begin them again. Not too many women wanted to spend their lives on assembly lines, although a few of the war workers did stay on."

"None of you did," said Maggie.

"No. None of us did."

Maggie glanced at Betty, who was now dozing, still holding the baby doll tightly to her breast. "Betty didn't work there."

"She did for a few months, at the end. But she was younger than the rest of us. She wasn't old enough to go," said Ruth. "One more thing she thought I'd been able to do that she'd missed out on."

Maggie searched the other photographs for familiar faces.

"I'm surprised you don't have a picture of your wedding here, Ruth."

"It was my wedding, not Betty's."

"And here you both are with your children, all four of them, in front of this house. Brian and Miranda are the little ones, right?"

Ruth and Betty were standing, each one holding a child of perhaps a year old, with a little boy and a little girl in front of them. The family. "Yes. They're close in age."

As they continued to circle the room the pictures of Ruth and Betty with the four children continued, with all six figures aging slightly in each view. Brian and Noah playing football. Stacy in a Girl Scout uniform. Miranda in a prom dress. Pictures of Noah's wedding. In between were one or two pictures of "the girls": Nettie, Mary, Gloria, and Susan with Ruth and Betty. And in later years, Doreen.

The history of Betty's life, in still photos on a sickroom wall.

Maggie had been so engaged in looking she'd forgotten about Miranda. When their tour of the room reached the door she left Nettie and Ruth to reminisce.

She found Miranda sitting at the kitchen table, drinking a cup of tea.

"Why did you come today?" she asked as Maggie entered.

"Because the investigation is continuing," Maggie answered. "People are being considered as suspects. Just because a person hasn't lived a perfect life they shouldn't be considered a murder suspect."

"You're not allowed to say who they're looking at."

Maggie shook her head.

"But it's someone in my family. That's why you're here."

Maggie didn't answer.

"I don't know you, Maggie Summer, and you don't know any of us. If it weren't for Aunt Ruth, I don't know what would have happened to Mother and me. She welcomed us into her home, and she and Mother brought all four of us up. We've headed in different directions over the years. We've had our squabbles. But we're all decent people. None of us are murderers."

"Aunt Nettie believes that, too. But Carrie Folk was killed. And so far, no one's found a serious suspect not connected to this house."

21

Haddock (Melanogrammus aeglefinus–Linnaeus).
Delicately colored 1904 chromolithograph of a haddock on off-white background. No artist named. One of several natural history lithographs bound with the *Annual Report of the Forest, Fish and Game Commission of New York.* 8 x 11 inches. $50.

WILL WAS standing at the door when they returned. "Where did you go? I got home sooner than I thought and I worried when you weren't here."

"We were over at Ruth Weston's," said Maggie, helping Aunt Nettie into the house. "We weren't gone long."

"You could have left a note. I was worried."

"We knew we'd be back soon," said Aunt Nettie. "Once in a while I go out, too."

"I can see that."

"How'd it go with the engineer?" asked Maggie.

"Turned out the only real question the guy had was about the clamshell plaster. He wanted to make sure I wouldn't insist on it being replaced in kind when new wiring was installed."

"I wouldn't think he'd even ask," said Maggie, hanging up her jacket and Aunt Nettie's.

"Hadn't occurred to me, either. But he had one client who wanted a house restored totally authentically. An estimate for that would push the price sky-high. The engineer didn't want to get burned again."

"Makes sense."

"It does. But I don't know why Jo or Art couldn't have explained that over the phone. I didn't really need to go over in person to talk to the guy. But maybe that's how things are done here. Making friends. Networking. In any case, it's taken care of for the moment. He said he'd finish his evaluation of the house and come up with his estimate tonight."

"So all's moving along well," Maggie said.

"Seems to be. How's Ruth?"

"Having a hard time of it. Taking full-time care of Betty isn't easy. We didn't stay long. Miranda was there, too," said Aunt Nettie. "And I've missed my nap. I'm going to lie down for a bit."

"We haven't had lunch," Maggie pointed out. "Maybe you should have something to eat first."

"I'm not that hungry. We had eggs again for breakfast. Maybe we can have supper a bit early."

"We can do that," said Will. "I'll fix your bed for you. And maybe while you're resting I'll take Maggie out for lunch. Would you mind?"

"Mind? Nonsense. The house will be quieter so I can rest. You two go on about your business."

While Will was getting his aunt settled, Maggie thought of the pictures they'd seen at Ruth's house. Last summer she'd seen Aunt Nettie's old pictures, too. She looked over in the corner bookcase where she remembered the old red morocco leather album was kept. Sure enough, it was still there. She opened it to one of the last pictures she'd remembered seeing: the handsome man in uniform who'd been Aunt Nettie's fiancé. The soldier who hadn't come home from the war.

That's where Aunt Nettie had closed the album last summer.

Maggie started there, and kept turning the pages. One picture was that of the four laughing young women who'd worked at the defense plant together. But in this picture they weren't in the factory. They were standing in front of a house, perhaps the boarding house they'd stayed at in Bath. It was winter; they were bundled up and the ground and stairs to the house were covered with snow. Then there was a black-and-white head shot of Nettie and Ruth with water and trees in the background. As Maggie looked more closely, Will came back into the room.

"Do you know where this was taken?"

He looked over her shoulder. "I remember seeing that picture when I was a little boy and asking her. I think it's in the Boston Public Garden. They were in one of the Swan Boats. I remember because I'd never heard of the Swan Boats before. I'd just heard the Hans

Christian Andersen fairy tale about the Ugly Duckling. I didn't know there really were swans."

"She and Ruth must have taken a vacation in Boston."

"Guess so."

Maggie turned the page. The next picture was of Ruth's wedding party. "What a gorgeous dress she's wearing. And there's Betty, her maid of honor. I'm guessing all the bridesmaids are 'the girls.' There's Aunt Nettie. The other three must be Mary and Susan and Gloria. The men look so serious. Ruth's husband, Jonas, was really tall and good-looking."

Will glanced at it. "And probably scared to death. Just got home from the war, and tying himself down for life." He reached down and closed the album. "Let's go get lunch. And talk about things happening in this century."

The Great Blue was as crowded for a December lunch as it was in the summertime. "People visiting for the holidays," Will said, glancing around. "There aren't many places open this time of year to choose from."

They were waiting for a table when the hostess came back to them. "The two ladies sitting in the corner over there offered to share their table, if you'd like to join them."

Will looked over her head. "It's Doreen and Zelda. Do you mind, Maggie?"

"Not at all; it might be fun."

"We'll join them, then," accepted Will, and they followed the hostess to the table in question.

"Hi!" welcomed Doreen Strait. "Zelda, you know Will Brewer, and this is his friend Maggie from New Jersey; Maggie, this is my granddaughter, Zelda. We decided to take ourselves out for lunch, and it looks as though the whole town of Waymouth had the same thought."

"Thanks for sharing your table," said Will. "Hope your Christmas went well."

"It did," said Doreen. "Sadly cut a little short when Nick got that call and had to go to work, but that's his life."

"We enjoyed hearing you sing Christmas Eve," Maggie said to

Zelda. The girl's face was healing, and she wasn't wearing makeup today. But her skin showed the yellow shadows of an earlier black eye.

"Thank you," said Zelda. She had a sweet smile. "I've been in the choir since I was twelve. The Christmas community sing and service are my favorites, I think."

"I'm glad your dad had the night off so he could hear you," said Maggie.

"He didn't have the whole night off," she answered. "After the sing he was on call for a few hours. He didn't get home until early Christmas morning."

Doreen nodded. "Poor Nick hardly had time to close his eyes before Owen called about Carrie, and he was off. He didn't get home again until late in the afternoon, so we waited to open our gifts until then." She shook her head. "It's hard on all of us, his having a job like that. Especially on a day like Christmas."

"I would think you'd be used to it by now," said Will.

"I don't think you ever get used to someone you love working such hours, and being in dangerous situations," said Doreen. "I worried about his father going out lobstering, and sure enough, one day he didn't come back. Nick deals with criminals who are even more dangerous and unpredictable than storms and waves."

Zelda reached over and patted her grandmother on the arm. "Don't get yourself worked up, Gram. That's who Dad is. You know you can't stop him."

This was the overly emotional daughter Nick was worried about? She was the calmest seventeen-year-old Maggie had met in a long while.

"What do you see in your future, Zelda? What do you want to do after high school?"

"Not nursing or police work." Zelda absently twisted a strand of her long hair as she thought. "I don't know exactly yet. I'd like to learn more about choices there are outside Waymouth. I don't think I'm ready for a school in one of the big cities, like New York, but I'd like to go to a university near a city, maybe in Maryland, or Virginia."

"You have an intelligent granddaughter there," Maggie said to Doreen. "That makes a lot of sense."

"It does," agreed Doreen. "I became a nurse because my mother was a nurse, and because nurses were needed. I didn't consider a lot of other options. That was well and good for the time, and for me. And Nick wanted to be in law enforcement from the time he knew what a policeman was. This is a new world. Zelda should explore it. Take time to decide where she wants to be and what she wants to do."

"I just have to convince Dad to let me go to a school outside Maine," said Zelda. "I've applied to a couple, but I haven't dared tell him. He's going to explode if I'm accepted and want to go."

"We'll figure out something, honey. That's why you and I've been putting money away all these years. You need to get out of here and see the world."

Will called over the waitress and they placed their orders: cheeseburger and fries with a blueberry soda for Zelda; lobster roll and onion rings and diet soda for Maggie; haddock sandwiches with sweet potato fries and coffee for Will and Doreen.

"Aunt Nettie and I visited Ruth this morning," Maggie said to Doreen. "She's having a hard time of it, taking care of Betty. But she said you're going to help her out. That's wonderful. She can really use a hand now."

Doreen nodded. "I thought as much. I'm going over later today. In a way I'm looking forward to it. I haven't used my nurse's training in a long time, except for binding up Zelda's and Nick's scratches and bruises. I wouldn't want to go back to work full-time at this point, but it'll feel good to help out a friend."

"Aunt Nettie said you worked here in town at Rocky Shores Hospital?"

"I did, for some years. And did private work as well." She looked at Maggie. "Did she mention that?"

Maggie shook her head. "No; she said you'd been a nurse, and your mother, Mary, had also been a nurse. And that when she was older, you'd taken care of your mother."

"Yes. Mother was ill for a long time, beginning when Zelda was a baby. Those were rough years." Doreen stood up. "I'm going to visit the ladies' room before our food is delivered. Maggie, can I show you where the rest rooms are?"

Maggie knew very well where they were, but she got the message. She excused herself and followed Doreen.

When the bathroom door closed in back of them Doreen glanced around to see if anyone else was in the room. No one was. "Maggie, I didn't want to talk in front of Zelda. Do you know if Nettie received a letter from Carrie Folk before Christmas?"

The Study Hour. Color lithograph of beautiful young dark-haired woman leaning on her hand and reading one of several books piled on her desk, which is also decorated by two red roses, some of whose petals have fallen off. Based on a print originally published in 1907, this copy was included in a collection of Harrison Fisher's illustrations (*Fair Americans*) in 1911. Fisher was a well-known illustrator of women in the first quarter of the twentieth century. 8.5 x 11 inches. Price: $65.

MAGGIE LOOKED at Doreen. "Nettie got a letter from Carrie last week threatening blackmail. So did Ruth. You got one, too?"

Doreen nodded. "I didn't know who to tell. I was stunned. The letter mentioned things that happened long ago; things my mother was involved in, more than I was, but that I knew about. I couldn't see why Carrie was dragging it all out now. I decided to wait and see if she approached me again; if she was serious. It seemed so strange. Anyway, maybe I was wrong, but I didn't do anything. I put the envelope in my desk, under other papers."

"And then Carrie was murdered."

"And Nick was investigating, and I realized that letter could make me a suspect. I knew I should give it to Nick, but it would only have upset him, and of course I hadn't killed Carrie, so I decided to destroy it. Forget it."

"And?"

"Christmas night, after Nick had come home and gone to bed, I went to get it. To burn it." Doreen looked stricken. "The letter was gone. I looked through that desk drawer a dozen times. I was frantic. I looked on the floor. I looked in the other drawers. It had disappeared."

"And you hadn't mentioned it to anyone."

"No one."

"How long had it been there?"

"Maybe three or four days? I'm not positive. Less than a week. And then I started wondering about other people. Whether anyone else had gotten letters. That's why I asked you. I was going to ask Ruth tonight."

"Nick's investigation includes Ruth's whole family. He was also looking at Aunt Nettie and Will; he may still be. Could he have found the letter and destroyed it so you wouldn't be a suspect?" Maggie asked.

"I suppose so. I hadn't even thought about that." Doreen paused, and then shook her head. "No. That would be destroying evidence. Nick's very strict about doing things the right way. I can't believe he'd break one of his own rules. But the only other person in the house was Zelda. She certainly wouldn't have been involved. If by any chance she'd found the letter she would have asked me about it. Zelda and I are close."

Maggie was about to say something when the door of the ladies' room opened and a middle-aged woman walked in and entered one of the stalls. Maggie turned the water on in one of the sinks and started vigorously washing her hands.

"Let's have lunch. But if you think of anything else, let me know. Nick and Owen have asked Aunt Nettie and me to talk with people connected to Carrie, to see if we hear anything helpful to solving her murder."

Their food had arrived by the time they got back to the table, and the rest of their conversation was about food, weather, and Waymouth's New Year's Eve celebration at the Town Hall.

Maggie kept looking at Zelda. Could she have left the house Christmas night and murdered Carrie Folk? Or could one of her friends, perhaps Jon Snow, have done that? Was there any possibility Doreen might be lying, and that she herself had killed Carrie?

What had Carrie Folk known that had so upset these ostensibly staid, elderly Maine women that murder was even a possibility? Doreen was younger and more mobile, but if she were the murderer why would she have told Maggie she'd gotten a letter?

Sitting here in early afternoon at The Great Blue, eating a lobster roll on a winter's day, from the outside it looked as though all these women seemed bound together by their friendship. By the memories they'd shared through the years.

And, Maggie realized, by their fear. What they had also shared through those years was the fear that whatever had united them all this time would be found out.

And when it had been, they'd closed ranks.

And Carrie Folk had died.

23
1988 signed calligraphic lithograph of lines from Edgar Allan Poe's poem "A Dream Within a Dream" ("All That We See or Seem Is But a Dream Within a Dream.") by calligrapher Robert Slimbach. Slimbach, who is also a type designer for Adobe Systems, has won international awards in typography. The roman script calligraphy demonstrated in this poster (white letters on a black background) formed the basis for his typeface Brioso. 10 x 20 inches. Price: $75.

THEY HAD AN early dinner, as they'd promised Aunt Nettie, and were checking the weather on WGME, her favorite Portland channel for news, when Will's cell phone rang.

"Darn. I hoped it'd be Jo, about my offer. It's Nick," he shared, before walking into the kitchen to take the call.

"I'd think Nicky'd be busy solving our crime," said Aunt Nettie. "It's been three days now. TV detectives would have had everything wrapped up by now."

"We haven't given him a lot of help," Maggie pointed out.

"He asked who else Carrie'd tried to blackmail. We told him Ruth had gotten one of those darn letters. That's all he asked us to do. And then you talked to Miranda. The way I see it, that was sort of a bonus for him."

"And now he's added Brian, and maybe Miranda, to his list of suspects." Should she tell Aunt Nettie about Doreen's missing letter? Doreen hadn't sworn her to secrecy. But the missing letter might put Zelda, and maybe even her friend Jon, on the suspect list. And receiving the letter in itself would add Doreen, which would take Nick off the investigation. It complicated everything. It wasn't her place to tell Nick he should add his mother and daughter to the suspect list. Although maybe someone should.

Will came back in, putting on his coat as he walked. "I'm not sure what the problem is. Maybe's Nick's already had a drink or two. He's mad as hell at me about something, and says we have to talk."

"That doesn't sound like Nicky," said Aunt Nettie.

"Well, it's him tonight," said Will. "I told him I'd meet him down at The Great Blue. I'm sorry, Maggie, but I think I should go. I've never heard Nick sound this way."

"Shall I come with you?" she asked, starting to get up.

"No, no. You stay here. Whatever it is, I have a feeling your being there would just complicate things. I'll be back as soon as I can. Promise." The door slammed on his way out.

"That was a surprise," said Maggie.

"I wonder what Nicky's got in his head," said Aunt Nettie. "Whatever it is, Will should be able to get him calmed down. Will's got a good head on his shoulders."

Maggie smiled. "He does."

"You need to make sure he points it in the right direction," she advised. "Sometime he gets distracted. Most men do."

"Aunt Nettie, earlier this afternoon I was looking at your book of photographs. The one you showed me last summer?"

"Whole history of the family's between those red leather covers."

"I saw a picture of you and Ruth, maybe in the 1940s. Will said it was taken in one of the Swan Boats, in the Boston Public Garden."

Aunt Nettie hesitated. "I'd forgotten that was in there. Yes, that was during the war. Boston was just far enough away so once in a while we girls would save our gas rationing stamps and our days off and take a little vacation. Ruth and Betty had a second or third cousin who lived in Arlington who let us stay with her."

"Was she the one who helped you when you were pregnant?"

"Yes. She was very understanding."

"And she helped Betty, too."

"I never said anything about Betty."

"No. But Miranda said she was born in Boston."

"I didn't realize she'd ever been concerned about her father," said Aunt Nettie. "Parents often keep secrets to protect their children." She paused. "And, perhaps, themselves."

Maggie plunged on. "At first, when I saw the picture of you and Ruth in Boston, and I thought of what you'd told Will and me, and what Miranda said, and I thought…I thought maybe…maybe you hadn't had an abortion. I thought maybe Miranda was your daughter."

Aunt Nettie looked at her, and then started laughing. And then the laughter turned to tears.

"Oh, no, Maggie. No. Nicky was right. You *are* a good detective. You put all the clues you heard together well. But you missed a few important things. Like dates." Aunt Nettie shook her head sadly. "Miranda's not my daughter. She's Betty's daughter. But you're right about one thing. I didn't have an abortion. Ruth went with me to Boston. I intended to have one, but the place we'd heard about was foul and loathsome, and the man who met me there was clearly in it only for the money. He didn't care who I was or where I came from, or even how far along I was. We were horrified at how the poor scared women waiting to see him were being treated. I couldn't go through with it. Instead, with help from Ruth and her cousin, I stayed in Boston and carried my baby to term. I was going to give him or her up for adoption. But my daughter, my little Julie, was stillborn. She died twelve years before Miranda was born."

"But why? Why did you tell Will and Nick and me you'd had an abortion?"

"Because that's what Carrie Folk wrote in that horrible letter. And it was true that I'd been pregnant, and I'd had a difficult pregnancy. My doctor said I couldn't have any more children. And my fiancé was fighting in Europe the whole time," said Aunt Nettie. "So many years later, it feels almost as though I'd gone through with the abortion. In my mind, my Julie disappeared. Exactly what happened to her doesn't seem important anymore. What was important Christmas morning, and what's still important, is finding the person who killed Carrie Folk."

"No wonder you gave me those wonderful books for Christmas."

"I know it's selfish, but I'm hoping you do adopt a little girl, Maggie, and that I live long enough to meet her."

"I hope so, too."

The two women smiled at each other.

"I think you should tell Nick that what was in that letter from Carrie wasn't the truth," said Maggie. "Because what might have been in the letters to other people might not have been true, either."

"We only know of one other letter, though," said Aunt Nettie. "The letter Carrie sent to Ruth."

Maggie hesitated. "There was at least one more. Today when Will and I were out having lunch we ran into Doreen and Zelda. Doreen told me that she'd gotten one, too."

"Oh, no." Aunt Nettie sat up straighter. "Did she tell Nick?"

"No. She hid the letter, and it's disappeared. She's afraid Zelda might have found it."

"She's at Ruth's house tonight, taking care of Betty," Aunt Nettie said, almost to herself.

"And Nick's with Will, and he wouldn't have left Zelda alone, so she's either with friends or with Doreen," said Maggie.

"Did you tell Doreen that Ruth received a letter?"

"Yes."

"Then maybe she'll talk with Ruth. They should connect," Aunt Nettie said. "Maggie, that's very important."

"They probably will," said Maggie. "But I don't think their talking will make a difference. Nick and Owen are looking at Brian as a potential suspect. He left the Westons' house at least once that night, and he's been having financial problems his mother may not know about. The police didn't find any money in the Folks' home." She hesitated a moment. "And, remember? Nick said Billy'd heard his mother talking to Santa Claus Christmas night. That was probably the killer. So the killer was a man."

"They might be jumping to conclusions. The killer might have been someone else. Or two people, and Billy heard one voice. Or thought he did."

"True." Maggie couldn't sit down any longer. There were too many possibilities. "I wonder what Nick wanted to talk to Will about tonight?"

"Maybe he wants advice about a lady friend. Or just wanted to get out of his house. I wouldn't worry about it, Maggie."

"His mother said he didn't have a girlfriend. But I'm restless. It's still early. Would you mind if I went for a walk, Aunt Nettie? Only for half an hour or so."

"You go ahead. I'll sit and watch *Jeopardy!* Maybe Will will even get back before you do," said Aunt Nettie. "Fresh air may clear your mind. We both have a lot to think about."

"Thank you. Don't worry. In this cold, I won't stay out long."

As Maggie pulled on her boots, wound her muffler around her neck, and put on her jacket and gloves and hat she felt a little crazy. Going for a walk when the temperature was probably close to zero? She refused to check the thermometer in the kitchen window.

But once outside, she was glad to be there. True, her nose felt frosty. She pulled the muffler up to cover the bottom of her face and walked down the silent snow-covered street toward the center of town. Snow crunched beneath her boots.

The sky was clear and bright. At her home in Somerset County, New Jersey she could sometimes see the North Star on clear nights, but light from other houses and a sky blocked by tree branches made star-gazing close to impossible. Here the open cloudless sky over the river was full of hundreds of lights; thousands, if you could count all those in the Milky Way. All were clearly visible and formed close to the same patterns they had for hundreds of years.

Each season's pattern was distinct. But tonight's sky looked like the ones pictured in Richard Proctor's 1887 *Half Hours with the Stars,* white-on-blue engravings, astronomical prints showing the night sky in various months throughout the year. Billions of people, all over the world, for generations and generations, had seen those same stars, she thought. And each of them thought their own lives, and their own problems, were significant.

And, who knew? Perhaps they were. It all depended on your perspective. Tonight, looking up at that sky, problems in Waymouth felt very small.

She turned from the river and walked up Main Street, past store windows, some closed for the night, some for the winter. In the distance a train's whistle echoed across the river. Somewhere a dog barked. A few minutes later church bells chimed eight o'clock.

On the next corner Maggie hesitated. Only half a block away was the Sunken Garden, where she'd sat on a granite bench one summer day and found quiet and peace. Now she knew it was also the place where Nick was haunted by the death of a young girl.

A girl about the same age his own daughter was now. The death of one, sadly unknown, girl, had changed the life of a young man, and resulted in his choosing a life pursuing the killers of others.

She started down that street, but turned back. This was not the time to visit the Garden. Its uneven stairs would be covered by feet of drifted snow; its paths and benches ghostly by-ways and hills hidden below the busy streets above. Spring and summer, and perhaps fall, were the Garden's seasons. Winter was its time to hold its past secure, and await its next renewal.

She walked another block on Main Street, enjoying her solitude, and the quiet and holiday lights.

Then, reluctantly, she turned and headed back after the cold began creeping into her fingers and toes. It was time to sip some cognac to help her warm up, and wait for Will to come home.

24   **"They Quaffed Their Liquor in Profound Silence."** Illustration by Arthur Rackham for *Rip Van Winkle* by Washington Irving. Six strange, small, bearded men (rumored to be the ghosts of Hendrick Hudson's crew) drinking deeply in a piece of woodland floating above the clouds. New York: Doubleday, Page & Co., 1910. Tipped-in lithography on green page; lithograph, 5.25 x 6.75 inches. Price: $65.

AT 9:00 MAGGIE helped Aunt Nettie into her bed for the night.

By 10:00 she'd finished two cognacs, a small plate of Stilton and wheat crackers, and read several more chapters in James Hayman's latest mystery. She was glad she'd waited until after their trip to Portland to read it. Hayman's Portland was fascinating, but definitely the darker side of the city.

By 11:00 she was trying to decide whether she should have another cognac, go to bed, or maybe call The Great Blue and ask Will whether he needed a ride home. She quickly decided the last option wasn't a wise one. But he'd been gone for hours. What if he'd had an accident?

The Great Blue wasn't far away. She could have walked there when she'd gone out, but she'd thought that would have been interfering. Nick had wanted to talk to Will. She hadn't been invited.

And Will had said he'd be home soon.

At 11:30 she poured that third cognac.

She started looking out the window, watching for cars. Very few people were out this late. Was The Great Blue even open after 11:00? Not many small-town Maine taverns were. Although maybe Christmas week they'd make exceptions. Not knowing didn't make the waiting easier. Twice she picked up her phone to call and find out, and then put it down. No. She didn't want him to think she was checking up on him.

But, yes. By now she was convinced something was wrong. Should she call the state police?

Except—he was *with* the state police.

At 11:50 Aunt Nettie's sedan finally pulled into the driveway. She watched it from the window and quickly went into the living room and picked up her book. She wasn't going to admit she'd been worried. He was a grown man. She didn't have any official claim on him. She should have gone to bed. Shown him she didn't care how late he stayed out.

She didn't move from the couch as she heard Will hanging up his jacket and turning off the light in the kitchen. He stumbled a bit as he walked into the living room.

"Maggie! Why're you still up?"

All her resolve not to question him fell away. "Where've you been? I thought you said you were going to be home soon. I've been worried."

"I've been with Nick, like I said I'd be. It just didn't work out that I'd be home early." Will came over, hitting the side table along the way, and slumped down next to her on the couch, putting his arm around her and knocking her book to the floor. "Nick and I were talking."

Maggie moved over. "I can smell how much you had to talk about."

"Maybe I had a little too much to drink. Just a little," Will admitted. "But not as much as Nick did!"

"That makes me feel a lot better. He must be in great shape," said Maggie. "I've never seen you like this. Why didn't you come home earlier?"

"My friend Nick needed me," said Will. "We men have to stick together."

"I see. So you men were out getting sloshed." She suddenly thought of the distance Nick had to drive to get to his home out in the country. "Was Nick driving home tonight?"

"Nope. State troopers aren't supposed to drive when they've been drinking."

"Good rule. Probably not only for state troopers," she added drily.

"The bartender was going to drive him home. We all left at the same time."

"So you closed the bar. Why doesn't that surprise me."

"It's a very friendly place, Maggie."

"So what was so important for you and Nick to talk about?"

"He's really pissed about you, actually," said Will. "That's why I had to stay. To defend your honor, as it were."

"Me? What do I have to do with your getting drunk?"

"You've been asking too many questions."

"What? Well, I think I have a right. You come home, lit up like a Christmas tree. I've been waiting here, worried, and you excuse your condition by saying you're defending my honor? Of course I can ask what you were talking about!"

"No, no, no, Maggie. Not questions now. Nick is mad because you're asking too many questions in town. About other people. He says it's none of your business. You're not a police investigator."

"That's ridiculous. Nick was the one who asked Aunt Nettie and me to ask questions. You know that. You were here when he did that, Christmas morning."

"He wanted Aunt Nettie to ask Ruth about that blackmailing. Maggie, between you and me, I'm pretty sure he thinks he has a case against her son Brian. But—shh!—it's a secret. He's putting it all together. But I think Brian is in big trouble. Very big."

Will tried to reach over and kiss Maggie. She pushed him away. "Hold on. I knew he was interested in Brian, but I didn't think he was that sure."

"He is. Believe me, Maggie. He says Brian was a pain in high school, and he's still a pain now."

"Being a pain doesn't make him a murderer. Let's go back a little. Just why is he upset about me talking to people? He's known I was helping Aunt Nettie from the beginning."

"He didn't know you'd be talking to his mother and Zelda." Will nodded. "Jo agreed. She thought maybe you'd gone a little too far."

"Jo? Jo Heartwood? She was there tonight, too?"

"She happened to stop in."

"I see. She happened to stop in and joined you two on your boys' night out?"

"Sort of like that. No big deal."

"No big deal? No big deal!"

"Nah. Her mom was visiting and said she'd baby-sit so Jo could go out for a while. So she was there. And we were all talking."

"And drinking."

"And we had a few drinks."

"And you talked about how your friend Maggie was messing up. How she was interfering with Nick's family."

"I didn't exactly say that."

"I assume I did these horrible things when we had lunch today. Because that's the only time I've ever met Zelda. And by the way, I wasn't alone at lunch. You were there, too. And how did Nick even know, since he wasn't there?"

"I don't know how Nick knew. But everybody does. And I told Nick and Jo you weren't asking questions at lunch about the murder. You were talking to Zelda about college and things like that."

"I see. You told Nick and Jo that."

"Of course I did! But that didn't make Nick feel better. In fact, he didn't like that at all. That was when he said he wanted you to stop talking to everybody in Waymouth." Will put his arm around Maggie again. She pulled further away. "Except me. You can talk to me anytime, Maggie."

"What did you say then?"

"I told him you were going home soon, so he wouldn't have to worry about you for much longer. That you didn't mean any harm. You teach at a college, so you talk about colleges. You didn't mean to interfere."

"You excused what I said? I was trying to help Zelda! Nick is browbeating her, and trying to keep her from finding out what the world is all about. He'd like to keep her at home in Maine for the rest of her life. That's not protecting her. That's keeping her from living her life! That's…child abuse!"

"Nick doesn't see it that way, Maggie. And she is his daughter. He wants you to stay away from his family. And he wants you to stop asking questions about Carrie Folk's murder." Will raised his hands. "That's it. That's what he wants. And he's the state trooper. He's the boss."

"He's not my boss. I'm not going to do it."

"We only have a few more days together before you have to go home. Nick's my friend. Why not make it easier for me? Why not do as he says?" Will asked. "Aunt Nettie won't mind if you stop questioning people. You and I can do other things. Fun things."

"Like your leaving here one of the few nights I'm in Maine to go drinking with Nick and Jo Heartwood? That kind of fun?" Maggie stood up. "The first thing you need to do is get a good night's sleep and sober up."

"Ah, Maggie, Maggie. I love you, Maggie. I'm not that drunk."

"You're not that sober, for sure." She reached out a hand. "I've never seen you like this before. And it's not pretty. Here. Let me help you up." She pulled him up to an unsteady stand. "Can you make it up the stairs by yourself?"

"Of course I can. I'm fine. I don't need any help," he said, lurching toward the staircase.

"I'm going to get you a glass of water and aspirin. I'll bring them upstairs. I'm sleeping in the guest room tonight," she added, as he headed upstairs. "And I don't care what Nick says. Or you say. I'm not going to stop asking questions."

25

Untitled tipped-in illustration for *Comus*, 1921, by Arthur Rackham. Shades of tan and brown; picture of gnarled, leafless tree, with snake coiled around it next to bony, ancient hag with long hair who is staring at viewer. Caption: "Some say, no evil thing that walks by night / In fog, or fire, by lake or Moorish fen, / Blew meager Hag, or stubborn unlaid ghost / That breaks his magick chains at curfeu time; / No goblin, or swart faery of the mine, / Hath hurtful power o'er true virginity." *Comus*, a masque in honor of chastity, was written by John Milton, and first presented on Michaelmas, the Feast of Saint Michael and All Angels, in 1634. Small fold mark on lower left corner. 5 x 7 inches. Price: $65.

MAGGIE HEARD the cowbell the next morning. Aunt Nettie's signal that Will had overslept. She groaned. No wonder. He was probably still out cold.

She pulled herself out of the guest room bed, threw on her bathrobe, and headed downstairs. This morning she'd help Aunt Nettie with her morning ablutions. After all, wasn't it Aunt Nettie who'd called her "one of the family"? Helping is what family did. It wasn't Aunt Nettie's fault Will had gotten drunk last night.

Half an hour later the sun was beginning to come up, coffee was perking, and the two women were plotting over bacon and toast with raspberry jam.

"If you're not supposed to talk with anyone, how are we supposed to find out anything?" asked Aunt Nettie. "I've been thinking about what you said about Brian. What do you think? Is he really the one who killed Carrie?"

"Maybe Nick's discovered something we don't know. That's his job, after all. He said the crime unit hadn't found fingerprints, though, so it isn't that. DNA? No. There hasn't been time for lab tests to come back," Maggie puzzled. "Let's think it through. Opportunity? Ruth told us that the night before Christmas Eve Brian went for a walk in the middle of the night. If he did that again early on Christmas Day no one would have thought anything about it. He could have gone to Carrie's house, killed her, stolen her money, and returned home to play Santa Claus."

"Possible," said Aunt Nettie, nibbling a slice of bacon. "But to do all that would take longer than it would take to walk around town for a bit. It's cold out there. I can't imagine Brian's taking a walk for more than a half hour or so. You went out last night. What do you think? How long would someone wander about in the cold?"

"I was gone for what? Thirty or forty minutes? And I was ready to come inside where it was warm. But we don't know that anyone was paying attention to how long Brian was gone. How far is Carrie's house from town?"

"He couldn't have walked there. Assuming he knew where it was, and he might have, since she's lived in the same place for years, it would take maybe eight or ten minutes to drive. She lived north of here, in the same direction as Nicky and Doreen live, but not as far out. Where she lived there are maybe a dozen houses, pretty close to each other, on the main road."

"I remember. Close enough so Billy went to a neighbor's house for breakfast."

"So maybe one of the neighbors saw something. That might be information Nicky has that we don't have. That could lead to a suspect: Brian, or someone else."

"Owen told me that, despite what Ruth said, Brian's having financial problems. New wife, new house, job not as spectacular as Ruth implied. He may have exaggerated when he told his mother, or she was exaggerating when she told us. In either case, he probably could use extra money. Jenny didn't marry him for his looks."

Aunt Nettie choked a bit on her toast. "That's nasty, Maggie."

"Did you see her ring? If Brian's finances are tight, that ring alone was a major stretch. And new babies run up bills."

"Maybe her ring's not real. Maybe it's one of those zirconias they sell on the Home Shopping Network," suggested Aunt Nettie.

This time it was Maggie's turn to chortle a bit. "Good thought. But having bills to pay, going for a walk, and even my seeing Brian looking through his mother's desk doesn't make him a murderer."

"Brian could have been protecting his mother. So no one would know what she'd done."

Maggie nodded. "Possible. Although Ruth had already agreed to pay Carrie."

"Maybe Brian wanted her to pay him instead."

"Take over the blackmailing?" Maggie shook her head. "What son would blackmail his own mother?"

"It would depend on what was in Ruth's letter," said Aunt Nettie, surprisingly. "But you're probably right. That isn't logical."

They were both quiet.

"So Brian doesn't have a clear motive. Even if he might have had the opportunity it still doesn't feel as though the case should be wrapped up."

"There must be someone else who makes more sense as the murderer," Aunt Nettie thought out loud.

"But neither of you are going to do any more investigating," said Will, entering the room and heading for the refrigerator. He poured himself a tall glass of orange juice and drank it in almost one gulp. "That's over. Done. Enough is enough. Nick and Owen Trask have jobs to do. They're figuring out who the killer is. They don't want you two involved anymore. Nick said it was a mistake to get either of you involved at all. So, stop. Just stop."

"Nick and Owen can continue investigating their own way," said Aunt Nettie. "I'm an old lady. They can't stop me from gossiping with my friends. There's no harm in chatting a little about the untimely death of an acquaintance."

"I didn't say you couldn't talk with your friends. But Maggie's got to stay out of it. I don't want to mess up my friendship with Nick because he thinks the lady in my life is interfering with his family." He looked from his aunt to Maggie. "I don't want to be in the middle of this mess, and I don't want either of you to be. Can't you understand that?"

"I understand Nick's decided he knows who killed Carrie Folk, and he's trying to prove it," said Aunt Nettie. "But he may not have all the information he needs to make that decision."

"Will, Nick doesn't want me involved in the investigation. I hear that. If he'd found Carrie's murderer, that would make sense. But Aunt Nettie and I aren't as sure as Nick that Brian's the guilty one."

"You don't get it," said Will. "At this point I don't care who killed Carrie Folk. And neither should you. That's Nick's job to find out, and he certainly knows more about this investigation than I do. Than even both of you do, no matter what you think. And if he says to stay out of the way, that's what you should do. It's that simple." He looked from one of the women to the other.

"Maggie or I will talk to Ruth about anything we choose," said Aunt Nettie. "We just won't let Nick know what we're doing. If he doesn't know, then he won't be upset."

"And although I'm not sorry for what I said to Zelda about her future, maybe I was out of line. I don't know her. Okay?" Maggie said. "I'll even apologize to Nick if it seems necessary. But if Aunt Nettie wants to talk to Ruth, or Betty, or Doreen, or any of her friends, she should be able to."

Will threw up his hands. "I give up. I woke up with a headache, and this talk is making the pain worse. I should have said something earlier. I shouldn't have let you both get involved in this whole murder situation."

"*Let* us? We didn't need your permission. Nick asked Aunt Nettie, and said I could help."

"That was Christmas Day. Now the situation is different. I think you're wrong to do something a state trooper specifically tells you not to do. Don't forget, officially, we're all still suspects ourselves. I hope you haven't forgotten that. But I can't put a gag on either of you." He glared at Maggie. "Although once in a while that sounds like a sane and reasonable option. You do what you want to do. Just don't expect me to back you up on anything to do with this investigation." Will picked up the cup of coffee he'd poured and stomped back up the stairs. "I'm going back to bed to see if I can get rid of this headache."

Aunt Nettie calmly finished the bacon she was eating. "Will seems a bit upset this morning. Maybe it's just as well we don't talk to Nicky today. But I need to talk with Ruth again, and I'd like you to drive me there. If you're still up for it."

"There's no reason I can think of for you not to talk with Ruth. I'd be happy to drive you there." Maggie glanced toward the stairway Will had taken to the second floor. "Maybe by the time we get home he'll be in a better mood."

A telephone call from Aunt Nettie confirmed that Ruth would not only be happy to see them, but she'd been about to call and ask them to come over. Maggie put the breakfast dishes in the sink to soak and got their coats. "I wonder if Doreen will still be at Ruth's? She was going to stay last night to watch Betty."

"I didn't think to ask," said Aunt Nettie. "But it might be better if she wasn't there. Wouldn't want you getting in any more trouble about talking to her."

"I'm not worried," said Maggie.

And she had no reason to be. Doreen had already left by the time they reached Ruth's house. "I'm glad you called," she said, opening the door and welcoming them in. "Doreen's gone home, Miranda left yesterday afternoon, and Nick arrived early this morning. He took Brian and Jenny back with him to the local police station to question them. Jenny insisted on taking the baby with her, so they're all gone."

Aunt Nettie and Maggie exchanged glances. "How is Betty this morning?" asked Aunt Nettie.

"She slept better last night, but she's napping now."

"We need to talk about this blackmail thing," said Aunt Nettie. "We hear Nick is focusing his suspicions on Brian."

"No!" said Ruth. "I knew he was being questioned, but I didn't think it was that serious." They settled at the kitchen table. "Brian wouldn't have killed Carrie. He's lived in Philadelphia for years; he hardly knows her. And he didn't know anything about the blackmailing."

"Nick thinks he did. That he overheard something here, or found the letter you'd gotten. That he decided to get in the middle of it all, maybe to protect you, or maybe for another reason." Maggie felt uncomfortable laying it all out for Brian's mother. "Ruth, the ten thousand dollars you gave Carrie is missing. Nick thinks whoever killed her stole that money from her house Christmas morning."

"Missing? The ten thousand dollars isn't missing," said Ruth. "Or at least I don't think it is. I didn't feel comfortable just handing Carrie ten thousand dollars, so we went to a bank in Portland where neither of us had accounts, so no one would ask questions, and she opened an account there for Billy, and deposited the money there. If she had cash in her house, it wasn't the ten thousand dollars I gave her."

"Did anyone else know you'd done that? Opened the account for Billy, I mean?"

"I didn't tell anyone. And no one's asked. When Nick questioned me yesterday afternoon I told him about the letter and the ten thousand dollars, as I'd told you."

"But you didn't tell him about the new bank account."

"Didn't think it was necessary. That money's Billy's now. Carrie was quite clear about that." Ruth hesitated. "She asked that if anything happened to her, I should make sure her lawyer knew about the account. I thought that was a little strange, but she wouldn't explain, and since she was murdered a couple of days later, I wasn't sure what to do. I planned to wait until all the fuss was over and then contact her lawyer."

"Remember you wondered whether Carrie or Billy were sick, since Carrie had taken several sick days this fall?" Aunt Nettie said.

"Whether Carrie needed the money to pay medical bills," Ruth agreed. "Or whether she put the money in Billy's name so any creditors she had couldn't get their hands on it."

"Nicky told us Carrie had stage-four cancer," said Aunt Nettie. "She wouldn't have lived long even if she hadn't been killed. From what they found in her home, the police are assuming she wanted the money to pay for an upscale facility where Billy could live after she died."

"She was that sick? She'd lost weight recently, but I didn't think anything of it. She must have been worried to death about what would happen to Billy. And that would explain why she said she needed the rest of the hundred thousand dollars by the end of January," said Ruth.

"Exactly," said Aunt Nettie. "And from what you've said, the ten thousand dollars isn't missing. Carrie's killer might have taken cash she had in her wallet, but there weren't thousands of dollars sitting around her house to be found and stolen."

"Not the ten thousand she got from me, certainly," said Ruth. "Of course, she could have gotten money from someone else."

"I didn't give her any," Aunt Nettie reminded her. "Did Doreen talk to you about her letter?"

"She did. That's one of the reasons I wanted to see you this morning. Of course, she hadn't given Carrie any money either."

Ruth and Aunt Nettie looked at each other. Finally, Aunt Nettie said, "I didn't ask what your letter was about. I told you what mine said; that I'd had an illegal abortion."

"Which was hogwash!" said Ruth, sitting up straighter. "Although no one would have blamed you for doing that after what you went through." She turned to Maggie. "Nettie was so brave, after the rape. She would have gone to the police in Bath, too, if it hadn't been that one of the men's brothers was in the sheriff's department."

"You were raped?" said Maggie.

"I thought you'd told her!" said Ruth

"I didn't tell her everything," said Aunt Nettie. "I didn't think I'd need to. But I guess the time for secrets is long gone." She turned to Maggie. "I was walking home by myself during one of the blackouts. I'd had dinner with Ruth and several other women we worked with. I remember we ate lobster that night. It wasn't rationed and you could get it locally. The others wanted to go on to the USO afterwards, but I was tired, so I left early. Two men who knew me from the Iron Works saw me, and followed me, taunting me. When I told them to get lost, they pulled me off the street, tore off my clothes, and took turns raping me. No one heard my screams."

"I'm so sorry," said Maggie, quietly. "How awful."

"I still have nightmares about it," said Aunt Nettie. "But it was so long ago, that's what it all seems. A nightmare. Which deepened when I realized I was pregnant."

"She was incredibly brave," put in Ruth. "She didn't tell anyone except the three of us from Waymouth—me and Mary and Susan— and she swore us all to secrecy. Even today I think many young women are embarrassed if they've been raped. But in those days, if she'd told anyone, she would have been thought 'easy,' and could have lost her job as well as her reputation."

"And you helped her by finding a doctor in Boston."

"My cousin did. But that man wasn't a doctor. He was a butcher."

"I told you that part," said Aunt Nettie. "Why I decided to have my child. By that time I'd begun to think of the baby I was carrying as mine. I tried not to think about how I'd gotten pregnant. I knew I couldn't keep my child, but I wanted him or her to have a good life. It wasn't that baby's fault I'd been raped. And I'd never have to tell my fiancé about what happened. It would all be over by the time he came home." She paused. "But of course, it didn't work out that way. My little Julie and my fiancé both died."

"And after that the four of us vowed to do everything we could to help women who were in similar situations," said Ruth. "But I wonder why Carrie thought you'd had an abortion?"

"She must have heard something from Betty. And she got the story confused. Or part of it wrong, anyway."

Maggie thought for a few moments. "Is that why Betty wouldn't tell Miranda who her father was? Was Betty raped, too?"

Ruth broke the silence. "Yes. Betty was raped, too."

Aunt Nettie said, "Maggie, you understand this is all confidential. Miranda doesn't know, and Betty never wanted her to know."

"I won't tell her, certainly," said Maggie. What would she say if her future daughter asked to know more about her birth mother? And father? She'd want to be honest. And positive. Although some stories would be hard to cast in a good light. "But I think Miranda may suspect that. Or that her mother didn't know who the father of her baby was."

"Betty certainly knew," said Ruth. "What an awful thing for Miranda to think about her mother."

"Miranda's a grown woman. I think she could cope with hearing pretty much anything about her father, as long as it was true. Not knowing would be much worse than knowing," Maggie said. "And, after all, Betty didn't have an abortion or give her up for adoption. She kept her baby, and loved her. That has to mean a lot."

"You're probably right," said Ruth. "But it's more complicated than that." Ruth's hands were clenched. "Miranda's father was my husband."

26

Untitled. Pen-and-ink lithograph by Charles Dana Gibson (1867–1944) creator of the "Gibson Girl," an ideal of American womanhood. Depicts well-dressed woman, all in black, greeting a gentleman. Dialogue underneath picture: *Young Widow: "How long should I wear mourning?"* *Answer: "I'm unable to say. I wasn't acquainted with your husband."* Originally published in *Life* Magazine, 1899. Reprinted in *The Gibson Book: A Collection of the Published Works of Charles Dana Gibson in Two Volumes,* 1907. 8.5 x 11 inches. Price: $60.

IT TOOK a moment for Maggie to absorb what Ruth had said. "Your husband raped your sister?" Ruth was still wearing her slim gold wedding band. In memoriam? Surely not a comforting reminder of a man she'd respected.

"My Jonas was handsome, charming, persuasive, and insistent on having his way, if persuasion didn't work. I'd put up with his penchant for women since shortly after we were married. He was a good father and provider, and it was the nineteen-fifties. Much as I hated what he did, he wasn't letting it interfere with our home life. He kept his pants on when he was in town, and never had a 'friend' long enough to threaten our marriage."

Maggie knew too well what it was like to be married to a man who cheated. Although she hadn't forgiven. She nodded, almost numbly. "But your sister…!"

"Betty came to me, and told me what had happened. It was all too simple and believable. He'd been drinking. She'd said 'no.' He wouldn't listen." Ruth's face hardened. "That was crossing a line I couldn't ignore. I couldn't be married to a man who'd hurt my little sister."

"Did you ask for a divorce?"

Ruth looked Maggie straight in the eye. "A funeral's cheaper than a divorce."

"Your husband died in a car accident," Maggie confirmed.

"He did," said Ruth. "And that's all I'll say about it. It was a long time ago."

"And Betty put an invented name on her daughter's birth certificate and then came here and raised Miranda with your children," Maggie said, almost to herself.

"I had Jonas's life insurance and savings and this big house. She was an unwed mother with an infant and no job. Miranda and Brian were close to the same age. It was the right thing to do."

"And no one ever knew what had happened?"

"A few, a very few, close friends knew. Nettie, of course. And Mary. They helped me, and supported Betty and me through it all. Without our friends, I don't know how we would have managed."

Maggie looked from Ruth to Aunt Nettie and then back. Another story complete with hazy details. There was more to this story, too, she was almost positive. These women and their friends had taken care of themselves through the war. They'd worked in a factory, welding and assembling destroyers for the United States Navy. She didn't want to know the details about Jonas Weston's death. But, given the timing, his accident seemed very opportune.

She forced herself to focus on the present rather than the past. "I think you should tell Miranda about her father. Betty can't now. But Miranda deserves to know the truth."

"We decided from the beginning never to tell either her or my children. Noah and Stacy have good memories of their father. It doesn't do any good to rake up the past or talk badly of him. If I told Miranda, I'd have to tell them all. What good would it do? It's over," said Ruth.

"Is that what was in your letter from Carrie?" asked Maggie. "About your husband and Betty? Or your husband's death?"

"It was a bit confused," Ruth said. "Confused with what she wrote in her letter to Doreen. But there was enough information to raise questions I didn't—don't—want raised. Now or ever. That's why I agreed to pay her."

"And you're sure Brian doesn't know anything about this."

"I don't know how he could. He hasn't even been in Waymouth for several years. Even if Betty were saying things that might be misinterpreted, he wouldn't have known about them."

"What was in Doreen's letter then?" asked Maggie. "If you can tell me. She said yesterday she'd gotten one, but not what was in it."

"I was afraid it was all related," said Aunt Nettie. "That's why we came to talk to you today."

"She told me last night," Ruth said. "We decided Maggie ought to know what the real issue was. Doreen would be here, too, if she hadn't agreed to spend the day with Zelda." She turned to Maggie. "You see, you've been asking questions, good questions, and a lot of them have needed answers. We needed to know why Carrie wanted money. Now we do. The police needed to know who Carrie was blackmailing. They know that, too. Or at least they know about two of us. But you understand that not everything I'm sharing with you is relevant to Carrie's murder. For example, letting people know about Miranda's father doesn't help solve the crime. It would put Betty and me in a very awkward position. It's a secret that could change how our children see each other, and my sister and me. But it's not a dangerous secret. Not one the police would be interested in."

Maggie decided to ignore the questions she had about Ruth's husband's death. He'd died in the 1950s in a car accident. Or perhaps it wasn't completely an accident. But how could anyone prove that more than fifty years later? Although there was no statute of limitations on murder. Accusing anyone of causing his death would only bring scandal and suffering to one or more elderly women who weren't dangerous to anyone. It could destroy the few years they had left.

"I won't tell your secret," she said quietly. "I understand why you haven't told anyone in all these years. I won't be the one to break your trust."

"Thank you, Maggie," said Ruth. "Nettie, now should we tell her the rest?"

"You said Doreen agreed we should."

"Doreen's very upset, and feels she isn't in a position to tell anyone officially, but she wants someone to know."

"And she won't tell Nick? He's her son!" said Maggie.

"Which is why she can't talk with him about this," said Ruth. "She's afraid of how he might react."

"Nicky Strait's always had a temper," Aunt Nettie said. "Most of the time he has it under control. But in the past year or two he's been more on edge. Doreen's tried to talk with him, but he won't listen. I guess, because of his job, he sees life, and people, in black-and-white."

"No one is all good or all bad," Maggie put in.

"Exactly. It's been hard for him as his daughter has grown up. She wants to do things her own way, like most teenagers do. I think she reminds him of her mother."

"Her mother was a piece of work," said Ruth, shaking her head. "All peaches and cream when she got what she wanted, and hard as steel when she didn't. Far as we could tell, she took to Nicky for his looks—he was a good-looking young man in those days—and because her wealthy parents didn't approve of a lobsterman's son. She was rebelling. And then she got herself pregnant. I've always wondered if she'd done that intentionally."

"Will said they were married when they were very young," said Maggie.

"They were. She was about eighteen, as I remember, and Nicky'd finished his freshman year at college. Her parents wouldn't give 'em any money, and that Emily wouldn't get a job. She was supposed to be taking care of Zelda, but she didn't have any natural-born mothering in her. She ran off when that baby was only six months old and went home to her own mother. Nicky had a scholarship, and he and Doreen agreed he needed to stay in school. He commuted to Portland several days a week and worked as a stern man when he could, and Doreen left off working at the hospital to take care of Zelda when Nicky couldn't. It was a hard, hard time for everyone, even before Mary got sick and Doreen had to take care of her, too." Ruth was silent, as though thinking of those days. "Anyway, Nicky's been coping with all of this for years now. Never found another girl he was interested in. Doreen sometimes wondered whether he was still carrying a torch for Emily."

"Or more likely, he'd had enough of women. He's been supporting his mother and daughter since he was a youngster," put in Aunt Nettie. "Although the three of them have gotten along remarkably well, considering."

"But recently Doreen's been worried for Zelda. Nick's been pretty hard on the girl. Maybe he's afraid she's going to run off, like her mother did. Or she'll get pregnant, same as Emily. Goodness knows what's in that man's head. But he's been trying to keep Zelda on a very short leash, especially when it comes to boys. Even good, responsible boys her age."

"She had a black eye when I saw her in the choir on Christmas Eve," said Maggie.

"He doesn't usually hit her. But Doreen told me he's done it more often recently." Ruth shook her head. "Nasty business, that. I'll admit I laid a smart hand to the backsides of my children a time or three when they were young. But Zelda's not a child, and hitting anyone in the face, especially a woman, is not a tap on the rear end."

Doreen had said she had to help Zelda get away from this place. Maybe what she'd meant was get her away from her father. It was an awful thought: Nick hitting his daughter. And who could the girl go to? Her father was the law. "I never imagined it was Nick who'd hit her. I assumed her boyfriend had done it."

"Not that sweet Jon Snow," said Ruth. "He's not the brightest bulb on the tree, but he's seriously religious, and Doreen says he's a good influence on Zelda. He keeps her calmed down when things get rough at home. He's not afraid to stand up to her father, either, which is why Nick can't stand him."

"So Doreen wouldn't tell Nick about the letter she got, because she was afraid of his reaction to it? Was she afraid he'd hurt her?"

"I don't think she's afraid of him for herself. Not physically. But she didn't want him seeing what was in the letter. It would have upset and embarrassed him. And with the mood he's been in lately, she didn't know what he'd do. It was safer not to tell him. She didn't think he needed to know. Until Carrie was killed, of course."

"She didn't tell me what was in the letter; only that she'd gotten one. Now she wants me to do something about it?"

"You're from away. It doesn't matter what Nick thinks of you. And you're free to have contacts she doesn't have," said Ruth. "You don't just talk to Nick."

"As of last night, Nick doesn't want me to talk with anyone," said Maggie. "He'd be furious if he knew I was here talking with you this morning." Will wouldn't be happy either.

"But you could talk to Owen Trask. Someone other than Nick, but someone involved with the investigation," Aunt Nettie pointed out.

"I guess I could," Maggie admitted. "Even if Nick and Will would be furious." She hesitated. This was to be the week she and Will tested their relationship. Right now that test didn't seem to be going very well. "I could call Owen if I felt I had information he needed to know."

"That's what Doreen and I were up late last night talking about," said Ruth. "She doesn't know what can of worms would be opened if you told Owen. But she feels law enforcement needs to know about her letter. All about her letter. She hasn't slept for days worrying about it."

"She told me she didn't know who'd taken the letter."

"That's what she told me. But I think in the back of her mind she's wondering if Zelda took it. I told her she knew that girl through and through. She couldn't be a murderer. It isn't in her."

Zelda seemed to be a sweet, intelligent young woman who had plans for her future. Plans that didn't involve her father, or even Maine. If she'd gotten involved with a murder, intentionally or unintentionally, that would be the end of any of her hopes and dreams. It sounded implausible.

"And if Owen had more information, maybe he and Nick would be less likely to suspect my Brian of killing Carrie," Ruth went on. "I told Doreen she had to tell what she knew. It affects us all, but it would be most important to her. Do you agree, Nettie? Is it time to tell someone? We never thought the past would be so important all these years later."

"The world's changed since then. I can't think why we shouldn't talk about it. At this point in our lives, what does it matter what anyone thinks anyway? We did what we thought was right, and we should stop hiding. If Doreen is willing to talk, even if it's through Maggie telling Owen, then we have to back her up." Aunt Nettie looked resolute.

"We're agreed, then," said Ruth.

Maggie looked from one of the women to the other. Neither was smiling. Both were tense, and weary. Sharing a secret that had been kept for many years was a serious decision.

"I've already told you I had an unplanned pregnancy," Aunt Nettie said.

So that period of time was relevant to this latest secret.

"Of course, abortions weren't legal then, but having a baby when you weren't married was totally unacceptable. If anyone had known my situation, I wouldn't have been able to hold my head up in Waymouth. Nor would my fiancé, despite his loving me, have understood. I would have had to give up everything in my life. I've told you Ruth went with me to a place in Boston we'd heard about."

"A dreadful place," Ruth put in.

"Not only did it change my mind about what I wanted to do, but afterward I kept thinking of all the other women we saw there. I wondered if they'd survived." Aunt Nettie stopped for a moment. "In those days, under those circumstances, some women died as a result of having abortions. And having seen one of those places, I could understand how that might happen. The place was dirty, to begin with. And although the man who was supposed to do the abortion said he was a doctor, I wasn't sure. Anyone could say that. Women who went to those places were so desperate that they'd believe almost anything they were told. In any case, I went ahead and had my Julie. But years later, when Betty found herself in a similar situation, Ruth and Mary and I decided to do something about the problem, even though Betty decided to have her baby. She didn't really have a choice."

"It wasn't fair that women had to risk their lives as well as their reputations because of pregnancy," said Ruth. "Betty and I were pregnant at the same time, although she stayed away from Waymouth. We told people she'd had a short marriage and was divorced. No one questioned her. That happened."

"Mary, Doreen's mother, was the one who really changed her life as a result of what happened to Betty and me. She went to nursing school and got her degree. Ruth helped out with her tuition, because we decided we were all in this together." Aunt Nettie paused. "I thought about joining her, about studying nursing, too, but I knew I didn't have the dedication needed. But I promised to help her in any way I could. We all did."

"So Mary became a nurse," said Maggie.

"Her getting her degree was the beginning," said Ruth. "After that she worked at Rocky Shores Hospital, specializing in maternity cases. She watched and listened and kept studying."

"But without Ruth's help, she couldn't have done what we'd

intended all along. Ruth had the money to set up a small operating room here, in this house," Aunt Nettie put in.

"You've seen Betty's room. It was in that space. In those days, the late fifties and sixties, those rooms were walled off from the rest of the house. One of my cousins from Boston came to Maine and helped with the carpentry and plumbing. We didn't want the children to know what was happening there. We told them it was a storage area. I think when they were teenagers they guessed something else was happening, but they didn't ask. And like they used to say in the army, we didn't tell."

"It wasn't that hard to keep it a secret, because Mary worked the day shift most years, especially after she married and had Doreen, and we scheduled most of the young women who came to her for help at night."

"She did illegal abortions here in this house?" said Maggie.

"Our goal was to create a place for women that was safe. Clean. Private. Kind. And in case there were any complications, which only happened twice, we weren't far from Rocky Shores Hospital, and Mary knew a doctor and nurses there who wouldn't question or talk. Ruth bought her all the medical equipment and supplies she needed, and she and Betty kept the children busy or out of the house or asleep. Whatever was necessary." Aunt Nettie smiled at Ruth. "And I helped by talking to the women. Holding their hands. Making sure they understood what was entailed, emotionally as well as physically, with making the decision to end their pregnancy. We wanted to make sure such a difficult decision had been thought out. And I stayed with the women after their operations to make sure they were ready to leave here."

"And this went on for how many years?" Maggie said incredulously.

"From about 1957, when Mary felt she had enough training to begin, until 1973, when *Roe versus Wade* was decided. Our services weren't needed when abortion was made legal," said Ruth.

"We drank a lot of champagne that night, didn't we, Nettie? And then I had the extra wall in the house removed, and Mary worked through another nurse to donate our equipment to a clinic in New Hampshire. Far enough away so no one would ask questions."

"Remember the party you held to wallpaper the re-done room, and hang pictures there? It became a downstairs living room, Maggie. A 'rec' room they called them in those days," said Aunt Nettie. "The children were pretty much grown up by then, but with a television, bookcases, and a Ping-Pong table, it became a room where they could entertain their friends when they were home. It helped us all erase what had taken place there, and celebrate living."

"And none of the children ever knew what the room had been used for before that?" said Maggie.

"Not one of our four who grew up here. The only one who knew for sure what was happening was Mary's daughter," said Ruth.

"Doreen," said Maggie. "Mary told her?"

"Mary was the most involved. And Doreen was small when it all started, so Mary would bring her here for one of us to look after when she was working. Then, when she was older, Mary explained to Doreen what she was doing. By then it was the early seventies, and Doreen was a teenager. She understood. That was the period of women's liberation, and abortion was one of the hot topics in the news. Doreen volunteered to do what she could to help."

"As a teenager?" Maggie said, incredulously.

"She wanted to, and Mary trained her and trusted her. She worked with Mary, handing her instruments, and doing some of the prep work that Mary'd always done herself."

"And when she was old enough she became a nurse, like her mother," said Maggie.

"She did. Of course, by then we'd closed down everything here. There was no longer a need for Mary's services. Women could be taken care of in clinics or hospitals. They didn't need to break the law. And neither did we."

"Which was an immense relief to all of us," said Aunt Nettie. "It was harrowing, all those years, knowing we could have been arrested at any time. But we were lucky. Those who knew what we were doing didn't tell the police, and we were able to do what we'd set out to do: provide a safe alternative to women in this part of Maine."

"And occasionally other states, too," added Ruth. "Word did spread."

"How many women did you help?" asked Maggie.

"We didn't keep records. We weren't that foolish. They would have proved our guilt if anyone reported us. But after word got out about what we were doing, about thirty or forty women found their way here each year."

"So it wasn't every day."

"Heavens, no. We tried to schedule people on one night a week. Usually it was one woman each time. We didn't want lines of cars outside the house. We kept it all very quiet."

"And I assume that was what was in the blackmail letter to Doreen," said Maggie. "The fact that you were all involved with illegal abortions."

"Yes. Although Doreen was only involved for a short time, and it was her mother who was the primary person."

"But abortion is legal today. There are restrictions in various states, but people who do what Mary did aren't arrested and put in jail," said Maggie. "That was over forty years ago. There's no way you could get in trouble today for what happened way back then."

"Not legally. But there are still people who believe women who choose abortion are evil, and those who perform abortions are murderers. And Nick Strait, unfortunately, is one of those. How do you think he'd feel if he found out what his grandmother and mother had done? Not to mention the fact that they were breaking the law at the time," Ruth said.

Nick, who saw the world in black-and-white.

Now Maggie understood why Doreen didn't want Nick to know. "But I suspect he'll find out somehow. Especially after what happened to Carrie. I just wish Betty hadn't said anything to her."

"She wouldn't have had to say anything for Carrie to know," said Ruth. "Carrie was one of the women who came to us back in those days. After Billy was born she didn't want to risk having another child with the same problems. She didn't think she could handle having two, and it was before genetic testing. She was scared, and her husband was about to leave her. She didn't see that she had any choice."

"Which was the way most of the women who came to us felt. Scared. Boxed in," agreed Aunt Nettie.

"So Mary terminated Carrie's pregnancy, so many years ago," Ruth continued.

"You'd think she'd have been grateful. That it would never occur to her to advertise what had happened."

"I've been going over it in my mind," said Ruth. "Carrie had cancer. Once again, she was scared. She didn't know what to do. So she lashed out. But telling people about what happened then would not only upset Nick, it might encourage people to ask who else we helped. What happened so many years ago needs to stay in the past."

"So, you see, you must tell Owen Trask. Tell him what really happened. See if knowing the truth will help to find whoever killed Carrie," said Aunt Nettie.

"I don't know if that can happen without Nick's finding out," said Maggie. "It doesn't seem possible."

"But at least he won't find out from his own mother," said Ruth. "That's why we need you, Maggie. You need to speak for all of us."

27

1. American Sparrow Hawk 2. Field Sparrow 3. Tree Sparrow 4. Song Sparrow 5. Chipping Sparrow 6. Snow Bird. Hand-colored copper engraving showing the Sparrow Hawk surrounded by five birds it preys on. "Drawn from Nature" by Alexander Wilson (1766–1813). Wilson, the "Father of American Ornithology," was the first to seriously study and draw American birds. His masterpiece, *American Ornithology*, was published between 1808 and 1814. This is an octavo print from the smaller 1832 edition, considered to have superior color to the first, larger folio. 5.5 x 8.5 inches. Price: $70.

"WHERE HAVE you been all this time?" asked Will as Maggie and Aunt Nettie came in. "I've been worried."

"Paying a call on a friend," said Aunt Nettie. "You went out last night. It was our turn."

Will looked less than pleased. "But at least I told you where I was going."

"We're home now," said Maggie. How was she going to talk with Owen Trask without either Will or Nick finding out? She couldn't just disappear. Will would ask questions. She needed to distract him. And after all, Will was the reason she'd come to Maine in the first place. They'd spent time together, but so far had avoided talking seriously about the future. Or, at least, about Maggie's future. "I just realized it's December twenty-ninth. I only have a couple of more days here. I thought maybe you and I could spend the afternoon together."

"I'd like that," said Will, calming down a little. "Walter English always has a big auction on New Year's Day. What about our checking out the preview?" He turned to Aunt Nettie. "Would it be all right if we left you for a couple of hours?"

"No problem at all," agreed Aunt Nettie. "It's time you spent time together doing something you both enjoy."

"Not to speak of the possibilities of finding inventory items for our businesses," agreed Maggie. "Although Will and I are both pretty picky. And I'm watching my budget." She didn't add that adoption could be expensive, and she was also putting aside money for when her daughter or daughters came home. Clothes, shoes, orthodontics, school supplies, sports equipment... She was pretty sure supporting a family of two or three would cost a lot more than her current budget for living alone.

Half an hour later Will and Maggie were on the road. "I'm surprised there's so much going on in Maine this time of year. I'd imagined the state pretty much closed down when the summer visitors went home," Maggie admitted.

"In many ways there's more happening in the winter and early spring than there is in the summer," said Will. "Summer along the coast is geared to boating and fishing, and of course, tourists. But in winter there are lectures and concerts and a lot goes on in the schools and churches. Some people ski or snowshoe. Kids play ice hockey and skate and snowboard. Hunting is big in the fall. Ice fishing is popular, too."

"I don't think ice fishing is my sport. Huddled in a small hut on a frozen lake or river?" Maggie shuddered. "No, thank you. But I'm glad to know there are activities for indoor types like me. Are there many antiques shows in Maine in the winter? Since I'm tied to my classroom, I've only done shows close to home. I haven't looked further."

"The big antiques shows, like Union, and the Maine Antiques Dealers' Association shows, are in the summer and fall," Will said. "But in the winter there are smaller shows at schools and churches on a regular basis, and a lot of the antiques malls stay open year-'round."

"As you're hoping to do," said Maggie.

"Exactly." Will pulled into the crowded parking lot outside Walter English's Auction House, the building where goods to be auctioned were displayed and the auction would take place. "Shall we do our usual: split up and meet at the desk in half an hour?"

Maggie nodded. "See you then."

She headed to the left, toward where Walter English usually hung prints and paintings, while Will walked in the other direction, in search of kitchen and fireplace ware. They both skipped the sections of glass, china, and furniture, at least for the moment. Maggie did admire a small pumpkin pine corner cabinet on her way by. It would have fit well in her living room.

But no, she told herself. Her van was full, and shipping costs would really add to the price. True, furniture usually went low at auctions. More people were downsizing than furnishing new homes now. But she shouldn't think of spending money on nonessentials, even if the corner cabinet was tempting. She kept walking.

She scanned the paintings quickly. Maritime scenes that would go too high for her business. Religious paintings that were out of style; they'd be very slow sellers. She paused at a beach scene from the 1920s. Now that she had space in Gussie's shop on the Cape it might be the time to start investing in harbor or beach scenes. But again, these were signed oils and would go higher than she wanted to pay.

She glanced through the books and prints. She loved Alexander Wilson's birds, but already had several dozen of his small prints. She could use more prints of nests and eggs, or anything eighteenth-century or before. But nothing in those categories was here. Not today.

This wasn't her auction. Or maybe everything else happening was distracting from her usual joy in sorting through antiques, although looking did keep her mind off what she'd have to tell Owen Trask.

The room where most of the items to be sold January first were displayed was large and crowded. Estate jewelry, which usually went at about half its appraised value, was too tempting to look at closely. But a rack of fur coats caught her eye. Why not look? There were four mink coats, of various sizes and lengths, and two other coats from animals she couldn't identify.

She'd never thought of buying a fur. There were too many stories about animal cruelty. But these animals had been gone a long time. She peeked at the estimates. Even the full-length mink was estimated to sell between four hundred and six hundred dollars; the other coats at even lower prices.

"Would you like to try one on?" asked a woman wearing a WALTER ENGLISH AUCTIONS name tag. "Doesn't hurt to see if any would fit. Winter is cold. Fur helps."

Maggie hesitated. It might be fun to have a fur coat. Not mink. She couldn't see wearing mink to the college or grocery store. And the full-length mink was really over the top. But there was a three-quarter-length gray fur jacket that was tempting. "What is this one made of?" she asked.

"It may be opossum," said the woman. "It's a beautiful shade. Why don't you try it on? We have a mirror."

Maggie gave in. She slipped off her heavy wool jacket and put on the fur one. Its silk lining was faded, and she suspected it might tear soon from age or wear. Maybe it could be relined. The fur itself was in good condition, though, especially considering it was probably at least forty years old. And it fit perfectly. She turned around, looking in the mirror. Would she really wear a fur jacket?

"I like that color gray," said Will, coming up behind her. He reached over and stroked it. "Soft. And would be warm, too. In Maine you'd need a warm jacket."

"But I live in Jersey," said Maggie, looking at him. There was a pause. He didn't reply. "But even Jersey has cold and windy winters." She checked the estimate of what the coat would sell for.

"Leave a bid," said Will. "Why not? If it's meant to be yours, you'll get it. You could pick it up the day after the auction, on your way home. If you don't get it, no problem."

"I suppose I could. Bid low and leave the decision to fate. Did you find anything of interest?

"One possibility. A standing iron candle and rush-light holder. It's eighteenth-century French. It'll probably go over fifteen hundred dollars, but just in case I think I'll leave a bid of eight hundred and fifty. I don't have anything like it, and the Victorian house would be a great place to display it. If I get the house. Most of the rest of this auction is dark furniture and crystal and such. But I think you should bid on the jacket."

Maggie put her old wool jacket back on. "I'm going to. I'll bid a hundred and fifty. If I get it, fine. If not, I'll live."

"Good plan," Will agreed as they walked to the desk so both of them could leave bids. "I hope you get it. You look beautiful in it."

Convinced by those words, Maggie filled out the form and added a plus to the hundred and fifty, so if someone else bid the same she'd go one bid higher. A good wool jacket nowadays would cost that much, and wouldn't be half as much fun.

She was back in the car when her cell rang. It was Owen Trask.

28

Moose Hunting. Wood engraving of bull moose fleeing in snow as Native American hunters cut throat of female moose downed by long rifles. Article above engraving describes "uncouth" (*sic*) animals, and says that when snows are deep, Indians on snowshoes can "run these large animals down, for their slender legs break through the snow at every step and plunge them up to the belly...a good runner will generally tire them out in less than a day." Cover of *Gleason's Pictorial*, a Boston newspaper, January 28, 1854. Page size: 10.5 x 15 inches; illustration 9.25 x 7 inches. Top of page is a 4 x 9.25-inch header for *Gleason's*, showing downtown Boston and Boston Harbor, including steam and sail boats. Price: $60.

MAGGIE HESITATED before picking up Owen Trask's call. She couldn't tell him what she wanted to with Will in the car. But on the other hand, she did want to be in touch with the deputy. "Yes?" she answered.

"I'm glad I reached you. We've been making progress on the case, but there are still open issues."

"I'd like to speak with you, too," replied Maggie, hoping that wouldn't aggravate Will. To appease him, she added, "But Nick's asked me to stay away from the case."

"He told me that. But before you disappear, I'd like to run a few things by you. Off the record."

Maggie glanced over at Will, who was frowning. "If it's that important."

"Nick's gone to Augusta for the afternoon. Could you come down to the Waymouth station? Now?"

"Will," said Maggie, "Nick's in Augusta this afternoon but Owen would like to see me for a few minutes to clarify some information. Would you mind stopping at the police station so I can make sure we're all on the same wave length?"

"You'll tell him you can't do anything more to help after this?" asked Will.

"Of course," Maggie agreed. She not only remembered what Nick had said…she remembered how angry Will had been in Cape Cod when she'd left him to help solve a mystery. She didn't want him upset again, but Aunt Nettie and Ruth and Doreen were counting on her to talk to Owen. It would be all be simpler if Will didn't know how involved she'd gotten.

"As long as this is the last time," he said.

"So you'll take me to the station?"

"I guess so."

Maggie turned back to the telephone. "I'll be there soon. Will's going to drive me."

Owen's voice hesitated. "I'd rather he wasn't with you."

"That's right," Maggie answered. "Could you drive me back to the Brewers' house after we talk?"

"I could."

"We're on our way back from Walter English's Auction House. I'll see you soon." She pressed the Off button and turned to Will. "Owen said he would drive me home after we talked. Would you do me a favor while I'm there? It won't be for long. But I've been dying to taste that Round Top ice cream we had last summer. Do you think you could find some while I'm taking care of this? Aunt Nettie loves sweets. We could have ice cream for dessert tonight."

"I don't like leaving you at the station," said Will. "Not after what Nick said this morning."

"Nick's in Augusta, remember? He won't know. And I've had this incredible craving for ice cream."

Will looked at her. "Are you sure?"

"I'm positive. Whatever flavors you can recommend. You know what Aunt Nettie likes, too."

"I suppose this craving of yours also includes hot fudge and whipped cream?" Will asked, smiling. "And a few cherries?"

"If you got bananas, too, we could make banana splits."

"I'm convinced. That all sounds crazy in December. But you're making me hungry. I may have to make more than one stop to find all the ingredients, though."

"Take your time," agreed Maggie.

A few minutes later Will had been safely dispatched to find ice cream, and Maggie was sitting across from Owen Trask at the Waymouth Police Station.

"We brought Brian Weston and his wife in this morning for questioning."

"His mother told me."

"I'm not surprised. And I have to tell you, Nick seems ready to arrest him. Did you know Brian got one of those blackmailing letters?"

"Brian? Not his mother?"

"Brian himself."

"Did he tell you that?"

"Under a little duress. We found a list of people who'd gotten the letters at Carrie's house, and he was on it. We didn't tell you, because we wanted to make sure. She could have made a list of possible blackmail targets and then changed her mind. But he admitted it. Carrie gave him the letter in person the first night he was in Maine."

"What information did she have about Brian? I can't imagine what Betty might have said about him. You said Brian had problems when he was young, but …"

"We had no idea, of course. Turns out this time what Carrie knew about him had nothing to do with Betty Hoskins. Brian blurted it all out as soon as we separated him from his wife. When he was in college he ran up a lot of debts. Thousands of dollars. Most of it, according to him, was because he was incredibly unlucky at playing poker with his fraternity brothers." Owen shook his head slightly. "To pay them back, he borrowed a car, drove up from Massachusetts, and broke into his own house when he knew his mother and aunt would be at a church event. He stole pieces of their good jewelry and silver. We checked. Ruth Weston had reported a burglary then, but no one was ever charged."

"How did Carrie Folk know Brian did it?"

"Seems our Carrie was working the night shift in a house across the street from the Westons' then. She happened to be looking out the window at the right time. She saw Brian go into the house, come back out with several cartons, and then drive away. Later she heard about the burglary, and put everything together."

"And she never said anything to anyone? That must have been ten or fifteen years ago."

"She kept her mouth closed. But in her letter to Brian she threatened to tell the police, and to notify the bank where he works."

"He's a lawyer. He could lose his job for even being accused of burglary," said Maggie.

"Exactly. Which is why he didn't tell anyone about the letter. He'd called his broker and cashed in a little stock he had, we think to give to Carrie, but the check from the broker hadn't come before Carrie was killed."

"And yet he told you about it."

"If there's a choice of being accused of burglary or murder, which would you admit? Brian's a lawyer. He knows the statute of limitations for burglary in Maine is six years, which was up a while ago. We couldn't arrest him now even if we wanted to and his mother agreed to press charges, which she probably wouldn't. But the accusation could still mess up his personal and professional life enough that he was willing to pay Carrie to keep quiet. Or kill her."

"Did Nick arrest him this morning?"

"I convinced him to wait a day. Brian's not my favorite guy, but he was pretty panicked when we talked to him. I'm not convinced he's guilty of murder, and he isn't planning to leave for Philadelphia until after New Year's Day. So we bought a little more time."

"Good," said Maggie. "Because I think there has to be another suspect."

"I hope you have an idea of who," said Owen. "Especially after Nick told me he thought you were confusing the issue. I wanted to hear from you what the confusion was." Owen hesitated. "I've worked with Nick on perhaps a dozen cases over the years, and this time he seems distracted. I don't remember a time when he was so focused on one suspect without overwhelming evidence. He may be right about Brian. But Brian's wife and mother agree he was only away from his mother's house perhaps half an hour on Christmas morning. That's not enough time to get to Carrie Folk's house, murder her, clean up, and return home. And a search warrant we executed a couple of hours ago on the Westons' home didn't turn up any bloody clothing or money or anything else linking Brian to the murder."

"Did you know Doreen Strait also received a blackmailing letter from Carrie Folk?"

"Nick's mother? No. I hadn't heard that." Owen looked at her closely. "Are you sure? Her name wasn't on the list we found."

"I can't explain that. But I believe Doreen when she said she got a letter. Why wouldn't she tell the truth? Maybe Carrie thought of her after the others and didn't add her to the list."

"Nick never said anything about his mother getting a letter."

"Doreen didn't tell him, or anyone, about the letter when she got it, and now the letter's missing. Whoever took it is likely involved."

Owen picked up a pencil and started making notes. "When did you hear this?"

"Doreen told me, yesterday, at lunch."

"Who does she think took the letter?"

"The only person in that house besides her and Nick is Zelda. If Nick or Zelda found it, wouldn't they have talked to her about it?"

Owen shook his head. "I can't imagine Zelda getting involved in anything like that. She's a sweet kid, and her boyfriend, Jon Snow, is one of the most reliable young men in town. Just last month his picture was in the *Waymouth Herald*. He'd killed his first moose. That's a big event in a kid's life. To be lucky enough to win a moose hunting permit in the state lottery, and then to actually shoot one? His dad was so proud of him. And you should have seen the smile on that kid's face."

"So he's a hunter." Maggie's father had been a hunter. He'd even taught her to shoot. But to end the life of a magnificent, harmless creature had never made sense to her. Unless the hunters were killing to fill their freezers. Then she could understand. And here in Maine, that was usually the case.

"If we started checking hunters, we'd have to call in half the men in town, and a fair number of the women. And Carrie Folk wasn't shot."

The telephone on Owen's desk was ringing. He glanced at it and then shrugged. "Excuse me while I pick this up."

The expression on his face changed a second later. "Stay in the house. I'm on my way."

He grabbed his jacket. "Looks like Nick didn't go to Augusta. That was his mother. He's at his house, and Zelda's friend Jon Snow has his rifle on him."

"What happened?" Maggie wasn't sure she'd heard right. But if she had, Owen would need all the help he could find. "I'll go with you," she said, following him. "Maybe I can talk with Doreen or Zelda."

Owen hesitated. "I really shouldn't…but we haven't time. And maybe you can help. C'mon."

In the car, which was breaking speed records on the back roads, all he added was, "Shit. How'd that kid catch Nick without his weapon?"

The Straits' driveway was full of vehicles. Owen reached for his gun. "You stay in the car until I tell you it's safe." He was headed toward the house when the sound of a gunshot came from the barn. Owen changed direction.

Who was in the barn? Owen had told Doreen to stay in the house. Had she done that? Where were Nick and Jon? And Zelda?

How could she be of any use sitting in the car? Maggie put her hand on the door handle.

But she didn't have a gun. Owen was by the barn now, getting closer and closer to the door. Could he hear whatever was happening inside? Was someone injured? Or worse?

If everyone was in the barn, maybe she could get to the house. Doreen should be there. And maybe Zelda. She opened the window so she could hear what was happening.

"Police! Nick, this is Owen. Jon, drop your weapon and come out with your hands above your head. Zelda, if you're in there, you do the same."

Nothing happened.

"I want everyone out of the barn, with their hands up. Now!"

Silence. Then Owen went into the barn.

Maggie couldn't stand not knowing what was going on. She ran toward the ell connecting the barn and the house. If she were closer, maybe she could help in some way. Do something. Anything. What was happening in that barn?

She looked back at the house. Doreen's face was at one of the windows. Good; Doreen was safe inside, where Owen had told her to stay.

Then she heard voices coming from the barn. And a tall young man, presumably Jon Snow, was backing out of the wide barn door into the snow-covered yard. But his hands weren't up, and he hadn't dropped his weapon. His rifle was pointed toward the barn doors.

Maggie gasped. Zelda was with him.

She heard Owen's voice. "Drop the gun, Jon. Zelda, move away. Whatever's happened, we need to talk about it."

"Jon was just trying to protect me," Zelda yelled. "He didn't mean to hurt Dad."

"I sure did," Jon called to Owen. "He hurt Zelda. She didn't deserve to be treated that way. I don't care if he is a cop."

Owen followed them out into the yard. He glanced at Maggie. For a second he looked angry. Then he shouted, "Maggie, call 911! Get an ambulance here, stat. Tell them it's an emergency. Officer down. Gunshot wound."

Maggie pulled out her phone and did as she was told. Then she ran toward the barn. "I have EMT training," she called to Owen.

"I could've killed him," Jon said loudly, backing further, getting nearer to where the vehicles were parked. "I didn't. I just kept him from beating Zelda."

"You've hurt him enough," said Owen. "He needs to get to a hospital. He's bleeding, bad."

Nick was on the floor of the barn. His belt was next to him. Jon's bullet had hit his left knee. Blood was seeping through his pant leg onto the concrete floor. Maggie grabbed the belt and tied it around Nick's thigh as a tourniquet. "That idiot kid," he swore, trying to get up. "Let me get at him. I told her to stay away from him."

"Don't move. You'll lose more blood," Maggie said, looking at the growing pool of blood under Nick's leg. "I've called an ambulance."

"What's happening?" Nick asked. "Did Owen get him?"

Maggie moved so she could see into the snowy yard. "Looks

as though they're talking." She didn't tell Nick that Zelda and Jon seemed united. Despite Owen's threats, they were both moving closer to a faded green Ford pickup.

As she watched, Zelda and Jon both turned and ran toward the truck, Zelda jumping into the passenger seat and Jon opening the door to the driver's side, which was away from Owen. Owen fired a shot—toward where? Maggie couldn't see.

The kids were trying to get away. Jon backed up his truck and turned it toward the road, his tires spinning in the snow as he accelerated. Owen ran toward them and fired another shot, but the truck kept going down the drive, sideswiping the Waymouth town ambulance that was turning in, pushing it into the snow so it blocked the entrance to the driveway.

Jon's truck spun out, but he kept it on the road and gunned it. Owen ran toward the ambulance as the truck disappeared down the road.

Doreen opened the door from the ell connecting the house to the barn. "How's Nick?" she said to Maggie, who was kneeling next to him.

"He's lost a lot of blood. But if they can get that ambulance out of the snowbank and take him to the hospital, I think he'll be all right."

Nick was still lying on the ground, moaning.

Doreen went over to him. "What in the hell happened out here?"

"That idiot Jon Snow shot me. I was trying to have a civilized talk with him and he grabbed that rifle from his truck and followed me in here. I didn't have time to get to my gun. The one time I wasn't carrying it."

"Zelda went with Jon?" Doreen asked Maggie.

Maggie nodded. "They took off. Owen could have shot him, but didn't."

"That's something," said Doreen. She bent down to check the improvised tourniquet and nodded. "Not a bad job, Maggie. Not what I would've expected from an antiques dealer from New Jersey. That should hold him until the ambulance crew gets in here. There's not much else you or I can do."

Doreen was a nurse. But although she'd checked out the makeshift tourniquet Maggie had created, she didn't do anything else to help Nick.

Owen ran up to them, followed by two men and a woman who must have been in the ambulance. Two carried a stretcher. "How's Nick?"

"Nick's mad as hell," said Nick. "Where's that damn ambulance?"

"Stuck in a snowbank," said one of the EMTs as he knelt to see what Maggie had done. "We've called for a second ambulance and a tow. In the meantime, are you allergic to any medications?"

"How the hell should I know," said Nick. "Just get this knee of mine fixed up so I can go after those dumb kids."

"He's not allergic to anything," said Doreen.

A trim woman wearing a faded blue L.L. Bean barn coat deftly cut his pants away from the bullet site. "Nice job with stopping part of the blood loss." She reached up to one of her partners, who handed her a hypodermic needle. "This should help with the pain while we get you on the stretcher and wait for the other ambulance." She shot the medication into his hip.

Nick groaned at the needle. "Why didn't you shoot him, Owen? He assaulted an officer."

"He's a kid. We'll find them both. I've already called in his truck description to the department. I doubt they'll get far."

"He could have killed me."

"But he didn't," said Owen calmly. "You relax and let these people take care of you."

"Why haven't you gone after my daughter? That kid is armed and he has her with him. He's kidnapped her."

"She went of her own accord. And I didn't go after them because my car is blocked in by the ambulance they hit. I'm stuck here until the tow truck arrives and pulls the ambulance out of the snowbank."

"Shit."

Nick's voice was getting quieter. Had there been something besides a painkiller in that injection? While they were talking the three EMT folks had managed to lift Nick onto the stretcher, fasten him down, and get an IV started.

"Owen, I've got hot coffee in the kitchen," said Doreen. "Can I offer you a cup while you're waiting?"

"Seems to me you just did," said Owen. "I've got several questions, and coffee sounds good." He looked down at Nick. "You're in good hands."

"Maggie, you come, too," said Doreen.

This wasn't the time to say she didn't drink coffee. With a last glance at Nick on the stretcher she followed Owen and Doreen into the house.

29 December. 1888 lithograph by Maud Humphrey (1865–1940), one of foremost American illustrators of babies and children in late nineteenth and early twentieth centuries. She's also remembered because she was the mother of actor Humphrey Bogart. This is one of a series of illustrations she did for Frederick Stokes and Company called *Babes of the Year*, illustrating each month with a picture of a toddler. The *December* girl is dressed in a white fur-trimmed coat and white feather hat, and is standing before a spray of holly. 7 x 9 inches. Price: $70.

"DOREEN, YOU'VE had more experience with injuries like this than I have. Is Nick really going to be all right?" Owen said as Nick's mother poured three pottery mugs of coffee.

"I'm a nurse, not a doctor," said Doreen calmly. "Jon got him in the knee. He'll probably need surgery, and then a lot of physical therapy. He's going to be off the job for a while. He may walk with a limp when this is all over. But he'll live." She offered milk and Owen nodded.

"Thank the Lord," said Owen. He paused. "I couldn't shoot Jon. Maybe I should have."

"I'm glad you didn't. We don't need two people in the hospital. Or worse." Doreen stirred two teaspoons of sugar into her mug. "Jon has a temper, and he was defending Zelda. Nick was lighting into her again, and this time he had his belt. If Jon hadn't happened to drop in, Zelda would have been in bad shape by now."

"And you knew that?" Maggie couldn't help saying. "And you didn't do anything to stop it?"

Doreen flinched. "I've done everything I could too often. This time Nick was angrier than I'd seen him, and I didn't know what to do. Call the police?"

"You could have called me. You did this afternoon," Owen pointed out.

"I called you when I saw Jon take that gun out of his truck. If I'd called to say Nick was upset with Zelda again and I thought he was going to beat her, would you have come as quickly?"

Owen winced a little. "I see your point. I'm a local deputy, but with Nick's being a state trooper there would have been questions. Not just from me. But from his superiors."

"Exactly. Which is why my goal was to keep them apart as much as possible, especially when Nick was on one of his tears, and then to help Zelda get away from Waymouth as soon as possible." She paused. "Nick wasn't always like this, you know. Oh, he spanked her when she was little and all. But it's only been the last six months or so, since she began going out with Jon Snow, that he's gone over the top."

"He's the one who gave Zelda that black eye last week," Maggie pointed out.

"She'd come in late a couple of nights in a row and he let her have it. I'll admit, she hasn't made this easier. It seems like she's asking for a confrontation with him. The more he tries physical force to discipline her, the more she resists. But I never thought he'd really beat her until this afternoon."

Owen put down his mug. "Doreen, Maggie told me you'd been one of those to receive blackmail letters from Carrie Folk."

"True," she answered, looking over at Maggie.

Maggie nodded her encouragement.

"Did she tell you that letter disappeared?" Doreen asked.

"She did. And that there's been no one in the house that you know of besides you and Nick and Zelda."

"And Jon, sometimes," Doreen added. "Although he hasn't been inside much recently. He usually waits for Zelda outside, or they meet somewhere else. To stay clear of Nick, of course." She hesitated. "I don't think he's been in the house since about a week before Christmas. Which was before the letter arrived."

"What was in the letter?" Owen asked.

Doreen glanced at Maggie. "I guess I have to tell you now. Carrie was threatening to disclose information about the abortion service my mother and a few other women in Waymouth ran from the late 1950s until 1973. I helped out there."

Owen's eyes widened. He pulled out his notebook. "I don't know anything about that. Did Nick know what you used to do?

Doreen shook her head. "I never told him. It all happened years ago. Those of us involved then swore not to mention it to anyone. That was the 'rule number-one' Betty was talking about at Nettie's party. Rule number-one was never to tell anyone about what we were doing unless we absolutely had to. And, even then, to insist on speaking with a woman, not a man. We thought a woman would understand. I can't imagine how Nick would have known anything about what we were doing. He certainly didn't hear it from me."

"It's quite possible, though, that he found that letter. He didn't say anything to you about it?"

"No. And I didn't mention it either. I'll admit, part of me was glad the letter disappeared. I kept thinking if the letter had disappeared, then the problem had. I wouldn't have to do anything about it."

Owen paused. "You know Nick was fixated on that cold case. That unknown girl whose body was found in the hidden garden in 1972."

"I haven't thought about that in years. As a boy he collected all the articles about the case, and used to say, when he grew up he'd find out who the girl was. And who killed her. He's still interested in that case?"

"He's practically memorized the case file. When I came on the job seven years ago that was the first thing he talked to me about. Since I was working in Waymouth, he made me read the file and promise to share any information, any leads or hints at all, that I might hear about it. He kept saying that someone in town knew more than they were telling, and someday he'd bring them to justice."

Doreen hesitated. "So you read the file."

"I did. And there's information there that wasn't released to the public." Owen looked at her. "That girl bled to death after having an abortion."

30 | **"On The Beach."** Winslow Homer wood engraving illustrating a story in *Harper's Weekly*, March 10, 1860. Pair of young eloping lovers run down the beach together, pursued by a tall man in a dark coat and high hat. 4.5 x 3.5 inches. Price: $125.

FOR A FEW moments no one in the kitchen said anything. Then Owen spoke again. "Maybe I should have connected the dots earlier. Nick's mentioned that cold case several times in the past few months. The girl who was found was about seventeen or eighteen, and that's the age Zelda is now. She's not much younger than Nick's wife was when she got pregnant, too."

Doreen nodded, slowly. "I thought of the connection with Emily, Zelda's mother. Nick's blamed her for a lot of things over the years. He loves Zelda, but his life would have been very different if Emily hadn't gotten pregnant, and he hadn't married so young and had to be responsible for a child. And of course, the current problems aren't all his fault. Zelda has been difficult."

"Emily didn't get pregnant on her own," Maggie put in. "And Zelda's a teenager. She's focused on her life. Not on her effect on others'."

"Of course not. And this isn't the first time I've seen a father wanting to protect his daughter from boys; from the way he remembered himself acting at their age." Doreen got up and walked over to the window, looking out toward the barn. "And now Jon's shot him, and it's going to mess up both their lives. Possibly permanently."

"Let's go back a bit. We need to talk about that letter you got from Carrie Folk. I'm very concerned about the possibility that Nick found it." Owen's voice was steady. "Doreen, you're sure he knew nothing about the abortion activities you were involved with before this?"

She shook her head and returned to the table. "I told you. I can't imagine how. Mother and I never talked about it. We'd helped a lot of women, young and not-so-young. But it was in the past. And we took the privacy of those who'd come to us very seriously."

Maggie put her hand out and covered Doreen's. "But you can see that when Nick found you and your mother were connected to abortions, he'd immediately think of that young women he's been obsessed with all these years."

"Of course. Now I see that." Doreen looked from Maggie to Owen and back. "He must have assumed we'd killed her! That's probably what both of you are thinking, too. But I don't know anything about that girl. I'm telling you the truth. I wasn't there every Thursday. But the last couple of years we were open I was there most of the time. Once I remember a woman bleeding too much. It wasn't a young girl; it was a married woman who already had seven children. Mother and I drove her to Rocky Shores as quickly as we could. It was scary at the time. Thank goodness, she didn't die."

"But you weren't there for every abortion."

"No. But even if one of our patients had died, we never would have taken her clothing. That girl they found was naked, wasn't she? And her body was left outside." Doreen pushed her chair back slightly. "We could never have been so callous."

"Not even if having it known would have closed your operation, and possibly sent all of you to prison?" Owen wasn't smiling.

"What happened to that girl doesn't make sense. And I have no proof, other than my word. Besides, that girl was never identified. Believe me; we knew who all our clients were. They came to us by personal referrals. We weren't like one of those butcheries in the cities where you could give a false name and as long as you had the cash, they'd operate."

"Like the place Nettie Brewer went," said Maggie.

"That happened before my time, of course, but Mother told me about it when she first explained what was happening in the Westons' house." Doreen took a deep breath. "We did it to help women, not hurt them. If that poor girl died of an abortion, it wasn't one she had from us. I swear." Her eyes filled. "What Nick must have thought when he saw that letter! He's been looking for that girl's killer all these years, and here he thought it was his own mother or grandmother." She shook her head. "No wonder he's been especially on edge the past week."

Owen paused. "It was all a long time ago. For now I'll take your word that you had nothing to do with that girl's death. Although now that I know about your organization it certainly raises questions I'm going to have to find answers to. But let's put that aside for a moment. I need to ask you something else. When I got the call from Carrie Folk's neighbor about her murder and called Nick Christmas morning, he hadn't been home long, had he?"

"No. He went to that party at the Westons' house," Doreen said. "Then he went to the midnight service at the church, to hear Zelda sing. I drove her home, and he went on duty."

Maggie looked at Owen. "And he's been the one investigating Carrie's murder."

"Oh, no." Doreen suddenly realized what they were thinking. "You think my Nick could have killed Carrie?"

"It would have been a way of keeping you from having this exact conversation. Of protecting you, if he thought you killed that girl in the sunken garden," Owen pointed out. "And we didn't find any fingerprints or other evidence in the Folks' home. Whoever killed Carrie Folk knew what they were doing."

Doreen picked up her napkin and wiped tears from her eyes. "Why didn't he come and talk with me about it? I could have told him I wasn't involved. I could have explained."

Owen shook his head. "I have to tell you, Mrs. Strait. I don't know for sure what Nick did. But I can understand how he felt. Not, you understand, that he should have killed Carrie Folk. But that he wanted to. Especially given his reaction to Zelda this fall."

The scream of an ambulance siren interrupted them. Doreen went to the window. "A second ambulance is here, and the tow truck almost has the first one out." She turned to the two at the table. "We've talked enough. Too much. My son is going in the hospital and I have to go to him."

Owen nodded. "Can I trust you not to say anything to him about our conversation this afternoon? I suspect he'll be in the hospital for at least a day or two. Right now I need to find Jon and Zelda.

Running isn't going to help Jon, and Jon didn't force her into that truck with him. She chose to stay with the man who'd shot her father rather than stay with Nick. She's an accessory to assault of an officer. Or attempted murder."

"Please. You need to find them before any other law enforcement people do," said Doreen, realizing what that meant. "Talk to them. Convince them to turn themselves in."

Owen got up. "I'm going to try."

"May I come with you? Zelda knows me, at least a little," said Maggie.

Owen hesitated, but only a moment. "C'mon then. Just keep quiet and stay out of the line of fire. Jon has a rifle. And he's already used it once today."

31

Buying Trotting Horses on the Androscoggin. Full page black-and-white wood engraving drawn by James E. Kelley (1855–1933) for *Harper's Weekly*, March 20, 1880. Kelley, a noted sculptor and artist remembered for his Civil War and other illustrations of American historical events, was also one of the founders of the Art Students League of New York. Illustration shows seven teams of horses racing sleighs on the frozen Androscoggin River in Maine. Men and boys (one African American) cheer on their favorites, and insets show a horse being trained by pulling a hay wagon on skids ("The Jumper"), a woman feeding a colt ("The Foster Mother"), and a man checking the legs of a horse while a woman with a whip holds the horse's bridle ("The Fair Jockey"). Small, almost invisible, tear in margin above print, extending about one inch into picture. Page: 15 x 10 inches. Price: $40.

AS THEY followed the two ambulances and the tow truck out of the driveway, Maggie realized that in all the excitement she hadn't called Will. She'd told him she'd meet him at home soon. Banana splits were now the furthest thing from her mind. She pulled out her phone.

"Hello, Maggie? Where are you? Aunt Nettie and I've been worried."

"I'm with Owen. A lot's happened. I'll fill you in as soon as I can. We're trying to find Jon and Zelda."

"I thought you were coming home after you talked with Owen."

"I was, but there was an emergency. I'll tell you all everything as soon as I can. But I need to stay with Owen now. Don't eat all the ice cream!" Maggie slipped the phone back into her pocket.

Owen glanced over at her. "Trouble with Will?"

"He doesn't like me getting involved with criminal cases. Especially when Nick told me to stop asking questions."

Owen grinned. "You? Stop asking questions? The man's a bit un-realistic. Do you need to go, then?"

"We need to find Jon and Zelda," said Maggie. "I'm here for the duration. Where are we heading?"

"Jon turned toward town when he left the driveway. He could be anywhere. But I'm hoping he headed for his own home. We'll go there first and see if his truck's in the drive."

"Wouldn't going home be too obvious?"

"Jon's a good kid. Attends church, does what his parents want him to. He's never been in any trouble before. I'm betting he's scared to death."

"He has Zelda with him. And that gun."

"But he was trying to defend Zelda. I don't think he'll hurt her." Owen frowned and kept driving. "But I'll sure feel better once we find them both."

He slowed down at a small house closer to the center of town. "That's his house. No truck. So my guess was wrong." Owen turned the next corner. "I'm trying to remember who his friends at school are. Who he might have turned to. Keep your eyes open for that old green truck of his. Luckily there aren't a lot like that in town."

"You said he went to church. Is he religious? Would he have turned to his minister for help?" Maggie suggested.

"Good thought." Owen turned his car away from town.

"You're not heading for the church," said Maggie.

"I am. *His* church. He and his parents don't attend the church on the Green. They go to a church outside of town." Owen smiled. "It's not the eighteenth century anymore. Not everyone in Waymouth goes to the Congregational church."

"Of course not. I thought, since Zelda went to that church…"

"That Jon would, too? Nope."

They weren't close to downtown Waymouth anymore. Owen turned off Route 1 and headed down a less traveled road. About a mile in, a small white building was set off the road. In front of it a sign read: REJOICE IN THE SEASON. LET JESUS INTO YOUR HEART THIS HOLIDAY.

"This is the place." Owen drove into a wide plowed driveway that curved around the building. "Reverend Adams's office is in the back. If he isn't here we'll check the high school. Jon's on the basketball team. The gym could be open for practices during the holiday."

Owen slowed down as he followed the icy drive around the back of the low building.

"There!" Maggie pointed. A green pickup was parked near the back door next to a black Subaru sedan.

Owen pulled in next to the pickup. "Stay here until I take a look at the truck," he said. "I want to see if his rifle's there." He got out and walked slowly toward the truck. He opened the driver's door and reached down. Maggie watched as he came back toward the police car holding Jon's rifle.

She opened her car door as he checked to see if the gun was loaded, and then put it carefully in the trunk. "So he's not armed now," she said. "Thank goodness."

"Let's go find them," said Owen. Maggie followed him into the building. The reverend's office was down the hall. Owen knocked. "Hello? Police."

Silence. Then, "Come in. Door's unlocked."

A tall, thin, balding man sat behind a wide desk piled with papers. In back of him was a bookcase packed with various editions of the Bible, hymnals, books on biblical interpretation, and books on counseling. A cross hung on the wall opposite the desk, over the couch where Jon and Zelda sat, holding hands. If Zelda's eyes hadn't been swollen from crying, they would have looked like any other guilty teenaged couple, perhaps caught in an embrace by a mother walking into the room.

"We were expecting you, Deputy Trask," said Reverend Adams. "It's been a hard day here in Waymouth."

"It has," said Owen, looking from the minister to the two young people. "Jon, I'm afraid you'll have to come with me."

Jon swallowed hard. "I did it to protect Zelda. He was going to hit her with his belt."

"And you shot him. You shot an unarmed Maine State Trooper," said Owen. "That's serious."

"How's my dad?" asked Zelda, not letting go of Jon's hand.

"He's in the hospital. Your grandmother went to be with him," said Owen.

"Jon didn't mean it. It's all my fault. I shouldn't have stayed out after my curfew. And I shouldn't have told Jon about what my father would do." Zelda turned toward Maggie. "I truly didn't think he'd come after Dad. I didn't."

"I'm not sorry. I know that's wrong, Reverend, but I'm not. Zelda's dad's been hurting her. You didn't have to tell me, Zelda. I saw the bruises. And the black eye. He was getting worse. I was wicked worried about her, Reverend. I wouldn't have killed her dad. I just wanted him to stop. I didn't want him to hurt Zelda again."

"I understand, Jon. But you know you have to go with the deputy."

"It wasn't like that Carrie Folk. She was going to tell people about Zelda's grandmother killing babies. She killed babies, Reverend! She's the one who should be going to jail. Not me."

Maggie stepped closer to the young people. "How did you know about the abortions, Jon? Who told you?"

"Zelda told me," he said. "She found a letter that woman…that Mrs. Folk…sent to her grandmother. She showed it to me."

"I didn't mean any harm to anyone," sobbed Zelda. "I didn't. I couldn't find my sticky tape, to wrap Christmas gifts with. I looked in Grandma's desk, and I saw the letter. It said awful things about Grandma, and her mother, too. Mrs. Folk was going to tell everyone in town what they'd done."

"They were murderers, Zelda. They murdered babies." Jon looked from her to Owen to the reverend. "They killed unborn children, Reverend. They should be the ones arrested."

"It was a different time," said Zelda. "I've heard that back then girls died from abortions. Maybe they were trying to help."

"Help by killing innocents?" said Jon.

"I told you not to talk like that," said Zelda. "I wanted to talk to Grandma and find out what it was all about. But I was afraid she'd be mad. I'd taken her private letter. And Mrs. Folk wanted money. I knew we didn't have that kind of money. Grandma's been saving so I could go to college, like we talked about the other day," she said to Maggie. "You remember?"

"I remember. We talked about your going to school outside of Maine."

"Away from my father," said Zelda. "Grandma understood. I was grown up. It was time to leave Waymouth. See the rest of the world. Be where my father couldn't worry about me. That's all he did. He worried about me."

"You wanted to leave me, too, then," said Jon. "You know I was going to stay here and work at my father's store."

"We could have seen each other on vacations," said Zelda. "But if Grandma paid that Mrs. Folk the money she wanted, then there'd be no money for me to go to college. I'd have to stay here in boring Waymouth for the rest of my life. Get a job at Bath Iron Works. Or work as a waitress." She shook her head. "I couldn't stand that."

"So what did you do?" asked Maggie gently. "To make sure the money would be there for you to go to college?"

"Christmas Eve, after Grandma was asleep, Jon came over, like he did lots of nights when Dad was working. I knew I could get away. I wanted to talk to Mrs. Folk. To tell her she shouldn't bother my Grandma. To tell her why she couldn't have the money she was asking for."

"And you did that?" Owen asked. "You both talked to Carrie Folk?"

Zelda nodded. "But it wasn't anything like I thought it'd be. She said she needed the money for her son. That it wasn't any of my business. That I was too young to understand." Zelda appealed to Maggie. "I'm not a child. I'm not too young to understand. I didn't want to be stuck in this town forever. College was my only chance to get away. To be free! She couldn't take that from me. I wouldn't let her!"

Jon spoke softly. "I tried to stop her. I did. But they were yelling at each other."

"What happened, Zelda?"

"I got so angry. I didn't know I could be that angry. I kept seeing her face, keeping me from living the kind of life I wanted to live."

"And ..."

"I picked up one of the logs she had piled next to her fireplace. And I turned and hit her with it. Just once!" Zelda sobbed. "I only hit her once."

"Jon?"

"She's telling the truth. She only hit her once. But Mrs. Folk fell down, and her head was bleeding all over the floor."

"I didn't know what to do. I covered her up with the afghan that was on the couch. I didn't want her to be cold. I didn't know she was dead. I was too scared to call anyone. My dad would have killed me if he'd known I'd sneaked out again."

"I threw the wood in the fireplace," said Jon, "and we got a dishtowel that was hanging in the kitchen and wiped everything we could. For fingerprints, you know? I've watched a lot of TV. That's what the detectives check for. We didn't want anyone to know we'd been there."

"And then we left," said Zelda. "Jon took me home and I went to bed. I hoped no one would ever know."

"We promised never to tell what happened," said Jon. "But it's right to tell now, isn't it, Reverend?"

Owen pulled out two pairs of handcuffs.

"Deputy Trask, before you take them away," said Reverend Adams, "would you mind if we said a short prayer?"

32

The Dark. 1909 Lithograph by Jessie Willcox Smith (1863–1935) showing a very young boy about to ascend a flight of steep, dark stairs. Smith, who studied with Thomas Eakins and Howard Pyle, was only the second woman (of ten) to be inducted into the Hall of Fame of the Society of Illustrators. Known as one of the "Red Rose Girls," a group of women artists who lived together near Philadelphia, she was known for her illustrations and paintings of children. 6 x 9 inches. Price: $60.

"ZELDA STRAIT killed Carrie?" Aunt Nettie shook her head in disbelief. "That nice young girl. And her friend Jon, shooting Nicky. I can't get my head around it all."

"Are you sure Nick's going to be okay?" Will asked.

"Owen checked with the hospital before he dropped me off. Nick's going to need surgery on that knee, and it will never be quite the same again. But he's in good physical shape, and despite the delay, he got to the hospital quickly enough so he didn't lose too much blood. After physical therapy he'll be fine," said Maggie.

"Poor Doreen. Her son in the hospital and her granddaughter in jail." Aunt Nettie shook her head. "I'll call her tomorrow and see if there's anything we can do to help. But her problems are the kind a casserole and flowers can't cure."

"And who knows how long the courts will take with this," added Will. "Nick must be furious. His own daughter. He always said that friend of hers was no good."

"But if Nick hadn't been abusive to Zelda, maybe this all wouldn't have happened," Maggie put in. "Although of course there's no excuse for murder or for shooting Nick. They're teenagers, and they overreacted to everything."

"What about those of us who were involved with the abortions?"

said Aunt Nettie. "Are they going to question us all about that poor girl's murder back in the nineteen-seventies?"

"I don't know," said Maggie. "I guess that'll be up to Nick, when he's better, or to someone else with the homicide division. Owen said that for the moment, anyway, nothing will be done about it. Doreen says none of you was involved; if they do question you and Ruth, I'm guessing you'll say the same thing."

"Certainly. No one ever died in our place. If anyone had, heaven knows, we wouldn't have left her body naked and out in the elements."

"If they have no more evidence than the fact that you were all involved with abortion, I don't see how they could put together a case," added Will. "Unless they had DNA evidence. And I remember Nick's telling me years ago that because the body had been outside in the rain, they found no evidence."

"I keep thinking of Doreen. And Nick. And Zelda, locked away tonight. She had such a bright future ahead of her. To do something like this," said Aunt Nettie.

"She must have been desperate to leave Waymouth," said Maggie. "And she and Nick both had tempers. Doreen admitted there'd been fireworks at their home during the past months. Zelda panicked, and snapped."

"And Carrie Folk died. Will, do we have any good sherry? I think I'd like a drink tonight."

"We do. Maggie's favorite, Dry Sack. I bought a bottle before she came."

"I'll join you, Aunt Nettie," said Maggie, as Will got up. "And if you have a little lemon to go in it, that would be perfect."

"Will do," came Will's voice came from the kitchen. "Two sherries coming up. And I think I'll have an Irish whiskey. I agree, this is a night for a drink. Then I'll go ahead and put the potatoes in the oven. When they're baked I'll broil the steak I bought when I was out buying bananas."

"Steak and potatoes…sounds like a man's winter meal," Maggie couldn't help smiling. "It sounds perfect. And simple. And then, if we dare, banana splits for dessert. But right now all I want to do is sip my sherry and be very glad I'm here with both of you."

Will handed around the glasses. "To us. And to our friends who're dealing with major problems tonight. May they be as strong as this whiskey."

Aunt Nettie and Maggie raised their glasses of sherry in response. "Perhaps a strange sentiment, but a true one, Will. And to Maggie, for helping so many people this week. At least now we know the answers to our questions. Whether we like the answers or not."

33 | **Santa Claus Knows His Business.** 1902 lithographed full-page illustration from *Harper's Weekly* by Clarence F. Underwood (1871–1929). Handsome young couple in evening attire (a flowing off-the-shoulder blue gown for her; a tuxedo and top hat for him) looking down at the red rose (a symbol of passion) he has just given her. In the background, a green-hatted Santa is pushing Cupid, complete with wings and arrow, into the room. 8.5 x 12 inches. Price: $50.

LATER THAT NIGHT, after Aunt Nettie had gone to bed, Will and Maggie sat quietly together on the couch, sipping cognac. For a while, neither of them said anything. Then Will spoke.

"After all that's happened today, and that big dinner, I'd really like to get some fresh air. How about taking a walk?"

A few minutes later they were outside. Light snow was falling as they headed down the street toward the town wharf.

"While you were solving crimes this afternoon, I was busy, too," Will said, reaching for Maggie's hand.

"I know. Getting all the ingredients for those banana splits." Maggie put her other hand on her stomach. "It was fun, and we needed a little fun tonight. I can't believe we ate so much. Thank you for doing that. And for understanding why I had to stay with Owen."

"I'm glad you enjoyed the dessert. And I do understand what you had to do. If there's someone in trouble, especially a young person, you want to help. That's part of what makes you Maggie. But that's not what I meant. Something else happened this afternoon."

"What?"

Will looked down at her. "I bought the house. It's all done but the closing, and that's set for next week."

"That's fantastic! Congratulations. Now I know what you'll be doing this spring," Maggie reached up and kissed him lightly. "I know you really wanted that house."

"I did. For a lot of reasons."

They kept walking, snow crunching under their feet and snowflakes dancing in the glow of the small lights on storefronts and streetlights.

"A lot of reasons? You mean so you'd have a project to work on this spring, and then open the mall you've planned," Maggie answered.

Will headed them toward the river. As they passed the snow-covered hidden garden, he squeezed her hand, but neither of them said anything.

A block or so farther, Will paused. "With all that's been happening in the past week, I don't want you to think I've forgotten the reason you came to Maine for Christmas was so we could talk." He swallowed hard. "In fact, I think about that every hour of the day and night."

"I do, too," said Maggie. "I suspect we've both been delaying the inevitable."

"I know I have. But for good reasons. Maggie, Christmas morning, when Aunt Nettie gave you those children's books, I almost opened my mouth. But it wasn't the right time. And then we heard about Carrie's murder, and all my plans seemed unimportant. You haven't said anything specific, but I assume you're going through with your plans to adopt."

Somehow it was easier to talk while they were walking. "It's very important to me, Will. I'd always regret it if I didn't. My home study was finished in December."

He didn't seem surprised. But then, he knew her well. "When do you think you'll have a placement?"

Maggie noticed Will was using the correct adoption terminology. He'd never done that before. "I don't know for sure. But I applied for one or two older children. Older children are waiting in both this country and overseas. I have an appointment to talk with my social worker in January. I'll know more then."

"I'm guessing you're planning to take a sabbatical from teaching after your child, or children, are placed with you."

"If I can afford to. And it will depend on when my daughter arrives." Maggie swallowed. *My daughter*. It felt so good, and yet so scary, to say that out loud. Especially to say it to Will.

"I checked with an adoption agency here in Maine. They said it would depend on the circumstances, but that if someone had a placement from a New Jersey agency, in many cases they could continue the post-placement supervision if the person adopting moved to Maine."

Maggie stopped. "You called an adoption agency?"

"Maggie, I love you. I want to be with you. And I've realized one of the parts of you that I love is the part that wants to adopt. Remember in October, when I asked you to marry me?"

"Of course. How could I forget?"

"That's what I want. More than anything. For us to be together. But I'm torn between caring for Aunt Nettie and loving you. And you're torn between adopting, and I hope, loving me."

"Yes." He'd said it perfectly.

"So instead of a full proposal, this time I have a proposition for you." Will turned and looked into her eyes. "I just bought a wonderful house. You've already agreed to display your antique prints in it."

"Yes?"

"How would you like to be my partner? My partner in business as well as in life." Will's words raced. "I'd hoped it would be settled before Christmas, so I could tell you, or ask you, then. But I've thought it all out. I can make the third floor of that house into an apartment, with space for you and even two children. After you have your placement you could move to Maine. Live here. You could be with your child, and manage the day-to-day operations at the mall. I'd be there, too, when I could, and we could hire someone else to help out. You wouldn't be tied down. But you'd have a place to live, close to me and Aunt Nettie. And Maine's a wonderful place to raise children."

Maggie was speechless as Will continued.

"If you're willing, I'll fix the apartment however you want it. It could be ready for you when your spring semester is over, if you have a placement. Or if you haven't had a placement by then you could have your home study transferred to the agency in Maine. But you could move here as soon as May, when school's over."

This wasn't what she'd expected. She'd been prepared to say good-bye to Will. To drive back to New Jersey alone, never seeing him again. "But if I move to Maine…my job …"

"If you take a sabbatical you'll have time to think about where you want to live, and look for a teaching job here, if you want to. You'd keep your options open. And we could see each other all the time, and I could get to know and love your child, too."

"Being in Maine, and near you, sounds wonderful. But what if… if it doesn't work out?"

"Then at least we'll know we tried. A year from now I don't know what my situation with Aunt Nettie will be. You don't know whether you'll have one child or two."

"But we'd be together. While all those issues are working themselves out."

"Exactly. That's why I wanted to make sure you loved that house as much as I did. I wanted to know if you'd want to live there. To look out over Waymouth from the tower. To bring your children home there. For now. Because I don't want to spend any more time away from you."

Maggie's mind flashed with images. Leaving New Jersey. Moving to Maine. Living in an apartment with a tower overlooking the harbor, in a house full of antiques. Space for one, or two, children. And the man she loved, close, if not present every hour.

"I thought you might be falling for Jo Heartwood," she admitted. "You were spending so much time with her, and she's so young and pretty."

"Jo? She's great. I hope you get to know her better. But she was helping me with the house. She even had a friend who connected me to the adoption agency. She's been helping me get all this taken care of before you left, Maggie. I love you. Only you."

"And I love you. And …" Maggie took a deep breath. "And I've always wanted to live in a tower."

"Then your answer is 'yes'?"

"Yes. You have a partner and a tenant for your antiques mall."

Maggie put out her hand to shake Will's, but the shake quickly turned into an embrace, which turned into a lingering kiss.

Will reached into his coat pocket and pulled out a small box. A ring box.

Inside was a simple gold ring, set with a green tourmaline. The stone Will always said matched her eyes.

"Will you, my dear Maggie, wear this ring? For now let's call it a promise ring. A ring that says I promise to love you, and be there for you, no matter what life brings to either of us. For now, and forever."

Maggie's eyes filled with tears of happiness as she nodded. Will slipped off her left glove and put the ring on her engagement finger.

In front of them, the Madoc River was filled with tiny lights. "What are they?" whispered Maggie. "It's as though there were fireflies on the river."

"I hoped we could see them," said Will. He put his arm around her as they looked at the river. "When I was out this afternoon on my quest for local ice cream in December, I heard about a farmer upriver. Every morning this time of year when he goes to his barn he finds the water in each cow's bucket frozen solid, except for the center. He empties them and saves the ice buckets, which look like enormous votive candle holders. Then, one night after Christmas, he invites his friends over for a party and they put a candle in the center of each ice bucket, and set them all afloat. That's what we're seeing. A river of lights, drifting downriver to the sea."

Maggie leaned against Will, and looked in wonder, her eyes shining like the lights. "They're beautiful. Unexpected. And magical. Just the way I hope our life together will be."

Acknowledgments

AS ALWAYS, writing a book takes the support and assistance of many people. I'd especially like to thank John and Susan Daniel and Meredith Phillips of Perseverance Press for bringing Maggie and her friends back, and Eric Larson for his inspired interior and cover designs. You've all been wonderful!

Among many sources of information I consulted about Alzheimer's, a special nod to Lisa Genova's book *Still Alice*. I recommend it to anyone interested in more information about this devastating disease.

For updates on Maine's services for the intellectually disabled, thanks to fellow Chatham College graduate Sabra Burdick for prompt and insightful responses. And thanks to Kathy Lynn and Sandy Emerson for their clarifications about law enforcement in Maine.

As always, this book is fiction, and any errors are mine.

And as always, thank you to my husband, Bob Thomas, who listened, advised, commiserated, cooked meals and mixed drinks, and in all ways made it easier for me to write this book. Every writer deserves a spouse as wonderful. But, sorry. I'm not sharing.

Most of all, thank you to all of Maggie's fans, who've encouraged me to continue her story, and to all the bookstores and libraries across the country that have opened their doors to me and to my books. I love you all.

About the Author

Mystery writer Lea Wait lives on the coast of Maine with her artist husband, where she also writes historical novels for young readers. She is a fourth-generation antiques dealer, and adopted four older children as a single parent. *Shadows on a Maine Christmas* is the seventh in Wait's Agatha-finalist Shadows mystery series. She participates in two authors' group blogs, and she may be visited at www.leawait.com, Facebook, and Goodreads.

More Traditional Mysteries from Perseverance Press
For the New Golden Age

Diana Killian
POETIC DEATH SERIES
Docketful of Poesy
ISBN 978-1-880284-97-1

Janet LaPierre
PORT SILVA SERIES
Baby Mine
ISBN 978-1-880284-32-2

Keepers
Shamus Award nominee, Best Paperback Original
ISBN 978-1-880284-44-5

Death Duties
ISBN 978-1-880284-74-2

Family Business
ISBN 978-1-880284-85-8

Run a Crooked Mile
ISBN 978-1-880284-88-9

Hailey Lind
ART LOVER'S SERIES
Arsenic and Old Paint
ISBN 978-1-56474-490-6

Lev Raphael
NICK HOFFMAN SERIES
Tropic of Murder
ISBN 978-1-880284-68-1

Hot Rocks
ISBN 978-1-880284-83-4

Lora Roberts
BRIDGET MONTROSE SERIES
Another Fine Mess
ISBN 978-1-880284-54-4

SHERLOCK HOLMES SERIES
The Affair of the Incognito Tenant
ISBN 978-1-880284-67-4

Rebecca Rothenberg
BOTANICAL SERIES
The Tumbleweed Murders
(completed by Taffy Cannon)
ISBN 978-1-880284-43-8

Sheila Simonson
LATOUCHE COUNTY SERIES
Buffalo Bill's Defunct
WILLA Award, Best Softcover Fiction
ISBN 978-1-880284-96-4

An Old Chaos
ISBN 978-1-880284-99-5

Beyond Confusion
ISBN 978-1-56474-519-4

Shelley Singer
JAKE SAMSON & ROSIE VICENTE SERIES
Royal Flush
ISBN 978-1-880284-33-9

Lea Wait
SHADOWS ANTIQUES SERIES
Shadows of a Down East Summer
ISBN 978-1-56474-497-5

Shadows on a Cape Cod Wedding
ISBN 1-978-56474-531-6

Shadows on a Maine Christmas
ISBN 978-1-56474-531-6

Eric Wright
JOE BARLEY SERIES
The Kidnapping of Rosie Dawn
Barry Award, Best Paperback Original. Edgar,
Ellis, and Anthony awards nominee
ISBN 978-1-880284-40-7

Nancy Means Wright
MARY WOLLSTONECRAFT SERIES
Midnight Fires
ISBN 978-1-56474-488-3

The Nightmare
ISBN 978-1-56474-509-5

REFERENCE/MYSTERY WRITING

Kathy Lynn Emerson
How To Write Killer Historical Mysteries:
The Art and Adventure of Sleuthing
Through the Past
Agatha Award, Best Nonfiction. Anthony and
Macavity awards nominee
ISBN 978-1-880284-92-6

Carolyn Wheat
How To Write Killer Fiction:
The Funhouse of Mystery & the Roller
Coaster of Suspense
ISBN 978-1-880284-62-9

Available from your local bookstore
or from Perseverance Press/John Daniel & Company
(800) 662–8351 or www.danielpublishing.com/perseverance